CARBON

BLACKWINGS MC BOOK FOUR

BY

TEAGAN BROOKS

Dedication

To my big sister and little brother.

CONTENTS

Author's Note

Chapter One begins four months before Ember showed up at the clubhouse in Dash (Blackwings MC Book One).

PROLOGUE

Harper

Victim.

I hated that word. I always felt like it carried a connotation of defeat. I wasn't defeated. I fought like hell, and for the most part, I won. No, I was not a victim. I was a survivor.

I fought hard to overcome the demons of my past. I was lucky to have a supportive family, even though it wasn't a traditional family. My mother passed away from cancer a few months before I was kidnapped. During the few weeks before my older brother rescued me, my father passed away.

When Duke found me and took me out of that

horrible house, he went straight to our Aunt Leigh for help, and she welcomed us with open arms. Her husband was my father's brother and died the year before Duke and I showed up in Devil Springs.

Duke only lived with us for a few months, just long enough for him to save enough money to get his own apartment. When he moved out, it was just me, Aunt Leigh, and her son, Judge, who was 15 at the time. He instantly became another brother for me, and Aunt Leigh took on the role of pseudo-mom. They did everything they could to help me deal with the loss of my parents and the kidnapping.

The first year was rough. When I wasn't crying, I was too scared of my own shadow to leave the house. After two disastrous attempts at trying to drop me off at school, Aunt Leigh and my therapist decided home-schooling would be a better option for me.

For the next few years, Aunt Leigh homeschooled me, and I continued to see a therapist twice a month. By the time I reached high school, I was on my fourth therapist and had learned how to manipulate them by saying the right things. After six months of listening to my carefully chosen words, my therapist told

Aunt Leigh I was ready to attend public school. Honestly, I was ready, even though I had to trick the therapist into agreeing with me. I loved my family and was greatly appreciative of everything they did to help me through my ordeal, but I was a teenager and needed teenage friends.

I also needed to be around people who didn't know about my past and didn't treat me like I would shatter into a million pieces if they said or did the wrong thing. Yes, I was fragile to some extent, but I wasn't that fragile. I had no desire to do anything to intentionally frighten myself, like watching horror movies or going to a haunted house, but I was perfectly fine going to school and hanging out with kids my own age.

I made it through all four years of high school with no traumatic events. Well, none that weren't part of the typical high school experience. Despite Duke's and Judge's best efforts, I even managed to go on a few dates.

After graduating from high school, I planned to attend college in Sugar Falls. Aunt Leigh was very supportive, Judge was skeptical, and Duke was totally against it, which didn't matter in the grand scheme of things because I was legally an adult and could do whatever I wanted.

During my first year of college, I lived in the

dorms on campus and became friends with several of the girls that lived on my floor. I did my best to fit in with them and have a normal college experience. And, for the most part, I did. I didn't care for the outrageous drunken frat parties, but I did join them when they went to clubs and other bars.

One particular night, my roommate, Courtney, was convinced her boyfriend was cheating on her and wanted to catch him in the act. Our suitemates joined us as we piled into Courtney's car and followed her boyfriend to a strip club. Instead of confronting him face-to-face, she wanted to do it by entering the wet t-shirt contest, but she didn't want to go up on stage alone. We all agreed to enter with her, and the next thing I knew, I was named the winner and handed five hundred dollars in cash.

As it turned out, Courtney's boyfriend, Brad, wasn't cheating on her. He worked at the club as a bouncer and didn't tell her because he didn't know how she would feel about it. She didn't care one bit, but he forbade her from entering any more strip club sponsored contests.

I, on the other hand, found the experience exhilarating. I continued to enter the contests and won first place every time. After my fifth win,

Courtney's boyfriend told me the manager of the club would like to speak with me in his office. I was hesitant to go, but Brad assured me he was a nice man and promised to wait right outside the office door for me.

Reluctantly, I followed Brad to an office in the back where he introduced me to the manager, Scott, who promptly offered me a job. After giving it some thought, I accepted the offer on a trial basis. The contests had done a lot to boost my confidence, and I thought performing on stage would, too. And that's how I came to be the headlining performer at The Booby Trap during my college years.

While it wasn't conventional by any means, working as an exotic dancer seemed to be just what I needed to bring me out of my shell. I fought hard over the years and managed to overcome most of my childhood traumas. I only had one major issue that I hadn't been able to completely overcome. Whenever men started yelling or fighting, I would curl into a ball or cower into myself and completely shut down as a flashback or panic attack consumed me. Thankfully, it never happened while I was performing. As the years passed, the time between flashbacks grew longer and longer, but they never completely went away, and I wasn't sure they ever would.

Carbon

I was getting angrier and angrier by the day. Fucking, fighting, and riding were no longer keeping the red haze just below the surface. After my family's unavenged murder, my only surviving sibling moved in with our grandmother, and I joined the Blackwings MC. My dad was a patched member, and I'd always planned to follow in his footsteps, but I never thought I would be doing it without him.

On the one-year anniversary of my family's murder, I lost my shit and nearly beat a man to death in a matter of seconds. Granted, he deserved a few hits, but nothing like the ass-whooping he received from me. If Phoenix and Badger hadn't been there, I would likely be spending my foreseeable future behind bars.

The next morning, Phoenix called me into his office and told me, in no uncertain terms, I needed to get myself under control, or I would lose my patch. Then, he said the words that ultimately saved me. "I think you should consider joining the military. Your patch will be here when you get back, and we'll look after your grandmother and sister."

I knew I needed help, so I took his advice and joined the Marines. He was right. The structure and discipline did help me learn some self-control. I also learned new skills, honed old ones, and found ways to channel my anger when I couldn't suppress it. Or so I thought.

As it turned out, I hadn't dealt with anything. I pushed it all to the back of my mind and managed to keep my anger locked down, only losing control a handful of times. Thankfully, my club was there to rein me in each time. Then, I lost another member of my family. Grandma's unexpected death was the catalyst that sent my bottled-up emotions into dangerous territory. I was drowning, but there was no lifeline in sight.

CHAPTER ONE

Carbon

I pushed the door open and let myself in, surprised by how quiet it was inside. "Mom? Dad?" I called out. Where was everyone? They knew I was coming over. Dad and I were going to look at a bike I was thinking about buying and Mom asked me to come over early to have breakfast with them. "Mason? Sage? Reese?" I yelled as I made my way upstairs. At the top of the stairs, I stopped dead in my tracks when I saw the blood...everywhere.

I shot up in bed, gasping for breath and covered in a light sheen of sweat. Even though I was expecting the memory to appear in my dreams, it still felt just as real as it did when it actually happened.

The memory of finding my family murdered in their home often haunted my sleep. At first, the hellacious scene played behind my closed lids every night. As time passed, the dreams didn't occur as often and finally dwindled down to only special dates like birthdays and anniversaries.

This particular one was the anniversary of my family's death, and I wanted to be alone. I just needed to get away from everything, and there wasn't any pressing club business to prevent me from riding out to clear my head. I usually spent the day with Reese and Grandma, but this was the first one since Grandma died and Reese said she wanted to spend it alone. I was hesitant to leave her, but she said she was probably going to stay in bed all day. So, when she was still in bed at lunchtime, I made sure she was okay; then, I got on my bike and rode.

I don't know how I ended up there. I was on my way back to Croftridge when the flashing sign on the side of the highway caught my eye, The Booby Trap. I chuckled to myself and decided to pull in for a drink. I'd been to my fair share of strip clubs over the years, and I suspected this one was no different than the others. I was wrong. Very, very wrong. This one was different, because it had *her*.

I had been sitting at a table for a half an hour or so, trying to decide if I was going to leave or order another beer when the next song that played made the decision for me. It was possibly the ultimate strip club cliché. I finished my beer and moved to stand as *Get Low* reverberated through the room. And there she was, center-stage, looking directly at me.

Immediately, I dropped my ass back into the chair and took in the magnificent creature dancing before me. I couldn't take my eyes off of her. She was breathtakingly beautiful, and she had an air of innocence about her. I wouldn't have thought that possible for a stripper, but there she was proving me wrong.

Her long auburn hair nearly touched the floor when she hung upside down from the pole. Her lightly tanned skin appeared to be flawless from what I could see, and I could see most of it. To my utter delight, her delectable tits seemed to be real. They bounced and jiggled while she danced, damn near lulling me into a trance better than any qualified hypnotist ever could.

I snapped out of my stupor when she finished her performance and quickly made a beeline for the stage to tip her—something I never did. I felt like a jackass. My hands were a little sweaty, and they most definitely were not shaking. I couldn't figure out what was wrong with me. I had never reacted this way to a female before.

When she stopped in front of me, I reached out and placed my hand on her waist. Her skin was soft and silky. I had to fight the urge to run my palm over her curves. With my other hand, I slowly slipped the bill in the very front of her G-string, dipping my fingers a tad lower than necessary. My fingertips met more smooth, silky skin and my cock twitched when I heard her soft gasp. I looked up as I pulled my hand back to see her plump lips forming a perfect 'O' and her dark blue, lust filled eyes staring down at me. I winked before turning and walking back to my table.

After finishing another beer, I made my way to the bar. I caught one of the girls working the floor and told her I wanted a private dance with the girl that was just on stage. She tried to get me to choose her for the dance instead, but I wasn't having it. I wanted the beauty from the stage, and no one else would do. She finally got the point and told me to wait at the bar.

A man in a suit came through the door I

assumed led to the back and approached me. He informed me that the girl went by the name of Pherra and she did not perform lap dances or private dances, she only danced on stage. That explained how she managed to be part sex goddess and part innocent angel. He offered me a discount on a private dance from one of the other girls. I didn't want that. I wanted Pherra, and I was going to have her.

"One thousand dollars," I offered.

His eyes widened. "For a private dance?"

"With Pherra. One thousand for a private dance with Pherra," I stated.

He sucked in a sharp breath and looked extremely uncomfortable. "I'm sorry, sir. Pherra doesn't do private dances. That was her choice, and I fully support it."

That was good to know, but it didn't help me out with my situation at all. "Two thousand. Go ask her," I barked.

He reluctantly turned and disappeared through the door. What the hell was I doing? I was about to drop two thousand dollars to have some bitch grind all over me and maybe finish me off with a sloppy blow job if I was lucky.

It was the date. It had to be. It was fucking with my head and causing me to act irrationally.

I was just about to turn and leave when the man returned.

"Follow me."

"She agreed?" I asked, hating the disbelief in my voice.

"She did. I feel the need to reiterate that this is not the norm for her; therefore, I will cover the rules with you myself. There is to be no contact other than what is initiated by her. You keep your hands by your sides and enjoy the entertainment you paid for. There are no 'carte blanche' services offered. Our rooms are monitored with a live audio feed. All she has to do is say one word and the dance is over, regardless of how much time you may have left. If she utters her safe word, a bouncer will escort you from the premises, and you will be permanently banned from the club. Any questions?"

"Nope," I said as he opened the door to a room in the back of the club. He closed the door, and I took a seat on the red leather sofa along the back wall. Thankfully, she didn't make me wait long. She came into the room, and my jaw dropped.

She was wearing a black leather bikini top, covered by a black leather vest, similar to a cut. On her lower half, she had on a very short black leather skirt. My eyes continued their descent down her body to land on black spiked heels that were the very definition of fuck me heels. I wasn't wearing my cut, so this had to be a damn lucky coincidence. Either way, she had my cock rock hard and ready to enjoy every second I had with her.

She reached out and pressed a button that turned on some music. Never saying a word, she stalked toward me and began to dance. She took her time and made it worth every penny. When she was down to just her G-string and shoes, I told her to put the leather vest back on. She looked a little confused, but did as I asked before climbing in my lap.

Her bare tits peeking out from behind that leather vest while she ground her warm pussy over my straining cock was almost too much for me to tolerate. Forcing my hands to stay at my sides was taking too much of my attention away from her. Man, she was gorgeous. Her hair, her eyes, her body, her scent, just everything about her was mesmerizing to me. I still hadn't heard her speak and she had me completely captivated.

When the next song started, she reeled me in even more. One of her hands slid down my arm and grasped my wrist. She slowly lifted my hand to her cheek for a brief moment before she slid my palm down her neck, over her collarbone, beneath the leather vest, and stopped when it was cupping her perfect tit. She did the same with my other hand, a little faster that time. Then, she started grinding against me like she was on a mission.

I sat there like a complete wanker with my hands on her tits, not moving them in any way. I didn't want to break any rules and risk not being able to see her again. She looked down at my hands, looked back at my face, and nodded. I tentatively squeezed one gently. Her lips parted slightly, and she nodded again. Assuming that was her permission, I started playing with her luscious offerings in earnest.

We weren't even having sex and I was in Heaven. I wanted to put my mouth on her so badly, but she hadn't indicated to me that I could. I hated not being in control. Hated. It. I was always in control, especially when I fucked bitches, but there I was, letting this girl call the shots.

A soft moan brought my attention back to the girl in my lap. She started moving a little faster, and a beautiful flush was making its way down her chest. Holy shit! She was about to come. I slid one hand to her hip and helped guide her movements. She moaned again, just barely a hint of sound leaving her lips. Then, she locked eyes with me, gasped, and started to come. It was as if lightning struck me, or maybe both of us. She kept her eyes locked on mine while she rode out her pleasure and simultaneously had me coming in my fucking pants like a pubescent boy.

We sat there in the same position, her in my lap, one hand on her hip, one hand still on her tit, while we caught our breath and came back to reality. She slowly climbed off my lap and took a step back. She smiled sweetly and brushed her lips against my cheek in the barest of touches. Before I could say a word or even respond in any way, she was gone. I wasn't worried about that though. I knew I would be back.

CHAPTER TWO

Harper

When I saw him in the club the next weekend, tingles of nervous anticipation shot through me. I tried to school my expression and continue with my performance as if I hadn't seen him. I didn't want him to know how much he affected me, how my body was aching to be pressed against his again. Keeping my eyes vaguely unfocused on the audience, I managed to make it through my performance without incident.

Walking to the edge of the stage to collect my tips, I dropped to my knees and started working my way from one end to the other. I wasn't sure if

I wanted him to be there waiting for me or not. It dawned on me at that moment how foolish I was being. Just because he came back, didn't mean he came back to see me. He could be looking for another girl to satisfy his needs.

That thought was crushing. I was ashamed to say that I thought about him almost constantly the entire week. And it wasn't just about the way he looked, though his sexy ass had been the star of every late-night fantasy since I first laid eyes on him. I was going to have to replace my vibrator in the very near future if I kept going at the same pace. There was just something about him that I was drawn to. Something in the way his pale green eyes tracked my every movement. The way his fingers dug into my skin while he rocked my hips over him. The way he expertly brought my body to climax with only the barest of touches. I even started calling him Boe—Best Orgasm Ever—in my mind.

I was suddenly embarrassed by my behavior, both during his private dance and the entire week after. Never had I fantasized about a client, let alone fooled around with one during a dance. Hell, as a rule, I didn't even do private dances. I was overcome with the need to bolt from the stage and hide in the dressing room until he left, but I couldn't, not just yet anyway.

Continuing to move down the stage, I collected my tips faster than usual. Typically, I tried to spend a few seconds with each man in hopes to lure them back to another performance. I had been working at The Booby Trap for a couple of years and had quite a few regulars. Even though I worked as a dancer for an entirely different reason, I made decent money from the tips alone, and I truly did enjoy my job, so I hoped I didn't offend any of my regulars, but I had to get off the stage before I had a panic attack in front of everyone.

My pace increased the closer I got to the end of the stage. When I finally reached the end, I looked up to find piercing green eyes staring back at me.

I gasped.

He smirked.

Then, he slid a bill into the very front of my G-string and, just like before, he dipped his fingers a little lower than he should to brush them against my bare skin. Tingles shot straight to my core and a shiver went up my spine. He winked and walked away, while I tried to remember how to stand.

Once I was on my feet, I left the stage and all

but sprinted to the dressing room, which was nothing more than a large room with vanities and racks of costumes. Collapsing into my chair, I dropped my face into my hands and shook my head. I couldn't have a panic attack, not at work. No one at the club knew about my past. No one had ever seen me have a meltdown and I desperately wanted to keep it that way.

I had been doing so well. I hadn't had a panic attack or flashback in months, maybe even a year, and I had long since stopped going to therapy. I desperately tried to recall some of the exercises I learned in school to work through an attack, but my mind was a jumbled mess of frantic thoughts, which caused even more feelings of panic to consume me.

A hand landed on my shoulder causing me to yelp and flinch away. "Pherra! Are you okay, honey?" another dancer named Ginger asked. Ginger was also dancing her way through college. I saw her on campus from time to time, but we didn't have any classes together. I didn't even know what her major was. It might seem wrong to some, but I tried very hard to keep my dancing life completely separate from the rest of my life. Ginger was a nice girl and someone I probably would have been friends with if she wasn't a part of my dancing life.

Taking in a large breath, I raised my head and answered, "I'm fine, Ginger. You just startled me is all."

She placed a hand on her cocked hip and appraised me. "Yeah, but were you okay before that?"

I nodded. "I'm good. Just tired. I had a tough week at school and I put in a lot of hours studying. I didn't get as much sleep as I should have."

"I bet Scott would let you go home early if you asked."

"I can't yet. I've got to be on stage two more times tonight because Cinnamon and Cherry both called in," I explained.

"Well, try to get some rest until you're up. I'll come get you a few minutes before if you want to try to take a power nap," she offered.

"Thanks, but I'll be all right. Only a few more hours left anyway."

I planned to stay backstage and out of sight until it was time for me to dance again. Rinse and repeat. After my last performance, I was going to hightail it out of there at warp speed. Then, I was going to go home and sleep. I was not going to think about the man from last week, who was currently in the main part of the club, and I was in no way, shape, or form going to touch on why his presence almost sent me spiraling into a panic attack.

"Pherra! You back here?" I heard Scott call from the front of the room.

My eyes darted wildly around the room, looking for some form of help or escape. Ginger answered him, "Don't see her. She might be in the bathroom. You need her?"

"Just remind her that she's up again in 10."

I exhaled with relief. I thought for sure he was going to tell me Boe wanted another private dance. Ginger strolled over. "You heard that, right?"

"Yeah, I did. Thanks for that."

She nodded and looked me over again. Hesitantly, she said, "You know you can talk to me if you need to. I know we're not exactly friends, but I'm a good listener if you ever need an ear." She extended her hand and patted my shoulder before strolling away. I would love to talk to her about my current issues, as soon as I figured out exactly what those issues were.

Several hours later, my two stage performances were done and I was ready to get the hell out of there. Despite my valiant efforts, my eyes landed on Boe multiple times throughout each performance. Part of me was hoping that he would leave and another part of me was thrilled that he was still there. However, all of me wanted out of the club before he had the chance to ask for another private session.

Pushing through the back door, I ran full speed ahead to my car and sped out of the parking lot with squealing wheels. I successfully avoided Boe and made it safely to my house, just as I wanted. So why did I feel like I missed out on something?

CHAPTER THREE

Carbon

She left the club before I could set up another dance with her. I could tell my presence unnerved her when she was on stage, but I had no idea why. I hadn't been able to get her out of my head all week. I craved more of her, which is why I drove a ridiculous distance to a strip club in a little college town instead of staying in Croftridge where there was a party at the clubhouse and guaranteed pussy.

I left The Booby Trap frustrated and pissed as hell. When I got back to the clubhouse, I was still pissed. Not in the mood for company or anyone's shit, I grabbed a bottle of whiskey and went straight to my room, alone. At some point before the bottom of the bottle, I decided that I would go back to see her, but I would have a plan so she couldn't get away before I'd had my time with her.

When I entered The Booby Trap, the first thing I did was find the manager. Lucky for me, he remembered me. I told him I wanted another private dance with Pherra and was willing to pay the same price as before. He informed me that she had another performance on stage before she would be free, if she agreed to the private dance. I knew she would. I had a feeling she enjoyed our time together as much as I did, which is why she did everything she could to avoid me the night before. Still, it would be foolish of her to turn down two grand for 30 minutes of her time.

I was almost giddy when the manager, I now knew as Scott, led me to the back hallway. "You remember the rules from before?" I nodded. "Good. She'll be in in a few minutes."

I sat in the same place as before and waited for her while my mind ran in overdrive. What would she wear? Would she speak to me? Would she let me touch her? Put my mouth on her? Would it end like last time? I was practically salivating when the door creaked open.

She waltzed in wearing a slutty schoolgirl outfit, complete with pigtails. I rubbed my hand over my crotch and groaned. I couldn't touch her unless she let me and I wanted nothing more than to bend her over my knees and turn her ass red until my palm hurt. She was pushing all of my buttons and she didn't even know it.

She turned on the music and started dancing, stripping off her top as she made her way to me. When she climbed into my lap, I was on edge. My hands were balled into fists at my side, every muscle in my body tensed. I was ready to push her off of me and leave before I did anything that wasn't welcome. Then, she laid her hands on my cheeks and stared into my eyes. Everything else disappeared and my body relaxed. She smiled and leaned forward, capturing the tip of my ear with her hot little mouth. She whispered, ever so softly, "Touch me."

No need to ask me twice. My hands came up and landed on her waist. She nodded her head in encouragement. I slid my palms up her torso and cupped her full mounds in my hands. That's when she started moving to the music again. I groaned. "You're a naughty little minx." She winked and continued her ministrations. "I want your tits in my mouth, baby. You gonna give that to me?"

She slid her hand up the back of my neck and wove her fingers through my hair. Using her hand, she guided my head to her chest. I greedily latched onto her nipple and sucked hard before gently biting at it with my teeth. She moaned and writhed in my lap. Oh yeah, she liked that. I played with one for a few minutes before giving the other one the same attention.

I was so caught up with her tantalizing tits that I lost all track of time. I had no idea how much time I had left with her, and I was going to be damn sure I made her come before the dance was over. I let her nipple go with a pop and brought my mouth to her neck. I didn't kiss or suck on her neck, just let my lips rest against her skin while I breathed her in. With my hands firmly gripping her waist, I guided the rhythm of her hips so she could get what she needed.

Both of her hands landed on my head, clutching fists full of my hair. She yanked my head back, dropped her forehead to mine, and stared into my eyes while she came and little gasps escaped her parted lips. It was by far the most erotic thing I had ever witnessed. While I watched in awe, she rode out her pleasure.

I was still admiring her when she put her

lips on my ear again. She ran her hand down my chest to the bulge in my jeans, rubbing me through my pants. I intended to stop her, to tell her that this wasn't about getting me off, but it felt so damn good I wanted to enjoy it for a few more seconds before I stopped her.

I don't know how she did it, but before I knew what was happening, she had my cock covered with a condom and sucked into her mouth. All. The. Fucking. Way. "Oh fuck," I groaned, leaning forward. "You don't have to," I gritted out. But I fucking wanted her to. Damn, her mouth felt good around my cock, even with it sheathed. And she didn't even bat an eyelash at my piercings.

I reached for her head and tried to ease her off of me gently. She subtly shook her head and moaned. The vibration had my balls ready to explode. She continued devouring my cock with her mind-blowing skills. "Baby, I'm gonna come," I warned. She kept going. I reached for her again, but she shook her head. "Last chance before I fuck that pretty throat of yours." She took me to the back of her throat and fucking swallowed my dick. That was it. Not even one thrust of my hips before I unloaded into the condom with a force that caused me to wonder if the tip was still intact.

When I recovered from the explosion, she was still on her knees, gently cleaning me. I cupped her cheek and tilted her head so she could look at me. "You didn't have to," I whispered.

"I know," she whispered back, her lips curved into a soft smile while a faint blush stained her cheeks. "I wanted to." She rose to her feet, kissed me on the cheek, and started gathering her clothes.

"Pherra," a voice called through the door. "Time!"

"I'll be right out, Scott." Her voice was soft and melodic, something I wanted to hear much more of. She turned back and glanced at my pants; I assumed to make sure I was back to rights. "Goodnight, Boe."

What did she call me? Before I could ask, she was gone.

***

I continued going to The Booby Trap once a week for several months. After the second private dance, she started charging me the standard fee; otherwise, I wouldn't have been able to keep coming back even if I wanted to.

After a few weeks, being the greedy man that

I was, I started scheduling her for two back to back private dances each week. Even that wasn't enough for me. I wanted more from her; I just wasn't exactly sure what more meant.

Each week, we went through much the same routine. She danced for me, got me off, I got her off, and then we did it again. We barely spoke. Most of the words we exchanged were whispered in the heat of the moment with her mouth at my ear or my lips pressed against her skin. I wondered if conversation was the more I was looking for. What would it be like to enjoy her mind for the allotted time instead of just her body? I wanted to know more about her, but I was afraid it would shatter the fantasy world I had been living in.

I couldn't explain it, but she did something to me. When I was with her, the rage that was always churning inside of me, ever so close to the surface, seemed to disappear. Her presence calmed me, but her touch quieted me. Every time she put me under her spell, I relished in it.

I didn't see it coming, so I wasn't prepared for the blow. I walked into The Booby Trap on a Friday night, anxious to see Pherra. I ordered a beer at the bar like I always did before grabbing a table. While I was at the bar, Scott appeared and slowly approached me with a grimace on his face. I studied him as he made his way to the end where I was standing, and I got the feeling I wasn't going to like whatever he had to say. Maintaining my mask of indifference, I lifted my chin. "What's up?"

He looked down at the bar and, with just a few words, shoved me back into a sea of rage. "Pherra doesn't work here anymore."

"What?" I croaked, trying to rein in my emotions.

"She graduated from college and gave her notice as soon as she found a job in her field." He reached into his pocket and slid a piece of paper across the bar to me. "She asked me to give this to you. Normally, we don't do things like this, but for her to ask," he paused and tapped the bar twice. "Well, you've been a good customer. It was the least I could do."

I continued to stare down at the folded paper long after Scott disappeared into the club. Ultimately, I took it with me, but I never bothered to open it and read her last message to me.

On the ride back to Croftridge, I realized I needed to let her go. I had formed some sort of unhealthy attachment to her. My anger hadn't calmed because she was something special. Hell,

I hadn't even fucked the girl. She just caused one hell of a distraction. Shaking my head, I focused on the road and the wind, determined to put all thoughts of Pherra out of my mind.

CHAPTER FOUR

Harper

Two months later

A phone ringing in the middle of the night was never good news. Never. When my phone rang at 4:30 am, I was already awake. I'd been waiting for the phone to ring, hoping for good news, but expecting the worst. I got what I expected. It was the hospital calling to tell me my brother was knocking on death's door and being taken into emergency surgery.

I called Phoenix, the president of the motorcycle club my brother belonged to, and told him what I knew. I was a mess and could barely get the words out. He offered to pick me up and take me to the hospital as I was in no shape to drive myself. I was grateful for his offer, but I didn't want to be around all of those big, burly men without my brother by my side. Over the years, I managed to overcome most of my issues, but when I was under a lot of stress or feeling vulnerable, it only took the slightest of triggers to send me into a tailspin. With that in mind, I agreed to allow Phoenix and my brother's best friend, Dash, to pick me up and take me to the hospital as long as Phoenix promised no one else would be there for the time being.

I don't remember much of the first few days at the hospital with Duke other than I never left his side during that time. My aunt and cousin tried numerous times to get me to take a break, just for a few hours to get some rest, but I refused. He had been attacked resulting in a skull fracture, brain trauma, and the associated complications from being stabbed eight times. EIGHT! I was a hot mess, frequently crying, getting very little sleep, and barely eating.

Finally, after Duke had been moved out of ICU, Phoenix put his foot down and ordered me to take a break from the hospital. He reminded me I could stay in Duke's room at the clubhouse where he promised I would be safe. He even offered to have one of his officers stand guard at the door while I slept. He wasn't giving me much of a choice, but I didn't try to argue with him. I knew I wouldn't be able to keep going much longer in my current state and I needed to be able to take care of Duke when he woke up. My only concern was that I didn't want Duke to be alone, especially if he woke up when I wasn't there. He promised to have someone stay by Duke's side while I was gone.

He must have already had his plan laid out because not even five minutes passed before a beautiful girl, who appeared to be a few years younger than me, came through the door with a grief-stricken face. "Reese, this is Harper, Duke's sister. Harper, this is Reese, Carbon's sister," Phoenix said. I remembered hearing Duke talk about Carbon and knew he was a member of the club, though I'd never met him.

"Hi, Harper. I'm so sorry about your brother. Is there anything I can do to help?" Reese asked. I wasn't sure if she was being polite or if she genuinely wanted to help, but I accepted her offer anyway.

"Actually, there is something you could do for me. Phoenix said you might be willing to stay with Duke while I go to the clubhouse for a shower and a few hours of sleep. I'm exhausted and I stink, but I don't want him to wake up with no one here. Would that be okay?"

Her words didn't match her expression. "That's fine with me as long as it's okay with Phoenix."

"That's fine, just make sure you stay in the room. You can ride back to the clubhouse with whoever brings Harper back. I'm going to walk Harper down and then I have a few errands to run," Phoenix said.

I assumed Phoenix was going to take me back to the clubhouse. He knew a little about my past and knew I wasn't comfortable around men I didn't know. So, when he told me Reese's brother was driving me back to the clubhouse, I started shaking my head in protest. "Harper, do you trust me?"

"Yes," I said, my voice shaky.

"I would never do anything to hurt you, and I would never knowingly put you in harm's way. The man giving you a ride back to the clubhouse is a man I trust with my life. Your brother trusts him with his life. He's one of my officers. He will keep you safe and stand guard outside Duke's door while you get some rest. I promise," he told me.

I reluctantly agreed and allowed him to lead me to the waiting car. When Phoenix opened the door, I slid into the front seat and froze. Sitting in the driver's seat of a beautiful black Mustang was none other than Boe himself. He didn't turn his head to look at me, just kept his eyes on the road. I settled into the seat and fastened my seatbelt while Phoenix thanked him for giving me a ride and reminded him to post up outside my door. He responded with, "No problem," and then we were moving.

He remained silent the entire way to the clubhouse. I tried to appear calm, but my insides were in complete turmoil. Boe's a member of my brother's motorcycle club. No, he's not just a member, Phoenix said he was an officer. Why didn't he wear a cut like my brother did? And why's he not talking? Did he not recognize me? I did look like shit. My hair was tucked up into a baseball cap, sunglasses covered my eyes, and I was wearing a very unflattering hoodie paired with ratty yoga pants. It was then I realized I didn't want him to recognize me.

We arrived at the clubhouse and he silently led me to what I assumed was my brother's room. I entered and closed the door without a word. It was rude not to at least thank him, but I didn't want him to recognize my voice if he hadn't figured out who I was already. I knew I wouldn't be able to hide from him forever, but I couldn't handle dealing with him on top of everything else that was going on.

After taking a long shower, I climbed into my brother's bed and prayed the sheets were clean. Despite being in a biker clubhouse filled with overgrown men, none of which were my brother, I fell asleep almost immediately. And it had nothing to do with the fact that it was Boe guarding my door. Nope, nothing at all. Unfortunately, it wasn't a dreamless sleep. My dreams featured Boe, aka Carbon, doing all sorts of filthy things to me.

I woke suddenly, covered in a light sheen of sweat and throbbing between my legs. The loud knock on the door startled me, and I realized that must have been what woke me. "Just a second," I called out.

I straightened my clothes and ran my hands over my hair before I opened the door. There he was, standing in the doorway, holding a plate of food. "Thought you might be hungry," he said and thrust the plate at me.

I took the plate and continued to stare at him, my mouth agape. I needed to say something, but I couldn't make my mouth work. "Eat and do whatever you need to do to be ready in an hour. Got shit to do so I'm taking you back to the hospital." He pulled the door closed and left me standing there wondering what in the hell was going on. Surely, he recognized me. He had to. My hair was a different color, but I didn't look that different.

He knocked on the door exactly one hour later. I silently followed him to the same car and climbed in. After 10 minutes of uncomfortable silence, I couldn't take it anymore. "Do you not recognize me?" I asked, my voice sounding shriller than I intended.

He kept his eyes on the road. "I do."

"You don't have anything to say?"

"If I did, I would've said it."

What an asshole! I couldn't believe how cold he was being. This man, Carbon, was nothing like the man I knew as Boe. The one I spent many Friday nights and countless fantasies with. Tears started to form in my eyes, but I would not let them fall, not in front of him.

When we pulled up to the hospital, I got out of his car as fast as I could and ran inside. I was barely holding it together. I dealt with his rejection reasonably well when I thought I would never see him again. To see him again and have him completely dismiss me, that hurt more than I ever could've imagined.

CHAPTER FIVE

Carbon

Fuck me. My Pherra was really Duke's little sister Harper. And she was in Croftridge. And I was being a complete dick to her. It was my go-to response when I was caught off guard or didn't want to expose my true feelings.

I hadn't recognized her at first. She was all covered up in baggy clothes and a baseball cap. I had never met Harper before, at least I thought I hadn't, but I'd heard about her over the years. According to Duke, she was shy and timid due to something that happened to her when they were younger. Either he didn't know her as well as he thought he did or she had overcome her issues.

The girl I knew as Pherra was by no means timid.

When I brought Harper something to eat and a blonde-headed Pherra opened the door, I thought I was hallucinating. She had crossed my mind many times since the last time I saw her. I didn't want to admit it, but I had missed her, a lot. The world I lived in was dark most of the time, and she was a bright spot in the darkness.

After I dropped her off at the hospital, I went back to the clubhouse and straight to my room. Phoenix needed me to do some stuff for him, but that shit would have to wait. Reaching into my nightstand, I pulled out the note from Pherra, the one the manager at The Booby Trap gave me. Yeah, I kept it. No, I never read it.

I unfolded the piece of paper and instantly felt like the biggest dumbass.

Boe,

I graduated with my degree a few weeks ago and was recently offered a job in my field, so my days at The Booby Trap are over. I couldn't bring myself to say goodbye to you after our last night together. I have enjoyed our times together more than you know. I want to see you again, outside of the club. If you feel the same, call me.

Pherra

At the bottom, she included her phone number, complete with a little heart.

Motherfucker! I'd been hung up on this girl for months, and I could've fucking had her if I'd just opened the damn note. I quickly saved her number in my phone and put the folded paper back in my drawer. I had things to do, but when I was finished, I was making it a point to talk to her.

***

As my luck would have it, I didn't get a chance to call or talk to her until a week later. I didn't even know if she was still in Croftridge. Shit blew up with the club that occupied my every waking moment. I was the Enforcer for Blackwings, and I was damn good at my job. I loved it, but for the first time in my life, I was getting frustrated with my role in the club because it was getting in the way of my personal life.

When things came to a head with Phoenix and his daughter, I was ass-deep in enforcing. I did some of my best work to Octavius and his associates. As far as I was concerned, there was nothing better than spending the night fucking myself into a coma after an evening of torturing, and that's exactly what I intended to do.

I pulled my phone out of my pocket and dialed Harper as I walked to my bike. She answered on the second ring, her sweet voice making my dick hard.

"It's Carbon. You still in Croftridge?"

"No, I left this morning."

"I need to see you. Tonight. Text your address," I ordered.

"Did something happen to Duke?"

"No. This has nothing to do with him."

"Is everything okay?" she asked.

"I didn't read your note until just now," I confessed.

"Why?"

"Does it matter?"

"I guess not."

"You gonna let me fuck you?"

She coughed and cleared her throat. "W-what?"

"I want to fuck you when I get there. Hard. Several times. If you don't want that, you tell me now."

I heard her intake of breath before she said the word I desperately needed to hear, "Okay."

"Be ready for me, baby," I said, softening my voice slightly.

She sent her address seconds after I disconnected the call. I climbed on my bike and rode like a madman to Sugar Falls.

She opened her front door when she heard me pull into her driveway. She was wearing a pair of short cutoff shorts and a thin white tank top that was obviously a size too small. Still, she was just as beautiful as she was when she was all done up in her dancing costumes. I stalked toward her hoping like hell she could handle me.

When I reached her, I put both hands on her ass and hoisted her up, never breaking my stride. Covering her mouth with mine, I stepped inside and kicked the door closed with my boot. As her soft lips consumed mine, returning my brutal kiss, I regretted not breaking the rules and kissing her at the club.

I knew nothing about her house, and I didn't have the willpower to pull my mouth from hers and ask where her bedroom was. I didn't need a bed anyway. Turning, I pressed her back up against the front door and shoved my thigh between her legs to keep her in place while I pushed her shirt up above her bra. I savagely yanked her bra down, causing her perfect tits to spill over the cups. Using one hand, I pinched and pulled her nipple while I set to work on removing her shorts with my other hand.

"Carbon," she moaned.

"Chase," I corrected. "My name's Chase."

Sliding an arm around her waist to hold her up, I let her feet dangle and yanked her shorts and panties off. They hit the floor, and her legs were back around my waist in an instant.

I pulled my mouth from hers and said, "I'm clean. Tell me you are and you're on the pill." She nodded rapidly and dove back for my lips. I unzipped my jeans, freed my cock, and paused. "You ready for me?"

She captured my lip ring between her teeth and gave it a little tug. "Fuck, yes." With that, I slammed into her all the way to the hilt.

Bliss. Pure and total bliss. My inner turmoil quieted, and all that existed was me and her. Me in her. I swallowed her moans and relentlessly pounded into her tight little pussy. Pulling my mouth from her, I locked eyes with her as I fucked her hard and dirty. "You gotta come, baby," I grunted. "Now, Harper. I want to feel you squeezing my cock. Fucking come all over me."

She clamped down on me to the point it

almost hurt. She screamed my name as she pulsed around me. "Chase! Oh, oh, don't stop. Please. Fuck me harder." I wasn't going easy on her by any means, but I couldn't refuse a request such as that. I gave it to her harder and faster, shoving myself impossibly deeper inside of her. She screamed. I came, my vision blurring and my knees weakening.

We ended up on the floor, still connected, me just as hard as I was before I filled her full of my come. She looked at me with glazed over eyes and smiled. I cupped her face in my hands and slowly brought my lips to hers as I started to move my hips again. "Not done yet," I murmured against her lips. "You okay?"

"Please, Chase," she whimpered.

"Please what, baby?" I wasn't sure if she was asking for more or asking me to stop. If she was asking me to stop, I would, but it wouldn't be easy. I needed this, and I needed it from her. I'd known it before, but I hadn't wanted to acknowledge it and, to be honest, I still didn't. Regardless, no other woman would ever compare to Harper Jackson.

"More. I want more, Chase," she pleaded before latching onto my lip ring with her greedy little mouth.

I thrust my hips forward, causing her to slide across the floor. I wasn't a gentle man, never had been and never would be. I liked to fuck hard and rough, and I needed to be in control. At The Booby Trap, I had to let her be in charge if I wanted to see her; but we weren't at the club anymore, and I had some time to make up for.

I slid my arms underneath her and grasped her by her shoulders to keep her in place while I hammered into her pussy on the floor right inside her front door. She bit down on the tendon between my neck and shoulder, sending a jolt of pleasure and pain down my spine.

I pulled out and roughly flipped her over. Smacking her bare ass, I ordered, "Hands and knees." She immediately complied, raising her pert little ass for the taking. My hands landed on her firm cheeks with a smack to hold her in place while I plunged back inside her.

"Harper," I groaned. "Fuck, you feel good, baby. Play with that pussy for me. Make yourself come." She balanced on one hand and stuck the other between her legs. When I thrust forward, her little fingers would caress my balls in the barest of touches. She was going to be the death of me.

I wrapped one hand around her neck and

lightly squeezed, watching for any signs of distress from her. When I didn't see any, I slightly increased the pressure and said, "You're being a bad girl. I told you to play with that pussy, not my balls. What do you think I should do about that?" I growled, letting her have some of my weight against her back.

She moaned and mumbled, but nothing coherent came out of her mouth. "Answer me, Harper," I barked, stilling my hips.

"Oh, oh, Chase. Ah, p-p-punish me," she managed to get out between moans. It was probably a good thing that she couldn't see the wicked grin that took over my face at her words.

"Gladly," I growled. I increased the pressure around her neck, careful not to cut off her air supply, slapped her ass two more times, and pressed the pad of my thumb against her rear entrance.

She squealed and jolted, causing the tip of my thumb to enter her. I hadn't meant to do anything other than apply a little pressure, but judging by the way her pussy drenched my cock, she liked it, so I left it there. After a dozen or so thrusts of my hips, I placed my lips against the shell of her ear and asked, "Do you want to come, naughty girl?"

"Please. Please, Chase."

"You've got 10 seconds to come, or I'm shoving my cock in your tight little ass and fucking it until I've had my fill," I growled.

That did it. She was pulsing around me and pulling me over the edge with her.

She.

Was.

Perfect.

I released her neck, and she slid down to her belly underneath me. Lowering myself with her, I rolled to the side and pulled her to me. We laid there until we caught our breath. Then, I rose to my knees, scooped her into my arms, and stood. "Where's your room?"

CHAPTER SIX

Harper

He kept me up all night fucking me. Several times I wondered if he had taken one of those erectile dysfunction pills. He would come and be just as hard as he was when we started. I'd never seen anything like it. Over and over he fucked me, never seeming to get enough. My pussy was beyond sore and in need of a vacation, but I couldn't bring myself to tell him to stop. I hadn't been able to stop thinking about him since I met him and nothing, absolutely nothing, was going to interfere with our time together.

When the sun began to light the sky, he

told me he had to get back to the club. I was disappointed, but I knew from things Duke and Judge had said, when the club needed them, they had to go. I kissed him goodbye at the door and watched him ride away, wondering when or if I would hear from him again.

I didn't have to wonder long. He sent me a text message later that night.

Chase: Don't make plans Friday night.

Harper: I might consider it if you asked nicely.

Chase: Do you want me to fuck your sweet pussy Friday night?

I couldn't think of a decent response. The man had a way of getting me so flustered I couldn't formulate anything beyond, "Yes, Chase. Whatever you want."

Chase: You know you do. I know you do. Say yes.

I huffed and sent my reply.

Harper: Yes

I didn't hear from him again until he was knocking on my front door Friday night. That became our pattern. Text, meet, fuck for hours, rinse and repeat. We did very little talking. One of the only conversations we had occurred during his second visit to my house, and it was regarding our relationship status and other people. We both agreed that there would be no one else while we were fucking each other, but neither of us wanted to be in a relationship; therefore, there was no reason to tell my brother anything. And that was how I came to be Chase's secret fuck buddy.

It had been just over a year of our unique relationship when I learned that my brother had a baby he failed to tell me about with none other than Chase's little sister. Aunt Leigh called to check in with me and mentioned the baby. I was beyond pissed at Duke, Reese, and Chase for keeping it from me. In a fit of anger, I packed a bag and drove my ass to Croftridge to let the three of them know exactly how I felt.

When I got there, I wished I had let Aunt Leigh explain more about the circumstances instead of hanging up on her like I did. The situation with Duke and Reese and their son wasn't anything like what I had assumed. Reese was quick to tell me my brother didn't know anything about his son until six weeks ago. She was adamant that I talk to Duke about it instead of her, so that's what I did. I also had words for Chase as well.

Reese arranged a babysitter for James, and Ember drove us to the clubhouse. She mentioned they would likely be having a party, but I wasn't sure what to expect. As my anger faded, my nerves escalated. I was ready to back out and go back to Sugar Falls by the time we pulled into the lot.

We walked into the main room to find Duke on a sofa, a whore in his lap, and Chase seated beside him, a whore rubbing his arm as she stuck her little tits in his face. "There's your brother," Reese snapped and stormed off down one of the hallways.

Duke shoved the girl off his lap, causing her to land awkwardly in the floor. He looked between me and the hallway, unsure of what to do. I made that choice for him. "Want to tell me why you have a son you didn't tell me about?" I yelled. Yes, yelled, in the middle of a biker clubhouse. I was pissed. And hurt.

"Harper, I...shit. Can we talk about this later? I need to go find Reese."

"No, we can't talk about it later! It is later as far as I'm concerned. Don't worry; I'll tell her I saw you push the whore off your lap." My eyes shot to Chase, who appeared to be whore-free for the moment. "I'm sure it didn't feel good to walk in and see a known whore crawling all over her man." At least I had seen Chase swatting the skank's hands away.

Duke sighed, and his shoulders dropped in defeat. "I'm not her man, but I'm trying to be," he said quietly and reached to pull me into a hug. "I don't know what to do, Harpie."

"I can't help you if I don't know what's going on."

He led me to the corner of the bar and gestured for me to have a seat on one of the barstools. He looked so lost and scared. "Why didn't you tell me about my nephew?"

"I didn't find out about him until six weeks ago, but I didn't call you right away because I knew you would want to come see him and it wasn't safe. It still isn't safe."

"Why isn't it safe?" I asked, trying to keep my composure.

"I can't tell you the specifics, but I found out about James when Reese didn't show up to pick him up from daycare. That was because someone intentionally rammed her car and pushed it off the side of a mountain with her inside. She's also been receiving some threatening letters. Anyway, I was going to tell you about James as soon as we got to the bottom of everything."

"Duke, if you'd explained the danger to me and asked me to wait until it was safe to visit, I would have waited," I explained.

"I'm sorry, sis. I was just trying to keep you safe."

"Am I in danger just being here?" I asked.

"Honestly, I don't know. Things have been—"

Duke stopped short when a deep voice shouted, "Carbon! Come quick!"

Chase was on his feet and down the hall in a nanosecond. "Reese!" he bellowed, sounding frantic.

Duke was on the move, right on Chase's heels, and I was close behind Duke.

"What the fuck did you do to her?" Chase yelled.

Ember, Dash, and Phoenix came down the hall and walked right into the room with everyone else while I waited outside the door. I didn't want to be trapped in the small room with everyone screaming and yelling the way they were.

I was quietly tiptoeing away from the door, trying to work my way down the hall without being noticed when Phoenix's voice boomed through the entire clubhouse. "ENOUGH! Everybody out of this room. Right the fuck now!"

And that was it for me. My back hit the wall, and I inched down it until I found a corner to curl into. My hands came up to cover my ears, and I started going through the multiplication tables in my head in a vain attempt to block out everything going on around me.

Familiar hands landed on my shoulders and pulled me against him, cocooning me in the safety of his muscular body. I inhaled deeply, his scent helping to calm me. Chase.

"You're okay, baby," he whispered against my ear. "No one here will ever hurt you. I promise. Just breathe."

I knew no one at the clubhouse would hurt me, especially Phoenix, but all it took was a stressful situation, a man yelling, and the threat of violence to send me into a tailspin. I didn't know how much, if any, Chase knew about my past, but it wasn't something I wanted to discuss with him, though I probably needed to.

"Come on; I'll take you to my room."

He scooped me into his arms and carried me to his room at the clubhouse. As soon as the door closed, he placed me on my feet, and I started babbling. "I didn't know we were coming here tonight. I mean, I did, but not until I got to the farm. I'm not stalking you or anything. I just found out about the baby, James, and wanted to see him. I was so pissed. I got in my car and drove straight to Croftridge without telling anyone. Me showing up here has nothing to do with you. I swear it."

Chase was leaning against the door, smirking at me. "You done?"

"No!" I shouted, my anger returning. "Why didn't you tell me about the baby?"

His smirk vanished, and he pinned me with his intense green eyes. "Probably the same reason you didn't tell me your brother was married."

"Why would I tell you my brother was married? As far as I knew, it had nothing to do with you. I didn't know he was screwing your sister. You, however, knew your sister had a child with my brother! A child she kept from him. And that does have something to do with me."

"I found out about the baby when Duke did."

"So? You still didn't tell me."

"I'm not trying to be an asshole here, but it isn't exactly like we did a lot of talking," he said carefully.

"You're right. We just fuck. Silly me. Well, now that we have that cleared up and you know I'm not here for you, I'll be on my way," I said and reached for the doorknob.

His hand landed on the door, and his big body caged me in. "Now, are you done?"

I nodded but didn't turn to face him. "Good. Didn't think you were here for me, but let's get one thing straight right now. I'm damn glad you are here."

I felt my cheeks heat. "Really?"

"Yeah, baby, really. Now get your ass on that bed so I can show you."

CHAPTER SEVEN

Harper

Chase and I had just finished redressing when someone started banging on the door. "Carbon! We gotta ride, brother. Now!"

"Stay in here until you hear the bikes pull out, then go to your brother's room and wait there until we get back," he said and took in my wide, panicked eyes. "At least two brothers will be here with you, Ember, and Reese. You'll be okay. I gotta go, baby." With that, he gave me a hard kiss and left me standing in his room with no clue as to what was happening.

When I heard the roar of the bikes fade into

the distance, I peeked into the hallway to see if the coast was clear. The moment I stepped out of Chase's room, I heard Phoenix call out my name seconds before rounding the corner with Ember trailing behind him.

"Hi," I said dumbly. "Uh, I was trying to find Duke's room."

"I need you to come with us first, sweetheart," he said, never breaking his stride. He looked tense while Ember looked scared, neither of which sat well with me. Ember took my hand and pulled me along with her as we followed her father on his mission.

He came to a stop when he found Reese putting a load of clothes in the washing machine. She turned around, and the look of utter devastation on her face had tears pricking the backs of my eyes. "What happened?" she croaked, then screamed, "Tell me!! Duke? Carbon? Who is it?"

I also wanted to know what was going on, but never in a million years would I have expected the words that came out of Phoenix's mouth. "It's James."

The screaming wail that erupted from Reese as she collapsed to the floor is a sound I hoped to never hear again, from anyone. My own chest ached as I took a staggering step back. Ember's arms surrounded me and held me steady as Phoenix scooped Reese off the floor.

"It'll be okay," she whispered.

We followed Phoenix as he carried Reese first to Chase's room, then to Duke's. He placed her on my brother's bed and began explaining the details of my nephew's kidnapping.

Kidnapped.

My nephew had been kidnapped.

I walked as fast as my legs would go on my way home from school. Dad was sick, and I needed to get back to take care of him. He'd been ill since we lost Mom a few months ago.

I watched the lines and the cracks in the sidewalk pass as I made my way home. I wasn't paying attention. I should have been paying attention.

The dark cloth that covered my head came out of nowhere. One second, I was watching my feet move along the sidewalk, and the next second everything was black as unforgiving hands lifted my body from the ground.

I cried out in pain when I landed on something hard. Someone wrapped something tight and sticky around my wrists and ankles. I tried to scream for help, but they quickly covered my mouth with something that felt like tape. What was happening to me?

Tears ran down my face as I tried desperately to plead for help or mercy through the substance holding my lips together.

"Do as I say and I won't hurt you," a man said.

I nodded my head. I didn't want him to hurt me, so I would do whatever he said.

"Good girl. You're going to a new home with a new family. And your name is now Vanessa."

"Harper, please answer me," Ember cried.

I blinked a few times, and the room came back into focus. I was sitting on the floor of my brother's room hugging my knees with Ember crouched in front of me.

"James?" I asked.

She smiled and nodded. "They got him. He's okay, and they're on their way back."

I nodded and exhaled a sigh of relief as more tears slid down my cheeks. Tilting my head toward the sky, I whispered, "Thank you. Thank you. Thank you."

Ember cleared her throat. "Harper, what just—"

I cut her off. "I don't want to talk about it. James is okay, and that's all that matters right now."

She nodded, rose to her feet, and extended her hand to help me up. "Let's go out to the common room with Dad and Reese and wait for them to get back."

After James's kidnapping, Duke was insistent upon me staying in Croftridge for an extended visit. I called work and told them I needed to take time off due to a family emergency. Luckily, I had enough vacation time available and agreed to stay for two weeks. It wasn't a hardship as far as I was concerned. I wanted to spend time with my brother and my new nephew. Spending time with Chase was an added bonus.

I didn't know how to act around him when we were around other people. I didn't particularly want anyone in the club to know about our relationship, or lack thereof, but I didn't want to completely ignore him either. It's not like I could. All the man had to do was enter the same room as me and my attention was solely on him, complete with wet panties and all.

During the first week of my stay, everyone was so wrapped up in the situation with Duke and Reese no one paid any attention to Chase and I. At least, I was pretty sure they didn't. During the day, I spent time with James, and usually

Reese as she was hesitant to leave his side after he was taken. Duke usually joined us for dinner before I went to my room at the farm and waited for Chase to text me. Then, just like a teenager, I would sneak out and spend the better part of the night fucking him in random locations around the farm property. I was exhausted most of the time, but it was so worth it.

The second week of my stay was much more eventful, starting when Reese asked me to help her sneak into the basement of the clubhouse to question the woman responsible for taking James. When my eyes landed on Melissa Massengill, anger like never before consumed me. This bitch had bullied me all through elementary school, had a ridiculous obsession with my brother, and, apparently, had just kidnapped his son.

I snapped. Unethical as it may have been, I used every bit of knowledge I had about human psychology against her and had her spewing her evil plans to us in minutes. The girl was certifiably insane. If I hadn't known it before, I would have the moment she started chanting about Nemo coming.

I looked to Reese, wondering if she knew what Melissa meant, when another voice spoke, scaring the shit out of both of us. "I can't take this anymore. Reverse it so she'll shut up. That's all you need to do!"

"Where in the fuck did that come from?" I whispered.

Reese asked who he was as we clung to each other and inched closer to the cell. When the man identified himself as Octavius Jones, Reese stumbled and fell to the floor, taking me down with her.

"We need to get out of here, Harper. Now!"

"Okay, okay. Let's go," I agreed and helped her to her feet.

Once she was up, we both ran to the stairs and all the way up only to be stopped by Chase, Duke, and Phoenix. And they looked pissed.

Reese pushed past them, telling them she would puke all over them if they didn't move. I wasn't sure if she was serious, but I followed her nonetheless. I would much rather deal with vomit than the three angry men staring at us.

They followed us to Duke's room and immediately began questioning us the moment Reese stepped out of the bathroom. We told them everything that happened. Then, Reese and Chase declared that Nemo was Omen which resulted in Phoenix calling the guys into Church.

All the while, I was wondering who in the hell Octavius and Omen were.

Later that night, I was in my room at the farm, when a knock at the door startled me. Opening the door, I found Chase standing on the other side, and he didn't look happy.

"What the fuck, Harper? What were you thinking going down to the basement with Reese?"

"Well, hello to you, too. Please, come in."

"Cut the shit. You could've been hurt, and you're damn lucky Phoenix didn't ban you from the club."

"Would you have preferred I let your sister go down there alone? Because I'm here to tell you, she was going whether I went with her or not."

He frowned and took a seat on the bed. "I appreciate you looking out for her, but I'd rather neither of you put yourselves in danger."

"Understood."

His head shot up. "Yeah?"

"Yes, I understand. I'm not making any promises, but, hopefully, something like this won't be an issue again."

"It better not be," he said seriously.

After a few beats of silence, his eyes flickered over me from head to toe, and the look on his face changed to one I was very familiar with. "Come here."

***

The next day, Duke picked me up first thing in the morning and drove me to the clubhouse. I expected him to use the time to give me a good lecture about what happened in the basement. To my surprise, that wasn't what he wanted to talk to me about.

"Are you doing okay?" he asked, his voice full of concern.

"Yeah, I'm fine. Why are you asking?" It was the tone of his voice that let me know his question had a far deeper meaning.

He shifted in his seat and blew out a breath. "My son was kidnapped, and Melissa is here. This whole mess has to be bringing up bad memories for you. I'm a shit for not asking about it sooner."

I placed my hand on his shoulder to reassure him. "Duke, it's okay. You've been focused on your son, as you should be. I'm not going to lie and tell you it hasn't affected me, because it has, but I can honestly tell you that I'm okay."

"Would you tell me if you weren't?"

"Yes, I would. I promise."

"Good." He was silent for a few moments before adding, "Shannon is coming to the clubhouse today. You can stay in my room if you don't want to see her."

"I never had a problem with Shannon. I mean, I didn't really know her," I explained.

"Okay, but if it gets to be too much for you, my room will be available for you."

"Thanks, Dukie," I said and snickered at my use of the nickname I knew he hated.

Shannon arrived with the president of another motorcycle club. Not long after the introductions were made, the men went into Church leaving us girls sitting awkwardly in the common room. Shannon sat off to the side quietly sipping her water while Reese left the room to change James's diaper.

I was trying to come up with something to say to Shannon when we heard a loud commotion followed by Chase's enraged voice shouting, "You mean your piece of shit offspring killed my family?" The doors to Church flew open, and my brother came out frantically searching for Reese.

While Shannon told him where Reese had gone, I got to my feet and walked into a room I had no business entering, but I could clearly see

Chase on his knees struggling against Phoenix's hold and knew he needed help.

Phoenix was yelling for me to stay back, but I kept going until I was directly in front of Chase. He stopped fighting and looked up at me with so much anger and pain in his green eyes. I cupped his cheeks in my hands and put my mouth to his ear. "You can't do this right now, big guy," I whispered. "Your family needs you to be strong and stay calm."

His big body relaxed, and his head dropped to his chest. I so badly wanted to pull him into my arms and comfort him, but I couldn't. Instead, I whispered, "You can use my body to work through it later." Then, I patted his shoulder and let him know I would be right outside the door if he needed me. Without making eye contact with anyone else in the room, I turned on my heels and planted my ass in a chair right outside the room, just like I promised.

The next thing I knew, I was being shuffled into a panic room with Reese, James, Shannon, and Ember while the guys went off to deal with club business. Several hours later we were being driven to the hospital in Devil Springs with no idea what awaited us.

When Byte said Chase had been hit, I fell to

the floor with Shannon before the rest of his words registered. It wasn't serious. Still, all I could do was look to Reese with pleading eyes and hope she understood my question. "Where is Duke?" she demanded.

Thankfully, my brother wasn't injured. Once I knew he was okay, I tried to focus on Shannon. Her man wasn't okay and might not make it from what I understood.

When Chase walked into the waiting room with a large bandage on his arm and locked eyes with me, I felt my entire body sigh in relief. He winked and turned his attention back to the room.

At some point, Chase was called out into the hall with my brother and Phoenix. Then, Duke was calling for Reese, and I just knew it was because of Chase. When Duke and Reese returned without Chase, it was all I could do to remain in my seat. I watched the doorway, waiting for him to return, but he never did.

Duke placed his hand on my shoulder. "Do you want to stay at the Devil Springs clubhouse tonight or do you want to stay at Aunt Leigh's?"

"Are you and Judge going to be at the clubhouse?" I asked.

"Yes, we are. Reese will be there, as well as

Ember and Dash. And you know Aunt Leigh will stay there, too, if you ask her."

"Okay, I'll stay at the clubhouse." I really would have preferred to stay at the house that was my home for eight years of my life, but I was hoping I would be able to see Chase at some point if I stayed at the clubhouse.

Once I was settled in my designated room, I locked the door and headed for the shower. Even though I was exhausted, there was no way I would be able to sleep knowing I was covered in hospital germs.

I found Chase on my bed, propped up against the headboard when I emerged from the shower. Dropping my towel, I went straight for him, completely forgetting that I was naked and still somewhat wet. I straddled his waist and brought my lips to his. "I've been so worried about you," I confessed. "Are you okay?"

"Yeah, I am now," he whispered against my lips and deepened the kiss.

He groaned, and I immediately froze. "Is it your arm?" I asked, worried that I had inadvertently hurt him.

"No, baby, it's my cock. You made him a promise earlier, and he's ready for you to make good on it."

I giggled. "And what exactly did I promise your cock?"

"That he could use your body to work through his troubles," he said as his lips slid down my neck. "Undo my jeans, Harper."

I could feel my body preparing for him. I loved it when he took charge in the bedroom, though I wasn't sure how much he could do with his injured arm.

"Now, Harper," he ordered with a light slap to my ass. I scooted back and set to work on getting his jeans open. Once I had him free, I wrapped my hand around his shaft and gently ran my fingers over the barbells that lined the underside of him.

"Stop," he commanded, and my hand instantly stilled. "Raise up on your knees."

I did and impatiently waited for the next instruction.

"Are you ready for me?" At my nod, he added, "Show me."

I kept my eyes locked with his as my hand trailed down my stomach to the apex of my thighs. I reached between my legs and slowly slid one finger inside myself. I moved it in and out a few times before holding it up for him to see.

He brought my finger to his mouth and licked it clean. "Fuck me, Harper," he growled.

No need to tell me twice. I grabbed ahold of his cock, positioned it at my entrance, and slid down his shaft. I started rocking my hips slowly and gradually increased my pace until I was bouncing up and down and our skin was loudly slapping together with each fall of my hips.

His good hand firmly gripped my hip as he ordered through gritted teeth, "Come."

And I did, completely forgetting to muffle my screams of ecstasy, as did Chase when he found his release seconds after mine.

I collapsed against his chest covered in sweat and panting for breath, but his next words had me shooting off the bed. "You were a little loud. You might want to make sure I locked the door."

CHAPTER EIGHT

Carbon

I was shocked when Coal was discharged from the hospital only five days after being shot, but I was damn grateful for it because I had a job to do, and I needed everyone associated with the club to be in Croftridge. Copper and his crew followed the convoy bringing Coal home but planned to return to Devil Springs the next day, which meant I had a small window of opportunity to do what needed to be done.

Harper spent the day babysitting James while Reese helped Ember and Mrs. Martin prepare for Coal's arrival. By the time all was said and done, it was late, and she was exhausted.

Phoenix offered her a room at the clubhouse so she wouldn't have to drive back to the farm and, thankfully, she took it.

After she went to her room for the night, I waited until the coast was clear and joined her. Usually, she snuck out to meet me somewhere on the farm, and we spent a few hours enjoying each other's bodies. This time, she was exhausted, and I needed her to fall asleep sooner rather than later. Crawling into bed with her, I pulled her to my chest and kissed the side of her face.

"Tired," she mumbled sleepily.

"I know, baby. Just want to hold you."

I held her in my arms and prayed it wouldn't be the last time I had the chance to. I buried my face in the crook of her neck and breathed her in before I carefully got out of bed and quietly walked to the door. I turned back to look at her one more time and almost decided to say 'fuck it' and stay with her. But, I couldn't. Because I knew I would regret it if I didn't do this.

Cracking the door, I peered into the hallway to make sure it was clear before I stepped out and walked straight out the back door. I couldn't risk anyone seeing me leave.

After weaving my way around the club property to avoid the security cameras, I finally made it to the fence. Hoisting myself up and over, my feet hit the ground running and didn't stop until I arrived at my condo where my Mustang was parked. Within seconds of arriving, I was in the car and on the road.

The next part of my plan was going to be tricky and had the potential to ruin everything, my life included. I pushed that thought to the back of my mind and focused on the task at hand. I knew I would only get one opportunity, so I couldn't afford to miss it.

I slipped into a janitor's closet unnoticed and kept my eyes on the man in the hall. He was sitting in a chair with his eyes glued to his phone looking bored, and tired. He yawned. He stretched. And within half an hour, he was asleep.

My chance had arrived. I left the closet and moved into the room without making a sound. When my eyes landed on him, my mind quieted, and everything around me ceased to exist. All I could see was him, but the rage I expected to consume me was strangely absent. Instead, I felt an overwhelming obligation to make the world a little less evil by removing this demon from it.

I wanted to make him suffer before I ended him. Make him pay for the beautiful, innocent lives he stole, leaving mine and my sister's forever tarnished. He deserved to have his teeth crushed one at a time with pliers held by my hand. I should get to hear his screams as I plucked each fingernail from its bed before pulling each knuckle from its joint. He should die lying in his own excrement after I broke every bone in his body I could get my bare hands on, and he should have to look me in the eye while I did it.

Sadly, he wasn't going to get everything he deserved. Life wasn't fair, and I was being forced to settle for a minuscule amount of what I felt was rightfully owed to me. The knowledge that he stared into my eyes while he descended to Hell would have to suffice.

I stalked to the side of the bed silently. Simultaneously, one leather-gloved hand shot out to cover his mouth and pinch his nose closed while my other hand reached under the covers and squeezed his balls. I didn't know if he would even feel the pain, but it wouldn't hurt to try. Or maybe it would. Ha!

The moment my hands landed on him, his eyes popped open, and he tried to fight against me, but I was far stronger than him when he wasn't injured, and I wasn't pissed. I kept my eyes locked on his and smiled. "Hello, Omen."

He bucked and wiggled as best he could, trying desperately to escape my hold. I had to fight to hold in my laughter. I shook my head and smirked. "You clearly didn't think I would come for you." I pulled my lip ring into my mouth and grinned. "You're making this so much better than I expected. Thank you."

His wide eyes fluttered before closing, and his body went limp. I immediately released his nose but kept my hand over his mouth as his body automatically sucked in some much-needed air.

It didn't take long for him to come around. When his body tensed and his eyes flew open, I brought my thumb and forefinger together again, effectively closing off his air supply. I didn't have an abundance of time, but there was no way I was letting him die an easy death. If anything, he was going to be well aware of what was happening to him and who was doing it.

I smothered him until he lost consciousness, over and over, one time for each member of my family, one time for his part in my nephew's kidnapping, one time for hurting Reese, and one time for Boar's father. But the last time, the time where I ended him, was for all of us.

I watched with glee as his eyes closed and

his body relaxed, but I didn't let go. I kept my hand over his mouth and nose while I silently counted out 180 seconds. My free hand came up and felt his neck for a pulse. When I was sure it wasn't there, I let go of him and took a step back, wishing I could at the very least spit on him.

With a sigh, I turned on my heel and approached the door. The hallway was clear of hospital staff and the police officer was still sleeping in his chair. I moved quickly and quietly, disappearing into the darkness as if I'd never been there.

By the time I made it back to Croftridge, I'd had plenty of time to process what I'd just done. He was far beyond my first kill, and I highly doubted he would be my last. Taking his life didn't bother me. None of the lives I'd taken bothered me, because I only took lives that deserved to be taken. It's not that I saw myself as judge, jury, and executioner, but I felt a need to protect the ones I loved and, more times than not, the justice system failed to protect. Our laws were focused on punishing a crime after the fact instead of trying to prevent them in the first place.

Feeling like I had finally written the end to this chapter of my life, I parked my car at my condo, trekked through the woods, hopped the fence, snuck into the clubhouse, and crawled into bed with the woman I was growing to care about more and more as each day passed.

CHAPTER NINE

Harper

At the end of the week, I reluctantly returned home to Sugar Falls. I thoroughly enjoyed seeing Chase every day, and I was really going to miss him, but our relationship needed to go back to the way it was, which was much more casual. I wasn't interested in a relationship and what I was doing with Chase was starting to feel like one. I had some weird trust issues. I trusted him with my body and with my safety, but I didn't trust him with my heart...and he was worming his way into my heart whether he intended to or not. Oh, my therapist would have a field day with this, if

I was still seeing her.

While driving to Sugar Falls, I decided it would be best to put some distance between the two of us. To do that, I would not initiate contact with him. When he called or texted to get together, I would tell him I was busy and brush him off for a few weeks. I figured that should be enough time to put things back to the way they were before my little visit to Croftridge. I felt good about my plan and fully intended to stick to it.

When I pulled into my driveway, I was mentally and physically exhausted. I really could have used a day or two to catch up on some sleep, but that wasn't an option. As tired as I was, I was still happy to be returning to work. I absolutely loved my job. Right after graduation, I landed a job as a licensed clinical therapist at a crisis center for children.

After my ordeal when I was a child, Duke moved us to Devil Springs immediately after he rescued me. We had family there, and both of us needed a support system. For me, I needed more than that. I needed someone to talk to that understood my feelings or was at least trained to help me work through them. Unfortunately for me, there was no one like that in Devil Springs. As I got older, I decided that I wanted to be that someone for other children. Working at the crisis center was literally my dream come true.

I was so lost in my thoughts that I didn't see it right away. It wasn't until I went to insert the key that I noticed my front door was open. I automatically took two steps back and surveyed the area while I removed the gun from my purse. I didn't see anything out of the ordinary, and I didn't hear any sounds, but I was still unsure of what to do. Finally, I decided to get back into my car and call the police to come check things out.

Thankfully, I didn't have to wait long for the police officers to show up. They asked me to remain in my car while they checked the house. I sat in my car and anxiously awaited their return. It took everything I had not to pick up my phone and call Chase. I didn't want to want him here with me, but at that very moment, I wanted him there more than anything.

A tap on my window had me jolting and letting out a high-pitched scream...and almost pointing a loaded gun at a police officer. "I'm sorry, ma'am. Didn't mean to startle you. You can step out of the car now. And, please leave your weapon in the car."

I nodded and placed the gun on the passenger seat before I exited my car on shaky legs and faced the officers. "I take it no one was in there?"

"No, ma'am, but we would like to clarify a few things with you. Follow me." He turned and walked toward the front door, his partner right behind him. What the hell did I need to clarify?

My question was answered the moment I stepped into my living room. In the center of the wall above my couch, someone had painted what looked like a game of Connect the Dots, in a color that I could only describe as blood red. What the hell? And where was the series of framed black and white photos that had been on the wall?

"Ms. Jackson?" I turned to face the officer, who apparently had said my name more than once. "I take it that this wasn't your doing?"

I shook my head. "No, sir. I had framed photos hanging there." I continued to stare at the wall in disbelief.

"If you'll follow me, just a few more things."

I followed him through my house as he pointed out broken picture frame after broken picture frame. Any frame that included a photo of Duke or my parents had been broken.

When we arrived in my bedroom, I found my bed covered in peas. Peas. What in the ever-loving fuck?

"Have you noticed anything missing?" the

officer asked.

"No, sir. Let me check my jewelry box and the places where I keep some of my small valuables." I returned a few minutes later to let him know that everything was accounted for.

"Well, Ms. Jackson, it appears that this is of a personal nature. Does any of this make any sense to you? Do you have any enemies? Recently had a disagreement with someone?"

"No, to all of those questions. I couldn't even tell you the last time I got into any kind of disagreement with someone." Well, there was the girl that tried to kidnap my nephew and kill Reese, but he didn't need to know about that. She was in custody, so she couldn't be responsible for this.

"Okay. If you notice anything missing or think of anything we need to know, give us a call. In the meantime, I'll finish up the report and send you a copy of it. We checked your door, and the lock is fine. Might not hurt to consider adding a security system. You take care, Ms. Jackson, and call if you need us."

I thanked the officers and quickly locked the door. When I was sure they were gone, I ran around the house and turned on every single light before I went back through the house and made sure every window and door leading outside were locked. Then, I sank to the floor and cried.

CHAPTER TEN

Carbon

This wasn't good. She hadn't been gone more than a few hours, and I was already missing her. I wasn't supposed to miss her. I wasn't supposed to have feelings for her... nothing more than that of a friend anyway. A friend would call and check to make sure another friend got home safely. So it was perfectly reasonable for me to call and check on her.

Once I had that rationalized, I grabbed my phone and touched her name. I was beginning to think she wasn't going to answer when she finally picked up.

"Hello," she said into the phone. Something in

her tone had my hackles instantly rising.

"Harper, what's wrong, baby?" I asked.

A loud sob followed by several gasps filled my ear.

"Harper!" I bellowed into the phone.

"I-I'm s-sorry. I'm okay," she said between hitching breaths. "I promise."

"Doesn't sound like you're okay. What the fuck is going on?" I demanded.

"I'm fine. Really, I am. I was watching a movie, and it's really sad. The main character just died when you called," she explained. I was damn sure she was lying to me. She didn't watch those kinds of movies. If I remembered correctly, she said they pissed her off.

"Oh, well, I was just calling to make sure you got home okay. I know you were pretty tired when you left. I'll let you get back to your movie," I lied right back to her.

"I'm home, and all is well. Thanks for checking on me, Chase," she said softly.

We ended the call, and I started gathering my stuff. My girl was not okay, and I was going to find out why. In less than five minutes, I had my shit packed and was climbing onto my bike.

Dash was coming through the gate as I was about to pull out. "Going somewhere?"

"Yeah, I'll be back in a day or two unless I'm needed before then," I answered.

"Where you headed?" he asked, raising a brow.

"Better if I don't say," I said flatly.

He shot me a knowing grin. "Have fun and tell Harper I said hello," he said before he revved his bike and rode past me. There was no way he missed the look of surprise on my face at his words. Fuck it. I'd worry about that later.

I rode hell-bent for leather all the way to Harper's place. Damn, she really needed to move closer. It wasn't that far, but it was too far when something was wrong, and something obviously was.

The first thing I noticed when I pulled into her driveway was that every light in the house was on, as well as her porch light and floodlights. The outside lights I could understand if it was dark out, but it wasn't.

I climbed off my bike and strolled to the front door. I rang the doorbell and waited. No answer. I rang it again and knocked twice. Still no answer. I knocked loudly and called her name. Nothing. After listening for a moment and hearing no sounds of movement inside the house, I lost it.

I beat on the door once more for good measure

before I raised my booted foot and kicked the fucker in. Then, everything happened so fast. I crashed through the door. A gun went off. I grabbed the shooter by the throat, knocked the gun out of their hand, and slammed them to the ground, following them to the floor. My fist was flying, halfway to its intended target, when I realized it was Harper beneath me.

I jumped to my feet and pulled her up with me. "Fuck! Are you okay? Did I hurt you?"

"N-no, you didn't."

"What the fuck was that, Harper? You fucking shot at me? I could have killed you," I roared. I was pissed—not about being shot at. I had been grazed or missed by bullets more times than I could count. I found it sort of morbidly fascinating that so many people missed a target as big as me. What had me raging was the fact that I could have seriously hurt her coupled with the obvious fear on her face.

"I didn't know it was you, you big beast!" she yelled right back, even as she clung to me.

"You would've known it was me if you would've answered the damn door! Or looked out a fucking window! What the hell is wrong with you?" I didn't intend for my words to come out as harsh as they did. She was scared, and I felt a primal need to protect her and eliminate the threat.

Her reaction was not what I expected. "I'm fucking scared, okay? I was already scared, and you scared me more!" she screamed as she pulled away from me, tears streaming down her face. "I'm sorry," she sobbed. "I didn't hurt you, did I?"

"Baby," I said softly, reaching out to cup her cheek, "I'm fine. Why are you so scared?"

She leaned into my palm, and her face crumpled even more. "Someone broke into my house while I was in Croftridge. The police said it appeared to be personal," she cried.

"Why do they think it's personal?"

"Follow me. I've cleaned up some of it, but I still have a good bit left." She turned, and I followed her through the house as she showed me the damage that was done to her home.

When we got to her room, I surveyed the area, rubbed my eyes, and looked around the room again. "Peas?" I asked.

"I know, right? If it hadn't happened to me, I might find it funny, but at the moment, I keep finding the fuckers everywhere. And let me tell you, you can't vacuum up mushy peas. No, they have to be picked up by hand!"

"So, let me get this straight. Someone broke

into your house, painted dots on your living room wall, broke a bunch of picture frames, and covered your bed in peas?" I asked, not believing the words coming out of my mouth. "Anything else?"

She chewed on her bottom lip before answering me. "The picture frames...only the ones with pictures of my parents and Duke were broken." She shrugged. "It's probably just a coincidence."

"I don't think so. I think someone is trying to send you a message." I pulled out my phone and continued, "I've got to call the club and let them know what's going on."

"No!" she shrieked and tried to grab my phone.

I yanked my phone away in time and held it above my head. "What the hell, Harper? You know I can't keep this from them, and you shouldn't want me to. Your safety is at stake here. We need to make sure you're protected."

"If you call the club, they'll want me to come back to Croftridge. I can't do that. I just took two weeks off work. I can't take any more time off right now. Plus, Duke and Reese have been through a lot of shit recently. I don't want my brother to worry about me. He needs to focus on his family right now. I have a gun, I'm getting a security system installed, and I called the police.

I want to handle this like normal people would," she explained.

"How do you think Duke would feel if something happened to you? How do you think I would feel, Harper?" I pounded my fist on my chest and stared at her.

"Nothing is going to happen to me."

"You don't know that! Do you think Reese thought a crazy woman would try to kill her and kidnap her son? Do you think Ember thought a madman would try to sell her into human trafficking and then try to kill her and her father? No! They didn't!" I roared. I was furious with her. What in the hell was she thinking? There was no way I was letting her stay in her house unprotected.

"Fine. I get it, all right? But I still don't want you to tell the club. What are my other options?" she asked, her tone much calmer than I expected.

I pinched the bridge of my nose and sighed. "I honestly don't know. I can stay tonight and tomorrow night. We'll have to figure something out after that. Have you already arranged to have a security system installed?"

"Not yet. I was going to call Judge, but then you showed up," she said, rolling her eyes.

"You realize your cousin is in the same club I

am, right?" I asked.

"Seriously, Chase. I was going to tell him that there had been some break-ins in the area and ask if he could come install a security system for me," she scoffed.

"No time like the present."

She called Judge and asked him to install an alarm system for her. He told her he would be there the following day to get it done while she was at work. Quite frankly, I was a bit surprised that he hadn't already installed one for her, but I didn't comment on it.

After she got off the phone with Judge, I helped her finish cleaning up the mess that had been made of her house. She wasn't lying; those fucking peas were everywhere. Once we had everything cleaned up, she offered to cook dinner for me, but I knew she was tired. I could see it in her eyes.

"Baby," I murmured against her skin as I nuzzled her neck. "As much as I'd love that, you're exhausted. Go take a shower, and I'll place an order for delivery."

"Mmm, that sounds wonderful," she breathed and turned her head to capture my lips.

She squeaked when I lightly swatted her ass and turned her by her shoulders. "Go," I ordered.

"I'll fuck you after dinner."

"Promises, promises."

As I waited for her to finish in the shower and for the food to arrive, I sat in a chair in her living room and stared at the wall. I couldn't for the life of me figure out what the damn dots meant. I even took a picture of the wall and did an image search, but I couldn't find anything like it.

The doorbell rang, interrupting my thoughts about the dots on the wall, but I was glad the food had arrived. I didn't know about Harper, but I was fucking starving. Swinging the front door open, I fully expected to find a delivery guy standing there with my bag of food. Instead, I came face-to-face with an attractive woman who appeared to be around the same age as Harper.

She took a step back at the sight of me. I was used to that reaction; most women did the same thing when they saw me. I was bigger than most men with a few visible piercings and an abundance of tattoos, all of which translated to scary for most females.

The girl blinked a few times and cleared her throat. "Uh, is Harper here?"

"Who wants to know?" I asked gruffly.

"Hilarie," she said, her eyes darting around wildly.

"She know you?" I asked.

"Yes. We work together, and we went to school together," she said nervously.

"Just a minute," I said and closed the door in her face.

I turned around to get Harper, only to find her coming out of her bedroom. "I thought I heard the door. Is the food here?"

"No, some girl named Hilarie is at the door asking for you."

She huffed and started stomping toward the door. "You didn't let her in?"

"Fuck no. I don't know her," I snapped.

She brushed past me and yanked the door open. The girl was still standing there. Guess I needed to work on my intimidation tactics. I thought for sure the girl would have turned tail and ran as soon as I closed the door.

"Sorry about that, Hilarie. Come on in," Harper said, holding the door wide open and gesturing for the girl to enter. "This is my friend, Carbon. He's a teensy bit overprotective. Carbon, this is my friend and coworker, Hilarie."

I met Harper's eyes and mouthed "Friend?" with my eyebrows raised in question. I wasn't her damn friend, and she knew it. She shrugged and turned back to our uninvited guest. "What brings you by?"

"I just wanted to check in with you. I haven't seen or talked to you in over two weeks. How was your trip?" she asked.

"You could have called her and asked that," I interrupted.

"Carbon," Harper snapped. "Stop being so rude."

"It's fine, really," the girl said. "I was on my way home and saw your car in the driveway, so I stopped. Am I interrupting something?"

"No," Harper replied at the same time I said, "Yes."

Harper cleared her throat. "We're waiting on our delivery order. You want to join us for dinner?"

I glared at the girl, willing her with my eyes to decline the invitation. It was subtle and brief, but I swear she smirked at me before she told Harper she would love to stay for dinner. It was official; I didn't like this bitch.

I followed them into the kitchen and took a seat on one of the barstools while the girls sat at the table. As I stared at Hilarie, I felt like I knew her from somewhere, or at least had seen her before. Oh hell, I hoped I hadn't fucked her. I had been through a lot of women in my past, and the majority of them were easily forgettable.

"How do you two know each other again?" I asked, studying the girl's face.

"Hilarie and I went to college together, and now we both work at the crisis center," Harper explained.

"So, you met at school?"

Hilarie answered that one. "No, we didn't have any classes together. We worked at the same bar while we were in school. That's how we met."

Ah, that's when it clicked. I'd seen her before and thankfully, had not fucked her. She was a stripper at the club where I met Harper. I snapped my fingers. "That's why you look familiar. You had different hair, but you were a stripper, too. Ginger, was it?"

Hilarie's cheeks flushed. "Yes, that was my stage name. The hair was a wig. I don't miss that at all." Both girls laughed at her statement, but I had no idea why.

"So, you work at the crisis center, too, but you two never had any classes together? That seems strange," I prodded; something was off about this girl.

"That's because I'm a licensed clinical therapist and Hilarie handles the finances and marketing. We have completely different degrees. Now, could you stop with the interrogation? You're acting like an ass," Harper snapped.

I placed my hand on my chest and pretended to be offended. "Excuse me for trying to get to know one of your friends. Clearly, I'm not wanted, so I'll be in the living room until the food gets here." I got up and obnoxiously stomped to the living room. In a way, I hoped they would talk more freely without me hovering over them in the kitchen. I couldn't put my finger on it, but something about Hilarie made me feel uneasy.

CHAPTER ELEVEN

Harper

"Sorry about him," I said to Hilarie. "I don't know why he's acting like that. I wouldn't say he's usually sweet, but he's normally much less of a dick."

Hilarie waved her hand in a dismissive motion. "Don't worry about it. I'm sure I've inadvertently pissed him off by interrupting his plans for the evening." She winked and waggled her eyebrows.

"The only plans for this evening are dinner and bed. I'm freaking exhausted. I could use a good 15 hours of sleep before the work week starts."

"Why are you so tired? Didn't you just get back from vacation?" she asked.

I sighed, "Yes and no. I went to visit my brother and his new baby, so I wouldn't exactly call that a vacation. A lot was going on the whole time I was there, so I didn't really get any downtime."

Hilarie straightened in her chair and gave me a pitying look. "I'm sorry. You deserve to have some time off that you can actually enjoy."

"I did enjoy my time off. I got to spend time with my nephew as well as my brother and his girlfriend. It just wasn't relaxing," I corrected.

She opened her mouth to say something, but Chase walked in carrying a bag of food. The smell quickly filled my kitchen causing my mouth to water. When I got up to get plates and silverware, Hilarie stood, too. "I'm going to have to take a rain check for dinner. I just remembered that I still have laundry to do before tomorrow. I'll see you in the morning."

I walked her to the door to see her out. When I returned to the kitchen, Chase had gotten the plates and utensils and was in the middle of dishing out our meal. I absolutely loved Hibachi style food and was blessed to live in an area where I could have it delivered to my front door, which I frequently did.

Chase and I ate in an uncomfortable silence. I had no idea how he was feeling, but I was a little irritated with his behavior. He was a total ass to Hilarie for no reason.

When I was finished eating, I rinsed my dishes and placed them in the dishwasher. He followed right behind me and did the same. Once everything was put back to rights, I silently checked the locks on the doors and padded to my bedroom. Our issues would have to wait. I was simply too tired to discuss it. It was all I could do to get changed into my pajamas.

"You going to give me the silent treatment for the rest of the night, baby?" Chase asked from the doorway of my bedroom.

"I just want to go to bed, Chase. I'm exhausted, and I have a full week of work starting in the morning," I explained.

He prowled toward me, placing his hands on my hips when he reached me. Leaning down, he nipped at my earlobe. "You going to let me sleep in here with you?" His lips moved slowly down my neck and back up to my ear as his warm breath caused goosebumps to erupt on my skin.

My traitorous body melted into his. "Yes," I breathed. His response was to scoop me up and deposit me on the bed. He crawled in behind me and wrapped his big arms around me. A few hours ago, I was sure I wouldn't get any sleep that night, but with Chase cocooning me with his big body, I quickly fell into a deep, dreamless sleep.

The next morning, I woke feeling refreshed and ready for work. When I was ready to leave, Chase met me at the front door, also dressed and ready to go. Damn. The man was sex on a stick, and he was looking at me with a hunger in his eyes.

Shaking my head to clear my naughty thoughts, which did not work whatsoever, I asked, "What are you doing?"

"Are you new? I'm taking you to work," he said.

"Why?"

"Seriously, Harper? One, because someone broke into your house and trashed it in the weirdest fucking way ever. Two, because Judge is coming to install your security system, and I didn't think it would be wise for him to find me piddling around your house."

I hadn't thought of that. Who could blame me? I was tired, and my mind was a jumbled mess. I still hadn't fully processed everything that happened with Duke and Reese while I was in Croftridge, and here I was with my own bullshit starting.

Chase drove me to work and told me he would be around, but I wouldn't be able to see him. I wasn't sure how he was going to pull that off, but I didn't ask. He insisted that I tell no one, not even Hilarie, that he was outside keeping an eye on the place. I didn't like it, but I agreed.

I couldn't help myself. Every chance I got, I was peering out a window to see if I could catch a glimpse of him. When lunchtime rolled around, Hilarie asked me if I wanted to join her for lunch at a restaurant down the street. I wasn't sure how to answer her because I didn't know if Chase would be able to follow me without being seen or not.

I was trying to stall and come up with an answer when none other than Chase came through the door. "Hey, baby. You ready to go to lunch?" he asked with a bright smile on his face. "Hello, Hilarie. Would you like to join us for lunch as well? You do have that rain check to cash in."

Was he high or something? This cheerful man standing in my office was most definitely not my gruff and grumbling Chase. He must have seen the confusion on my face because the big beast winked at me and continued to smile at Hilarie.

"Uh, sure," she stammered out. "Are we ready

to go now?"

"I'm ready whenever you two ladies are," Chase said cheerfully. He was starting to freak me out. He looked like one of those people who appeared to be happy all the time, but you just knew that they were really a closet psychopath waiting for the perfect opportunity to burst into the world.

I shot him a stern look and grabbed his hand. "Let's go."

Lunch was uncomfortable and awkward, to say the least. I would rather be probed and prodded at the lady doctor after having a fresh Brazilian wax than have to sit through a meal like that again. There was an almost palpable tension between Hilarie and Chase, and I didn't have the first clue as to why. They both made ridiculous small talk and kept these horrific fake smiles plastered on their faces. By the end of the meal, I wanted to scream at both of them and demand they tell me what in the hell their problems were with each other. I wanted to, but I didn't. Instead, I kept my mouth shut and returned to the office.

Chase walked in with me. I moved down the hall toward my office when one of the receptionists stopped me. "Harper, your cousin is waiting for you in your office."

Shit.

Shit.

Shit.

I turned my wide eyes to Chase.

"Go on. Keep him busy for a few minutes while I slip out of sight." He gave me a quick kiss on the lips and then he was gone.

I slowly walked to my office, trying to force myself to relax. I lived with Judge from the age of 10 until he moved out when I was 15 years old. Judge was like a brother to me, a brother who could easily tell when I was lying to him or hiding something from him. I knew he was coming to install the system, but I wasn't expecting to see him. I assumed he would leave instructions on the kitchen table or email them to me.

"Hey, Brother Judge! I wasn't expecting to see you today," I said excitedly. I was excited in a way. I hadn't been able to spend any significant time with him in a while, and I missed him.

He stood and enveloped me in a bear hug. "Sister Cousin Harper! You didn't really think I would drive all this way and not see you, did you?" He smiled down at me. "I came to take you to lunch, but the girl at the desk out there said you were already out for lunch."

"I wish I had known you were coming. I would have rearranged my schedule for that," I said.

He shrugged. "I didn't know I was coming to take you for lunch either until I finished installing everything early. Your house had a security system at some point in the past. I was able to use most of the existing setup without having to start from scratch. Saved me a shitload of time."

"That's awesome! Thanks for getting it done for me on such short notice."

Judge went over how to operate the security system and gave me the security code he had chosen. He also gave me a set of keys as he had replaced every lock in my house. He was nothing less than thorough. We talked for a half an hour or so, and he left with a promise from me to call him soon.

The rest of my day seemed to drag. All of the patients I saw that day were doing well, which was great for them, but meant my day was basically spent socializing with teenagers. By 5:00 pm I was anxious to see Chase. Right on cue, he strolled through the front door with that fake smile once again plastered across his handsome face.

"Hey, baby," he greeted me, bending down to kiss my forehead. "How was your day?"

I quirked an eyebrow at him. "Good. How was your day?"

His creepy smile widened. "Great. I was wondering if Hilarie could take you home. I've got to run an errand before I get back to your place."

I didn't see why I couldn't just go with him to run the errand, but I didn't question him. He had been acting strange all day. As soon as Hilarie said she would give me a ride, Chase took one of the new keys to my house, pecked me on the lips, told me not to wait for him for dinner, and disappeared again.

"Do you want to grab something to eat on the way home?" Hilarie asked.

"Sure. Why not?" I replied, somewhat dejectedly. I had so been looking forward to spending the entire evening with him. I usually loved spending time with Hilarie, but she wasn't who I wanted to be with right then.

Dinner wasn't as stilted and awkward as lunch, but it didn't have the natural ease that I usually had with Hilarie. My mind kept straying to Chase, trying to figure out what kind of errand he could be running. Hilarie seemed off as well.

"Is everything okay with you?" I asked. I was being a shitty friend and asked, not because I was genuinely concerned, but because I wanted to get my mind off of Chase.

"Since you asked, no, not really," she snapped. "You were gone for two weeks and didn't even bother to call me the entire time you were gone nor when you got back. Not only that, you came back with that monster of a man who guards you like a pit bull, and you seem perfectly okay with it! Are you going to be one of those friends who just disappear the second they are in a relationship?"

Her voice had grown much louder toward the end of her rant. "Hilarie, please lower your voice. I'm sorry I didn't call, but in my defense, a lot was going on when I was in Croftridge. When I got back, I had a list of things to get done before this morning. As for Carbon, I didn't know he was going to show up last night. On that note, I'm not going to be one of those friends who disappears when they are in a relationship because I am not in a relationship."

She scoffed. "You might want to tell him that."

"I don't have to. He knows we aren't in a relationship."

She rolled her eyes. "His actions say otherwise. Anyway, so what happened in Croftridge that kept you too busy to use the phone?"

Crap. I couldn't tell her what went on there. She didn't know Chase, my brother, and several other members of my family were in a motorcycle club. It wasn't information I readily volunteered. When girls my age found out about my association with a well-known motorcycle club, they tended to either look at me like I was a piece of trash, or they were a biker fangirl and tried to become my new best friend.

"Just a lot of stuff with my brother, his girlfriend, and their son. Sorry, Hilarie, that's all I can give you. It isn't my story to tell," I explained, hoping she would understand.

"Fine, keep your secrets," she huffed.

I tried to change the subject and keep some sort of conversation going, but she wouldn't engage. She was obviously upset with me, but I wasn't sure what she wanted me to do. I apologized for not calling, even though I really shouldn't have. I didn't answer to her or anyone else for that matter.

When she pulled into my driveway, I invited her to come inside, but she declined. I hoped she couldn't tell how relieved I was that she decided just to drop me off. I pulled out my new keys and unlocked my front door. When I pushed the door open, a scream erupted from me at what I saw.

"Harper, baby, calm down. It's okay," Chase said as he rushed toward me.

"What the fuck is that?" I screeched.

"Your new dog," he said excitedly.

"My what?" I asked incredulously.

"Your dog. He's a trained guard dog. I got him to protect you if I wasn't around. He's also a certified service dog, so you can take him to work with you. Do you like him?"

I just stood there, looking back and forth between the two beasts standing in my doorway. "Um...I don't know what to say. He's beautiful and big, really big, but you didn't have to do that. You really shouldn't have..."

Chase's face fell. "I can take him back," he muttered.

I felt like such an ass. "No, don't do that. I'm sorry, I just wasn't expecting anything like this. I've never had a dog before. I have no idea how to take care of one."

It must have dawned on Chase then that I was still standing on the front porch. He stepped back and motioned for me to come inside. "It's not hard to take care of a dog. I'll make sure you know everything you need to know before I leave."

"You're leaving?" I asked, instantly hating the

shock and disappointment in my voice.

He pulled me to his chest and closed the door. "Not until Wednesday morning, baby. I'll head out when you go to work."

"Tell me about the dog," I mumbled against his chest.

"His name is Titan. He's a four-year-old Cane Corso and has been professionally trained by a friend of mine. He will guard and protect you with the same ferocity that Duke or I would. You won't have to command him to defend you. He will take his cues from your body language as well as the situation and respond accordingly. If he does subdue someone, he will not release them and stand down until you give him the command. Also, the collar he is wearing must stay on him at all times. Ruben is a well-known trainer in the Southeast and has worked with many law enforcement offices to educate the officers on how to identify service dogs and subdue a protection dog without using deadly force. When one of his dogs is matched with a client, he personally calls the head of each nearby law enforcement division to let them know one of his dogs is on duty in their area. If they aren't familiar with his program, he emails an information packet and sets up a time for him or one of his associates

113

to come speak with the officers. So, if something happens in Sugar Falls or Croftridge, as long as he has that collar on, he won't be harmed by law enforcement," he explained.

"I think I can handle that. He is beautiful—scary, but beautiful." I paused and leaned back so I could meet his eyes. "Thank you, Chase. It was very thoughtful of you, and I do appreciate it."

He smiled down at me. "Since I can't stay and you won't come back with me, I had to do something to make sure you're safe when we aren't together."

"Chase—" I started, but he cut me off.

"No, Harper, let me finish. I know this isn't what we talked about well over a year ago, but regardless of what we said back then, we have formed a relationship, and you can't deny that. When I heard you on the phone, scared and crying, I knew you were lying to me, and I couldn't get to you fast enough. All I could think about on the ride here was that I couldn't lose you. I don't know how you did it or when you did it, but you wormed your way in and I don't want to let you go." He spoke with such sincerity and honesty; I felt tears welling in my eyes.

"Then don't," I rasped out.

He didn't, not until he was forced to so I could go to work the next morning. Once again, he disappeared into the shadows while I worked. I don't know what he thought he would see while he was hiding out there, but he was adamant that it was necessary.

Personally, I thought he was going a bit overboard. Yes, someone broke into my house. Yes, it scared the hell out of me. But there was minimal damage done, nothing was stolen, and no threats were made. It was probably just some bored teenagers.

The first part of the day was pretty much the same as the day before, including another awkward lunch with Hilarie and Chase. I had back to back sessions after lunch which made the afternoon go by faster. Chase picked me up from work and drove us back to my house. We ate a quick dinner and spent the rest of the evening and night wrapped up in each other.

The next morning, after he helped me get Titan in the car, it was time to say goodbye, and I was struggling to keep my emotions at bay. I didn't want him to leave. I knew he would be back in a few days, but that did nothing to ease the ache in my chest. I cared about him, probably loved him, and he was leaving, because he lived in a different city—hell, a different state—and he had his own life there.

"Harper, look at me," his deep voice rumbled by my ear. I lifted my head and met his soulful green eyes. "You okay, baby?"

I sniffled. Damn it. I didn't want to cry in front of him. Clearing my throat and trying desperately to swallow over the lump that had formed there, I barely managed to answer, "Yes, I'm fine."

He chuckled. "Bullshit. Whenever a woman you're involved with says she's fine, it means she isn't. Now, tell me what's wrong."

"I don't want you to go, okay?" I mumbled into his chest.

"Say again."

We each repeated the same thing three more times before I finally yelled, "I don't want you to go!" With that, the floodgates opened. Once the first tear fell, the others took that as the okay to follow.

Chase went right into full protector mode. "Are you still scared?" I shook my head. That wasn't it at all, but I didn't want to tell him the real reason. I didn't have to because moments later, he figured it out on his own. "Oh, this is just about me. You're going to miss me?"

I wiped the tears from my face with my hands.

"Of course I am, you big beast."

He smiled a genuine, breathtaking smile. "I don't want to go either, baby, but I have to. We'll talk every night, and I'll be back Friday night. So, really, that's just one day you won't see me."

"You're right. I'm being silly," I said, shaking my head at my ridiculousness.

"Nah, baby, you're not. I love that you're already missing me and I haven't even left yet. Now, quit your crying and kiss me."

I did just that. After he helped me into my car and kissed me once more, he climbed onto his bike, and I watched him ride away with tears still in my eyes. I was still staring off in the direction he'd gone when a cold, wet nose nudged my cheek. I looked over to see Titan staring at me, his head cocked to one side like he knew something was wrong, but he wasn't sure what it was. I patted him on his big head to reassure him and then drove the two of us to work.

I was a little nervous about taking Titan into the office. I hadn't mentioned anything about getting a service dog to any of the employees at the crisis center. I knew I was allowed to have one; I just didn't want to deal with all the attention he would draw when we entered the building for the first time. Taking a deep breath, I pushed through the front door with Titan by my side.

Jackie, the receptionist, jumped out of her chair with an excited squeal. "Oh! Who do we have here?"

"This is my new service dog. His name is Titan."

"Can I pet him?"

At my nod, she crouched down in front of him and started talking to him in a voice similar to the one people used when talking to a baby while she lightly scratched behind his ears. Her antics garnered the attention of most of my coworkers, who trickled over one by one to see what was going on. I looked around and sighed. "Everyone, this is Titan, my service dog. He's well trained and very obedient. He will be accompanying me to work from now on. He'll be by my side at all times and shouldn't be a bother to any of you. If you have any issues with him, please come speak to me directly so we can address it."

"Oh, who could possibly have any issues with him? He's absolutely adorable!" Jackie squealed again. Adorable? Titan was not adorable. Beautiful? Yes. He reminded me of a black panther, beautiful, yet deadly.

I looked around the office again. "Where's Hilarie?" I asked, directing my question to Jackie.

"She's not here yet. She called about an hour ago and said she would be in late this morning. She didn't give a reason or a specific time when she would arrive, but she assured me that everything was okay," she told me.

I went on to my office and got started with my scheduled sessions. The day passed by quickly. All of the kids seemed to love Titan. I was beyond impressed with his behavior in my office. I wasn't sure what to expect from him. He picked a spot as soon as we entered my office and stayed put. He didn't make any noise throughout the day, and I almost forgot he was there a few times.

At the end of the day, I assumed Hilarie would want to go somewhere for dinner since we didn't eat lunch together. That was our usual routine. We either ate lunch together or dinner together during the work week. Grabbing my purse, I called Titan to my side and walked out to the front office to find Hilarie.

"Jackie, do you know where Hilarie is?"

"She went home early. Said she wasn't feeling well."

Before leaving the office, I tried to call her to make sure she was okay and to see if she wanted me to bring dinner over, but she didn't answer. After my second unsuccessful attempt to call her, Titan and I climbed into my car, hit a drive-thru for dinner, and went home.

I tried to keep myself busy as I anxiously waited for Chase's call. By 10:00 pm, he still hadn't called, so I gave in and called him. I was trying not to be clingy, but I missed him, and one phone call wouldn't be considered being clingy. The call went straight to voicemail, which typically meant the person had their phone turned off. Maybe he was in Church. I knew Phoenix usually asked them to turn their phones off while they were meeting.

I waited an hour and called him again. Same thing, straight to voicemail. I told myself not to worry. They were probably still in Church. This wasn't the day they usually met, so a meeting meant something was up, and Church might last longer than usual. Once I had myself convinced of my concocted story, I climbed into bed, turned on the television, and waited for his call.

I groaned when I heard my alarm clock. I had tossed and turned all night long, never really falling asleep. Reaching over and grabbing my phone, I checked the screen for any missed calls or texts, even though I knew there wouldn't be any. My phone was right beside me all night, and I would have heard it if he called or sent a text.

I tried calling him again on my way to work. Straight to voicemail. Okay, maybe he lost his phone and hadn't gotten a replacement yet. It had to be something like that. I tried again at lunch with the same results. When I still couldn't get a hold of him on my way home from work, worry set in.

He wasn't the kind of man to ignore phone calls or try to avoid someone. If he didn't want to talk to me, he would answer the phone and tell me just that. But what if something happened to him? No one from the club would think to call me, that is, if they even knew.

Shit. There was only one way to know for sure, but that meant having to answer questions I didn't want to answer just yet. I mentally debated the pros and cons before I finally decided to call Phoenix and hope he would keep as much of this to himself as possible.

"Phoenix," he answered sharply.

"Hi, Phoenix, this is Harper. Um…are you free to talk right now?" I asked, trying to stay on top of my nerves.

"Just a minute," he replied. I heard some rustling and then a door close. "I'm alone in my office now. What's going on, Harper?"

"Uh, I haven't been able to get a hold of Carbon since yesterday morning. I wanted to make sure he was okay, and I didn't know who else to call."

There was a long, uncomfortable moment of silence before Phoenix spoke again. "He's not where he can get to a phone, but he's fine."

"What exactly does that mean?" I asked.

"Sorry, sweetheart, it's club business."

"Are you kidding me right now?" I snapped. "I've been worried sick for well over 24 hours and all you can say is 'club business'?"

"Don't forget who you're talking to, Harper," he scolded. "Now, if you were his Old Lady or a family member, I would gladly fill you in, but you're not. On that note, why exactly are you calling about Carbon? I wasn't aware that you two were close."

The moment he raised his voice, I felt my hands dampen and my breathing pick up. Phoenix would never hurt me. Phoenix would never hurt me. I repeated that over and over in my head. I knew that, but it didn't change the fact that I was already on edge and Phoenix just reprimanded me in a not so gentle way. Suddenly, I was in another place.

"Don't you forget again!" he roared.

I screamed when I felt the streak of fire across my back. He was using his belt like a whip, striking my bare back with lash after lash.

"I'm sorry!" I wailed. "Please, stop. I promise I will do better."

"That's what you said last time. You need to learn your lesson, girl!"

He showed me no mercy. The lashes continued to come, covering nearly every inch of my back. I screamed, begged, cried, pleaded, promised, anything to get him to stop, but it all fell on deaf ears.

"Harper! Talk to me, sweetheart. Are you okay? Do you want me to get Duke?" Phoenix's frantic voice broke into the nightmare of my past.

"No. Don't do that. I'm fine," I croaked.

"Bullshit. What happened just now?"

"Flashback. It's over, I'm good."

"Aw, shit, darlin'. Because I yelled at you," he said, more to himself. "I'm sorry, sweetheart. I guess I forgot who I was talking to. You sure you're okay?"

"Yes, sir. I'm fine now. Sorry about the way I spoke to you earlier."

"No worries. Now, you want to tell me what's

going on with you and Carbon?" he asked.

"I don't exactly want to, but I feel like maybe I should. I'm sure you've noticed how he's been disappearing once a week or so for the last year..."

Phoenix laughed. "Sort of. I mean, he's rarely ever here on Friday nights, but I assumed he was...well, I'm sure you know what I thought he was doing without me saying it."

"Um, you weren't entirely wrong."

"Go on," he encouraged.

"He's been coming to see me. And before you ask, my brother doesn't know. As far as I know, no one does. It started as just a casual thing, but somewhere along the way, things changed. I care about him, and I'm really worried, Phoenix. Will you please tell me what's going on?" I pleaded, hoping my honesty would be met with the same from him.

"He's in jail," he blurted.

"What?" I shrieked. "Why?"

Phoenix sighed. "I'm guessing he was on his way back from your place yesterday morning when the cops pulled him over. He was about halfway between Sugar Falls and Croftridge. Anyway, there was a fight between two street gangs in Atlanta Tuesday night. Everyone scattered when the cops arrived. They found a gun registered to Carbon, with his prints on it, next to a dead body. When I talked to him, he told me it was his gun, but swears it was locked up in a closet at his condo. He said he hadn't touched that particular gun in months, and that was just to clean it. We've got the club's lawyer working on it, but due to the severity of the charges, we can't just go and bail him out right away. He has to see a judge first and, depending on the judge, bail might not even be an option," he explained.

"I can help!" I screeched excitedly. "He was with me the entire night before."

"That's good, but I think we are going to need a little more than just his secret girlfriend's word, Harper."

"Judge installed a security system in my house on Monday while I was at work. I set the alarm when Carbon and I got home Tuesday evening. Isn't there some kind of log or something that would show if the system had been deactivated during the night?" I asked, crossing my fingers that I could help prove Chase's innocence.

"Yeah, there is. If it's one of Judge's systems, you can sign in to your account and download or print the activity log. Email me that log, and

I'll forward it to our attorney as soon as I get it. Maybe that and your statement that he was with you will be enough of an alibi for him. Are you willing to go in and give an official statement?"

"I'll do anything to help him. Oh, I have some pictures, too, on my phone. We took a couple of selfies that night, but you can definitely tell that we are in my house and they're time-stamped," I said, my excitement growing. I could prove it wasn't Carbon and get my man out of the clink. My man? Nope, not going there.

"Send those to me with the alarm report. In the email, you need to add a statement along the lines of 'Chase Walker was in my presence at my personal residence' and include the dates and times. I'll call the lawyer now and let her know what we're sending. Hopefully, this will be enough to get the charges dropped."

"If it is, when will he be released?"

"They have to release him immediately after the charges are dropped, and I'm going to do everything I can to make sure that happens first thing tomorrow morning."

"Thank you, Phoenix. Please keep me posted. And if you talk to him, please tell him I was worried, but I'm okay."

"Will do, sweetheart."

"Oh, one more thing. Um, can we keep this conversation between the two of us for now? I'm not asking you to keep it from Duke so much as I'm asking you to give Carbon and I the chance to tell him and Reese ourselves," I begged.

"You intend to tell him soon?"

"To be perfectly honest, we hadn't planned on making our relationship public knowledge any time soon, but we will now."

"As long as you two don't draw it out, I'll keep it to myself."

"Thank you. We won't draw it out," I promised.

"All right, darlin'. You get that email to me as soon as you can, and you'll hear from one of us tomorrow."

I immediately got to work on my tasks. After sending the report, the pictures, and my statement to Phoenix's email, I also sent the pictures to his phone via text. Then, I sent them to myself via email. To be absolutely certain I could access copies if needed, I backed up my phone to my computer and then backed up my computer to the external hard drive I kept locked in a fireproof safe.

After all was said and done, I felt much better about the entire situation. I didn't like the fact that Chase was in jail, but I knew he could handle himself. He was so big and intimidating; I doubted anyone would have the balls to mess with him. It was at that moment I realized I had never been afraid of Chase. I had been uncomfortable or nervous around him, but never afraid.

CHAPTER TWELVE

Carbon

I rang the doorbell and waited. I heard paws clicking across the hardwood floors followed by the sound of human footsteps. Seconds later, the door flew open and Harper squealed my name before launching herself into my arms.

I held her there, breathing her in and absorbing as much of her as I could. She felt...right. She filled a hole in my heart that I wasn't even aware was there. I was coming to realize that I needed her in my life more than I had ever anticipated.

"When did you get out?" she asked.

I walked into the house with her legs wrapped around my waist. "Around lunchtime. Got a hotel room so I could shower and clean up. I picked up some new clothes and shit and came straight here. I hope you're hungry because I'm starving. Jail food sucks."

I heard a sniffle, followed by, "I missed you. I was so worried about you."

I smoothed her hair with my hand and squeezed her a little tighter. "I know, baby. Phoenix told me you called him. I'm glad you did because you single-handedly saved my ass. You know that, right?"

She kept her face buried in my neck and mumbled, "I did what I could to help. I hope you're not mad that I told Phoenix about us."

She was worried about that? Hell no, I wasn't mad that she told Phoenix, for two reasons. One, my ass would have been sent up the river for a long time if she hadn't. Two, I was ready to move to the next step with her. I had a lot of time to think during my concrete vacation, and most of my thoughts were about her. I was ready to tell everyone that she was mine.

"No, baby, I'm not mad about that. Never was. Told you I was glad you called him."

We'd been standing in her living room for several minutes, and she'd given me no indication that she wanted to get down. "Baby, as much as

I love you being in my arms, I want to see your face." She slowly dropped her legs to the ground and pulled back, staring up at me. I swear she got more beautiful each time I saw her.

I reached out and cupped her cheeks in my hands. "You're mine, have been for a while now. I think it's time we both acknowledge it and stop hiding it from our friends and family."

"Okay," she replied simply.

"That means you're my girl. That means telling your brother and my sister," I explained. I didn't want to scare her off, but I needed to make sure she understood what I meant.

"Okay," she said again.

"Okay? That's all you have to say about it?"

She grinned and nodded, blinking up at me with her big blue eyes. I pulled her to me and kissed her, slow and sweet. My girl. I broke the kiss before things could get out of hand and smiled at her. "Let's go get something to eat."

Over dinner, we talked about how we were going to break the news to Duke. I wasn't worried about Reese. She would be happy as long as I was happy. Duke, on the other hand, wouldn't be happy about his sister and I being in a relationship. He would have to get over it though, just like I did when he knocked up my sister behind my back.

We decided it would be best to break the news to our friends and family members in person. We also thought it would be best to do that sooner rather than later, particularly since that's what she'd more or less promised Phoenix. I needed to get back home anyway, so Harper packed a bag, put Titan in her car, and followed me back to Croftridge.

I wasn't sure what to expect when we arrived. It was a Friday night, which usually meant a party at the clubhouse, but it was anyone's guess whether or not Duke and Reese would be there. I called Phoenix before we arrived and let him know our plans. He said Duke and Reese had decided to stay home, so we bypassed the clubhouse and dropped our things off at my condo before heading over to their house to talk to them.

I climbed in the driver's seat of Harper's car and called my sister.

"Hey, big scary brother," she answered.

"Hey, Reesie Piecie. Is it okay if I stop by?"

"Yeah. Is everything okay?" she asked nervously.

"Everything's fine. I just didn't want to drop in unannounced in case you and Duke were doing things I'd much rather not know about."

Reese laughed. "What? Like making another niece or nephew for you?"

"Shut it, Reesie. See you soon," I said and disconnected before she could say anything else.

As we got closer, I could tell Harper was letting her nerves get the best of her. I placed my hand on her thigh and gave it a light squeeze. "You worried, baby?"

"A little," she confessed.

"Tell me what you're worried about. What do you think is going to happen?" I asked.

"I don't want this to ruin your friendship with my brother," she quickly answered.

I believed there was truth to her answer, but I didn't think that was the only thing she was worried about. "What else?"

She chewed on her bottom lip before finally answering me. "I know you two fought when you found out about Duke and Reese. I don't want you guys to fight again. I don't handle that kind of violence well. You know, maybe we should wait and do this at the clubhouse or call Phoenix and ask him to come over to Duke's."

"Baby, Duke and I didn't get into a fight because of his relationship with my sister. I beat his ass because I found out he had a wife while he was fucking and impregnating my sister. I don't have a wife I've kept hidden, and you're not pregnant, so everything should be fine. You're not pregnant, right?"

She laughed. "No, I'm not pregnant." She was silent for a few beats before she said, "He's still going to be upset. He's very protective of me, and he's not going to like this one bit."

"What aren't you telling me, Harper?"

"Too much to tell you right now," she said with a sigh. She was right. I had just pulled into the driveway to see Duke and Reese waiting on the front porch.

I squeezed her thigh once more. "Let's not keep them waiting."

We exited the car and silently made our way to the porch with Titan glued to Harper's side. Duke's arms were crossed, and the scowl on his face was aimed directly at me. Reese, on the other hand, was grinning and glancing back and forth between the two of us and the dog.

"Hey, Harper! Is that your dog?" Reese asked.

Harper's response sounded meek and timid, nothing I'd ever heard from her before. "Yes, this is Titan. He's a service dog."

"He's beautiful. Can I pet him?"

I glanced at Titan. He focused on what he

perceived as a threat, and that was Duke. "Uh, I don't think that would be a good idea right now, Reesie Piecie," I said, and darted my eyes to Duke.

Reese followed my gaze and formed her own scowl when her eyes landed on Duke. She glanced back at me, then to Harper, seeming to finally register this was not an average visit. "What's going on, Carbon?" she hesitantly asked.

I took a few steps forward and suggested, "Maybe we should go inside and sit down."

"No. Here's fine. Start talking," Duke ordered, anger radiating from him.

Duke's animosity was met with a growl from Titan as he placed his body in front of Harper and kept his eyes on Duke.

The tension was mounting by the second. Focusing my attention on the dog and Duke, I didn't see what was happening with Harper until it was almost too late.

Reese gasped. "Harper!"

I turned back to see her swaying on her feet, her eyes wide and unfocused. Duke lunged for her, leaving me only a split second to make a decision and I prayed it was the right one. Instead of trying to catch Harper, I went for Duke, taking us to the ground. A flurry of activity was happening around us. Reese was screaming. Titan was barking. Duke and I were rolling across the yard. When we came to a stop, I jumped to my feet and spun toward the girls. Reese was kneeling a few feet away from Harper who was on the ground on top of Titan. I breathed a sigh of relief and made a mental note to get that dog a steak for dinner. He'd used his body to keep Harper from hitting the ground when she fainted.

"What the fuck, man?" Duke snarled.

"He thought you were going to attack her, which means he was going to attack you. I knew if I went for you, he would take care of her," I explained as I stalked back to Harper.

"Harper, baby, are you okay?" She was on the ground, sitting up with her arms wrapped around her knees and shaking like a leaf. She buried her face in her arms, but I knew she was crying because I could see the tears running down her bare legs. As I got closer to her, Titan's warning bark turned into a deep growl. I stopped moving forward and put my arm out to stop Duke, who was two steps behind me.

"Harper, I need you to call off Titan. He won't let anyone get near you, not even me."

Titan's body instantly relaxed and the barking

ceased when she murmured, "Calmati."

I was at her side immediately, pulling her into my arms. I ran my hands over her hair and down the sides of her face. "Are you okay, baby?"

She nodded and sniffled. "Yeah, I think so. Is Titan okay?"

My sweet girl was worried about the dog. "He's fine. He doesn't know it, but he's getting a big juicy steak for dinner tonight."

She smiled, but it was weak. That coupled with her tears was it for me. I slowly rose to my full height and faced Duke. "We came here tonight to tell you that we are in a relationship. Out of respect for you, we wanted to do that in person and break the news gently. She was worried about how you would react. She said she didn't want to mess up our friendship. We were hoping to sit down and talk about it like mature adults. After what just happened, fuck all that. She's my Old Lady. Deal with it. We're going home."

I scooped Harper into my arms and placed her in the passenger seat. Titan pushed his way around me and climbed in the front floorboard to sit between Harper's feet. I stalked around the car and glanced at my sister. "Love you, Reesie Piecie," I said before slamming the door and peeling out of their driveway.

When we arrived at my condo, I carried her straight to my bedroom and placed her in the center of my bed. Cupping the sides of her face, I gently kissed her lips. "Do you want to talk about what happened back there?"

"No, but we probably should."

"Does it have anything to do with your past?"

Her head shot up. "What do you know about that?"

I held my hands up in a placating manner. "I don't know anything other than something happened to you when you were younger that somehow altered your responses to certain situations. At least that's what I'm getting based on what I was told and what I've seen for myself."

She slumped in defeat. "I should've told you before now, but I hate talking about it."

Holding her hands in mine, I softly said, "You don't have to tell me if you don't want to. All that matters to me is that you're okay."

"I don't want you to treat me differently once you know." Her cheeks flushed, and she turned her face away from me.

It took only a second for it to register in my brain. I swallowed thickly and managed to ask, "Are you referring to how I treat you in the bedroom?"

She kept her eyes pointed away from me when she nodded just one time. I sucked in a sharp breath. The sudden pain in my chest was excruciating. Had she been...? I couldn't even think that word in regards to her. I was rough in bed, rougher than most. And I was a big man. Much larger and stronger than her tiny frame. And she'd been through something so traumatic at such a tender age. I couldn't breathe. All I could feel was pain...and shame.

Her voice managed to break through the barrage of emotions slamming into me, but not enough to completely pull me back to the present. "I wasn't raped, Chase."

She rose to her knees and grabbed my face with both hands. She placed her nose against mine and repeated herself, "I wasn't raped."

Those words only relieved part of the horror churning inside of me. "Have I ever hurt you?" I asked as one tear rolled down my cheek.

"No, baby. Never," she whispered against my lips. "I swear it."

Sweet relief washed through me. I slid my arms underneath her and gazed into her eyes. "I love you, Harper Jackson."

She gave me a genuine smile. "I love you, too, Chase Walker."

"Did you mean what you said at Duke's?"

My brows furrowed in confusion. I wasn't one to say anything unless I meant it, but I had no idea what she was referring to. "I said a lot at Duke's. Can you narrow it down for me?"

"About me being you're Old Lady. I understand if—"

"I didn't say it out of anger. I fucking meant it," I said and pressed my lips to hers.

"Okay," she said without breaking our kiss. When her lips left mine, she sighed. "I guess we should get back on track."

"In a minute," I said as I tightened my hold around her and buried my face in her neck. We had a serious discussion to get through, but I wanted to hold her close and savor her for a few more minutes. I didn't know what she was going to tell me, but I knew it wouldn't change the way I saw her or the way I felt about her. I loved her, and she loved me; we could get through anything.

CHAPTER THIRTEEN

Harper

I didn't want to tell him. I didn't want to relive the memories my nightmares were made of. I knew that I had to share this part of myself with him if I wanted to have a relationship with him, but knowing it didn't make it any easier to get the words out.

"Baby, I know this is hard for you. Do you think it would be easier for you to give me a brief summary of what happened and then I could ask questions?" he gently asked.

That was a perfect example of why I had so effortlessly fallen in love with him. He understood me; he seemed to know what I needed without me saying a word. "Yes, that would make it much easier. Thank you."

He kissed my cheek. "Take your time. I'm not going anywhere."

I took a few moments to gather my thoughts and prepare myself to venture back to the most horrendous time of my life. I just needed to give him an idea of what happened. I could do that without going into detail. It was the details that got to me every time I tried to talk about it.

I took in a deep breath and started, "When I was 10 years old, I was kidnapped. The man that took me had 10-year-old twin daughters, and one of them died. The surviving twin was having a hard time with her sister's death, and nothing was helping her deal with the loss. I looked almost exactly like them. I don't know how they found me, but they did, and they took me. As long as I remembered to act like *her*, everything was fine. I was there for almost three months before Duke found me and rescued me. He moved us to Devil Springs immediately after my rescue. Aunt Leigh and Judge took us in. I lived with them until I was 18 years old. I moved to Sugar Falls for college, and here we are."

He gave me a few minutes to myself before he spoke. "May I ask you a few questions now?"

I nodded. Surprisingly, I was okay. I had never made it through a long or short version of that story without turning into a hiccupping mess of snot and tears.

"Did anyone hurt you while you were there?"

"Define hurt."

"Were you sexually abused in any way?"

"No."

"Were you physically abused?"

I swallowed audibly and felt the color drain from my face. "Yes," I whispered. "If I didn't act like her, I was punished."

I watched the rage build inside of Chase. His muscles tensed. His fists balled. His nostrils flared. "How?" he asked through his clenched jaw.

"Corporal."

He stood and began to pace. I watched him warily. I wasn't scared of him, but I didn't know what to expect from him either.

"The thought of someone hurting you infuriates me. I'm just trying to work off some of my rage. Let's keep going."

"Okay," I whispered.

"What happened to the family?"

I didn't like reliving this part of the story either. "I don't believe anyone knows this part, other than Duke and me and I'm only telling you because you're a Blackwing. Okay?"

He stopped pacing and met my eyes. "Okay."

"Duke killed the father. The mother killed herself not long after her husband's death."

"You sure he killed him?"

I could feel the bile churning in my gut. "Yes. He didn't make me watch him do it, but he made me look at his dead body before he took me out of the house. Duke said I needed to see him to know that he could never come after me again."

"What happened to the other little girl?"

I swallowed thickly. "She went to live with her aunt and uncle in another state. She struggled after losing her entire family and ended up in a mental hospital for years. When she was 18, she was found dead in her apartment from an overdose. Not sure if it was accidental or intentional."

Chase had resumed his pacing, from one end of his bedroom to the other, over and over. "Tell me about the punishments."

I frantically shook my head. "I can't do that. Please don't make me do that."

"I only want to know what he used."

I managed to utter, "A paddle or a belt," before the memory consumed me.

The only warning was the sound of the paddle slicing through the air before a line of fire streaked across my backside. Before the scream could leave my throat, the next strike landed.

"What is your name?" he bellowed as the paddle continued to harshly land against my skin.

"V-V-Vanessa," I wailed.

"You. Are. Vanessa." he screamed, each word punctuated by a strike of the paddle.

He left me there when he was finished. He always left me there, tied to a support beam in the basement. Sometimes it was just a few hours, and sometimes it was over 12 hours. As I watched my tears drip to the floor, I wondered how long I would be left there this time.

"Harper! Baby, please!" I heard Chase's desperate pleas and felt myself being cradled in his arms.

"I'm okay," I mumbled. I was never completely coherent immediately after a vivid flashback.

"No more, baby. We don't have to talk about it anymore." He placed kisses all over my face and head. I tried to move but found myself wedged between Chase at my front and something at my back. Reaching back with my hand, I discovered Titan was pressed firmly against my back.

"He jumped on the bed and used his body to maneuver you to your back when the flashback started," Chase told me, a hint of pride in his eyes.

"Impressive, Titan. Good boy," I praised while petting his head. I was skeptical about Titan and his supposed abilities at first, but he'd proven me wrong two different times in one night.

"Are you sure you're okay?" he asked, searching my eyes for the answer.

"I'm sure. I have flashbacks or panic attacks from time to time. It happens more when I'm stressed or if I'm in a tense situation with raised voices, particularly male voices. My go-to response is to cower and mentally withdraw."

"That's what happened at Duke's tonight, isn't it? You fainted right after we started yelling."

"I'm not sure. That was different. I didn't have a flashback, and I'm not scared of you or Duke. It was weird. One second I was fine, the next I felt lightheaded and then I was going down."

Chase was on his phone before I could protest. He handed the phone to me. "It's Patch. He's a club member and a doctor. He wants to ask you a few questions."

I spoke to the man on the phone and answered his questions. In a few short minutes, he determined that I needed to eat something with some protein and get some rest. Chase took those words to heart. He made steak for both of us, as well as the dog, took a very chaste shower with me, and tucked me into his bed.

***

I was surprised when Duke showed up at Chase's place the following morning. Not because he was there, but that it had taken him so long to show up. I thought he would have been there within an hour or two of us leaving his house.

Chase opened the door and blocked the view with his body. "Look, man, if you're going to say or do anything to upset her, I can't let you in. She doesn't need the stress right now."

"I'm here to apologize, to you and to her. May I please come in?"

"Let him in, Carbon," I called from my place on the sofa.

Chase reluctantly opened the door to let Duke in. However, it appeared he needed to apologize to Titan as well. My beautiful dog was standing in front of me, a low growl coming from his throat.

Duke froze mid-step. "Harper, can you call off your beast?"

I laughed and raised an eyebrow. "Which one?"

Duke snorted. "That one," he replied, pointing to Titan.

"Calmati," I softly said, and Titan's growling instantly stopped. He glanced back at me, as if double checking my decision, then resumed his position on the floor by my feet.

Duke kept his eyes on Titan and slowly made his way to the love seat. He leaned forward, placing his elbows on his knees before meeting my eyes. "I'm sorry about last night. I would've been here sooner, but I honestly didn't know if it would make things worse for you." He looked at his feet and took in a shaky breath. "I've never been the cause of a flashback. I'm so sorry, Harper."

I was on my feet and across the room in seconds. My brother was hurting, and I couldn't have that. Grabbing the hand closest to me, I held it tightly while I spoke, "You weren't the cause last night. I didn't have a flashback at your house. I fainted. Patch thought it sounded like my blood sugar was low. He told me to eat some protein and go to bed. I guess he was right because I feel much better today."

"You would tell me if I was the cause of one, wouldn't you?"

"Duke, there is only one person to blame for my flashbacks, and you killed him a long time ago."

Duke's head shot up. "I told Carbon everything last night. He needed to know to understand your reaction and, in turn, my reaction. I should've told him before now, but you know how much I don't like talking about it."

Duke's eyes widened in disbelief. "You told him everything?"

"I didn't go into extreme detail, but yes, I told him all the major points of the story. I hope you're okay with that." I'd seen my fair share of therapists, psychologists, and psychiatrists over the years, but no one besides Duke knew the whole story.

"It's your story to tell, Harper. If you're okay sharing it with him, then so am I."

"I only told him about your part in it because he's a Blackwing," I assured him. I was well aware of the trouble my brother would face if our story got out. Regardless of the reason, my brother killed a man, didn't report it, and fled to the other side of the country. I didn't want him to think I would share our story with just anyone.

Duke nodded and remained silent for a few moments. Finally, he asked, "Are you happy with him?"

"Very much so," I said with a broad smile on my face.

"That's all I've ever wanted for you." He pulled me into a hug and kissed the top of my head. "I love you, Harpie."

"Love you, too, Dukie."

A throat clearing broke up our family moment. "Harper, I think there are some other things we should share with Duke," Chase said with a raised brow.

Shit. Another discussion that I didn't want to have, even though I knew he was right. I took in a deep breath and met Chase's eyes. "Fine, but you can do the talking this time."

I sat quietly while Chase filled Duke in on everything from our relationship to the break-in to Titan. Duke listened to him intently and took things better than I expected. When Chase finished, Duke turned to me and asked, "Why did you go to him about the break-in and not me?"

"It wasn't like that. I didn't go to him. He

called and could tell that I was crying when I answered the phone. I told him I was watching a sad movie and ended the call. He didn't buy it and showed up at my house a few hours later." I felt my cheeks redden as I started the next part. "I had to tell him about the break-in so he would understand why I shot at him when he entered my house."

"You shot him?"

"I shot AT him," I explained.

"I wanted to get the club involved, but she refused. I was lucky to get her to agree to have Judge install a security system," Chase added, casually taking the focus off me shooting at him.

I held up a hand to stop Duke before he got started. "I didn't want to involve the club because they would want me to stay at the clubhouse until who knows when. I've taken a lot of time off work recently, and I can't miss any more right now. The other option would be for me to have one of the club members follow me around everywhere I went, and I didn't want that either. Judge installed the security system, and Carbon showed up with Titan. Problem solved."

Chase's phone pinged with a message, followed by Duke's phone doing the same. "We've got Church in 30 minutes. Do you want to stay here or hang out at the clubhouse?"

"I'll stay here."

"Okay, baby. I'll be back as soon as I can."

CHAPTER FOURTEEN

Carbon

Duke and I were the last to arrive for Church. When I walked through the doors, I could feel the charge in the air. We already knew something was going on because Phoenix had called us in for an unscheduled meeting, but the tension in the room had my hackles rising.

Standing at the head of the table, Phoenix waited for Duke and me to take our seats. He banged the gavel once and started pacing, which did nothing to dispel the unease churning in my gut. I had only seen Phoenix lose his shit one time, and that was when Ember showed up.

There was only one reason I could think of that would explain his current state.

"I found her," he said, almost sounding pained. Holding up his hand to keep us quiet, he continued to pace.

"I'm leaving in the morning to go get her. I'll be gone for two weeks or so. As far as everyone else is concerned, tell them I've gone on a run and will be back when I get back. Badger will run things while I'm gone, and Copper is only a phone call away. For the next two weeks, I am not your president. Until I return, do not breathe a word about this to anyone. If Ember or Coal gets wind of it, you'll pay for it with your cut." He slammed the gavel on the table and plowed through the door, leaving the lot of us sitting there stunned speechless.

"Before any of you say anything, I'm just as concerned about him as you are, but he's a grown man, and this is something that he needs to do by himself. He doesn't need us there to witness their reunion, be it good or bad. What he needs is for us to be here ready to support him when he returns to Croftridge, especially if he comes home alone," Badger informed us.

Duke asked me to join him at the bar before I went back home to Harper. "About the break-in, do you agree with the cops? Do you think it was personal?"

My jaw clenched at his words. "It had to be. Nothing was stolen and the damage done to her house was odd, to say the least. It doesn't sit well with me, brother."

"Me either. Thanks for getting her the dog. After seeing him in action, even though it was against me, it makes me feel a little better about leaving her in Sugar Falls on her own. I wish she would move here or back to Devil Springs."

I smirked. "I sure wouldn't mind having her living in Croftridge."

"Don't even go there, man."

I laughed. "Payback's a bitch, isn't it?"

"Seriously, what do you think we should do about this?"

I sighed and pinched the bridge of my nose. "There's something else that hasn't been mentioned yet. I thought it was the reason Phoenix called us into Church today, but it looks like it got sent to the backburner since he located Annabelle." Duke nodded and waited for me to continue. "Someone broke into my condo and stole one of my guns. It was found at the scene of a murder a few days ago. I was pulled over and arrested on the way back from Sugar

Falls. Harper got a printout from the security company showing the alarm was set all night. She also had a few pictures that proved I was at her house with her that night. Otherwise, I would still be in jail."

"What?!" Duke bellowed, pushing back from the bar. "When exactly did all this happen?"

"They dropped the charges yesterday. We came back to Croftridge as soon as she got off work."

"And you're sure it's your gun?"

I looked at him incredulously. "Of course I'm sure. It's registered to me. I just don't understand why that was the only gun they took. It was the little .38 I bought for Reese years ago so she could use it for target practice. I'd meant to give it to her, but never got around to it."

"Was anything else missing?" he asked.

"Nothing as far as I could tell. I went over the whole place last night after Harper fell asleep. There were no signs of forced entry on any of the doors, including the locked closet where I keep my weapons. If I hadn't been pulled over and arrested, there's no telling how long it would have been before I realized that gun was missing. That doesn't sit well with me either."

"And you left my sister at your place by

herself?" he shouted.

"No. I left her there with Titan, and Kellan is outside, but she doesn't know about that."

"We need to talk to Badger," Duke said.

"Talk to me about what?" Badger asked from behind me.

I started at the beginning and filled him in on the details of Harper's break-in as well as my own. Badger listened intently and remained silent for several minutes after I had finished. He leaned back in his chair and crossed his arms over his chest before declaring, "You need to file a police report with the Croftridge Police Department and let them dust for fingerprints and whatever else they need to do."

"Phoenix did that on my behalf right after I was arrested. They didn't find any prints that didn't belong there, and there were no signs of forced entry," I told him.

He nodded and scratched his head. After a few minutes of silence, he added, "Call Judge and get him down here to install some cameras at your place, today if possible. Wouldn't hurt to add cameras to Harper's place as well. Seems odd that her place was broken into while she was here with you and then your place was broken into a few days later while you were at her place.

You two piss anyone off recently?"

"No, not that I know of. I've been around here dealing with club issues and going to see her on the weekends. We rarely left her house when I was there. As far as I know, Harper goes to work during the week and spends her weekends with me unless she is here visiting or I'm tied up with club business. We haven't been around anyone to piss them off," I explained.

He clapped me on the shoulder and stood. "Call Judge and get him down here. You and Harper stay vigilant. Keep your eyes and ears open while we get this sorted."

"Thanks, Badger," I said. Rising to my feet, I pulled out my phone to call Judge and head back to my girl.

Pulling up to my condo, I scanned the area for Kellan. He was either good at staying out of sight, or he was slacking on his job and going to get his ass kicked. I stomped to the front door, trying to rein in my temper before I entered. My efforts proved futile when I opened the door to find Kellan sitting on my sofa in his t-shirt and boxers. What the fuck?

A growl from me was his only warning before I lunged. Wrapping my hands around his throat, I pressed him into the sofa and demanded, "Where is my girl and what the fuck are you doing in my house without your pants on?"

Titan came running into the room, snarling and growling, ready to attack. He took one second to look between the two of us before he leaped onto the couch and continued his growling only inches from our faces.

Tightening my hands around Kellan's neck, I demanded through clenched teeth, "Where. Is. She?"

"Carbon!" Harper shrieked. "What in the hell are you doing? Let him go, you big monster!"

At the sound of Harper's frantic voice, Titan inched his face closer, his growl progressively getting louder. "Call off the dog, Harper."

"Just so you know, if I wasn't worried about Kellan's safety, I wouldn't call him off," she snipped with her hands on her hips. "Calmati."

Titan stopped his growling, jumped off the couch, and moved to stand in front of Harper. "Let him up and tell me what the hell is going on."

I released Kellan and took two steps back. Glaring at her, I insisted, "Not until you tell me why this little fucker is on my couch in his boxers!"

Realization dawned on her. "Fuck you,

Carbon!" she yelled and stomped up the stairs.

"Carbon, man, it's not what it looks like. I was sitting behind some bushes when she took the dog out. He fucking pissed on my leg and then tried to rip my throat out. I explained who I was and what I was doing here. She offered to wash and dry my jeans for me. She's been upstairs the whole time while I was down here watching television," Kellan rushed to explain.

I stepped back. "Shit!" I pinched the bridge of my nose and took in a deep breath. "Sorry, man. I've got a lot going on, and I snapped when I saw you in here like that. I need to go talk to her, and I'll see if your pants are dry."

"Not a problem. Shit happens," he shrugged like he hadn't just been seconds away from having his neck snapped by the Blackwings' Enforcer.

I found Harper on the floor of my bedroom, curled into a tight ball, quietly crying. I scooped her up, and my gut sank when I felt her body stiffen in my arms. "Baby, I'm sorry. I overreacted. It had nothing to do with you and everything to do with me. I'm already concerned about your safety. Then, I found another man in my house in his underwear and you were nowhere around. I thought something happened to you."

"If you thought he was capable of hurting me, why would you send him over to watch me?" she asked, without raising her head.

"I don't think he's capable of hurting you. He's a good kid, and I trust him. I just reacted. Like I said, this is on me. It's something I thought I had worked through, but it looks like there is still some work to do."

"Is this about your family?"

I tightened my arms around her. "Yeah, baby, it is. I love you, Harper. It would kill me if something happened to you."

"Did you apologize to Kellan?"

"I did."

"Okay." She raised her head and gave me a small smile before she started to wiggle out of my arms. "I need to go see if his jeans are dry."

"That's it?" I asked.

"I have a fucked up past, too. I get it. So, yeah, that's it."

***

After sending Kellan on his way, Harper and I spent several hours in bed making up. We would have likely spent all day in bed if we hadn't been interrupted by someone knocking on the front door. "Fuck, I forgot to tell you Judge was coming by to install some security cameras this afternoon. I'm guessing that's him at the door," I said while quickly getting dressed.

"Damn it, Chase. I need to take a shower. I have sex hair and probably smell like a brothel!" She jumped out of bed and scurried to the bathroom.

"Take your time; we'll be downstairs."

I opened the door to find Judge standing there with a knowing smirk on his face. "Took you long enough."

"Sorry, brother. Come on in."

"That better be my little sister cousin you've got up there, or I'm going to have to beat your ass in your own living room," he said, completely serious.

I stood there, speechless, shocked by his knowledge of my relationship with Harper.

"Don't look at me like that. Did you forget that we have the same training? I've seen the way you two are around each other. Plus, I spotted you at her office last week. Then, Ruben tells me you bought a dog from him the same day I installed a system at her house. If you two thought you were being covert, you were very, very wrong."

"Well shit. We did think that, but it doesn't

matter now. We told the club last night," I said.

Judge held out his hand. "Congratulations. Not that you need it, but you have my blessing. Just know that no one will be able to find your body if you hurt her."

"Well aware, man. I would expect nothing less."

About halfway through the installation process, Harper tiptoed down the stairs, looking nervous as hell. I nudged Judge with my elbow and jerked my chin in her direction.

Without lifting his head, Judge said, "I've known since I installed your alarm system. Now, quit freaking out and come give me a hug."

Harper grinned and rushed over to hug Judge. "You're not mad?"

"Why the fuck would I be mad? I don't care who you choose to spend your life with. If you're happy, I'm happy. If he hurts you, I'll kill him, but I have a feeling you already knew that."

She giggled. "Yeah, I did."

By the time Judge was finished with the installation, we were all hungry. We opted to pick up something to eat on the way to the club. The club wasn't as packed as I assumed it would be for a Saturday night. When I spotted Ranger at one of the tables, I asked, "Where is everyone?"

He chuckled. "Shaker and a few boys went to Cedar Valley to chase some pussy. Dash and Duke are out at the pool with their girls. Phoenix is on a run. As for the rest of them, I ain't their keeper."

I couldn't help but laugh at the man. I wasn't sure how old Ranger was, but he had been around as long as I could remember. He was the youngest of the original members and followed the mother chapter to Croftridge with Phoenix. His wisdom and experience were priceless to the club.

"Judge! Didn't see you there with Carbon's big ass in the way. What brings you to Croftridge, boy?"

Judge smiled fondly at Ranger. "Good to see you, old man! I came down to install some cameras at Carbon's place. Thought I'd stick around for dinner before I head back."

Ranger gestured to the table in front of him. "Have a seat. What're we having for dinner?"

CHAPTER FIFTEEN

Harper

Leaving Croftridge Sunday night was harder than any of the other times one of us had to return home. This time, I was leaving knowing that I wouldn't see him in a few days. I hated that we couldn't be together during the week, but we both had lives established in different places. We couldn't be together without one of us having to give up something we loved. When things were casual between us, it worked well only seeing each other on the weekends. I wasn't sure that would be the case now that our relationship was different.

The night before, during dinner, Ranger

asked why we were increasing security at both of our private homes. After we told him about the break-ins, he made a suggestion that I hated, but had to admit was a good idea. He suggested that Chase and I stay away from each other for a few weeks to see what happened. Depending on what, if anything, happened to one or both of us, we would know if the break-ins were random, intentional, or somehow related.

After a tearful goodbye and an even more tearful drive to Sugar Falls, I was pleasantly surprised to see a familiar motorcycle parked in my driveway. Judge opened the front door of my house and helped me carry my things inside. "What are you doing here?"

"Nice to see you, too, Sister Cousin."

"Oh shut it. I wasn't expecting you to be here is all."

"I finished with the cameras a few hours ago, but I did something else for you and I wanted to be here when you saw it," he smiled, but it didn't reach his eyes.

Nervously, I asked, "What is it?"

"I'll show you." I followed Judge to the front porch. He flipped a switch that turned on my very bright floodlights. My driveway was on the side of my house, so I hadn't seen the front yard when I pulled in. My entire front yard was now covered in beautiful, lush sod.

Turning back to Judge, I asked, "Why did you do that? Don't get me wrong; it's beautiful, and I appreciate it, but there has to be a reason you redid my entire front lawn."

He shrugged. "I had to bury some cables for the cameras, and I didn't want it to be obvious that something had been installed recently. If anybody was watching, it looked like you were having your yard resurfaced, not having a security system upgrade."

"Clever. Well, thanks, Judge. It looks great. Do you want me to make you something to eat before you go?"

"No, thanks. I picked up something while I was out. Wish I could stay, but Copper has a few things he needs me to take care of, so I've got to get going."

The following three weeks were nothing short of miserable for me. I felt like a part of me was missing as I went through the motions of what used to be an enjoyable life for me. Even when Chase and I were just Friday night fuck buddies, I wasn't miserable and lonely during the week. If it weren't for Titan, I believe I might have completely lost my mind.

During the week, my patients kept me reasonably occupied while I was at work. After work, Hilarie and I ate dinner together a few times a week like we usually did. I wasn't great company to have, but she didn't seem to notice. She prattled on and on about some guy she met at a club. Apparently, they were hot and heavy because she was nowhere to be found on the weekends. A large part of me wanted to throw her own words in her face about being one of those friends who disappeared the second they found a man, but confrontation was hard for me, especially with someone I was close to.

Without Chase or Hilarie, I was left to entertain myself on the weekends. The first one I spent at home by myself, barely getting out of bed and not bothering to shower. The second weekend I treated myself to a spa package and spent the following day shopping. At the beginning of the third week, I was desperate to see Chase. We talked on the phone and sent texts throughout the day, but I needed to see him, to feel him. Even though he assured me we wouldn't have to be apart for much longer, I was already trying to put together a plan for us to see each other without anyone knowing.

After dinner with Hilarie on Wednesday of the

third week of our forced separation, Chase called shortly after I arrived home. "Hey, baby. I've got some good news for you."

"Oh, please tell me this ridiculous separation is over. I'm dying of loneliness here," I whined.

He chuckled. "It's sort of over." My growl of frustration prompted him to continue. "Dash and Ember are getting married a week from Saturday. You're invited to her bachelorette party this weekend, and she wants you to be a bridesmaid."

I squealed with excitement. "That means I will have to come to Croftridge two weekends in a row!"

"Does that mean I can tell her you accepted both of her invitations?"

"Yes!" I yelled into the phone.

***

Color me surprised when Hilarie asked me at dinner the following day if I had plans for the weekend. My inner bitch wanted to ask if the guy she had been wrapped up in finally got sick of her, but I didn't. Keeping my irritation at bay, I replied, "I do. My friend, Ember, is getting married next weekend and her bachelorette

169

party is this weekend."

Hilarie scrunched her nose. "So, you'll be in Croftridge two weekends in a row? What am I supposed to do?"

I wanted to slap her but managed to refrain. "I would assume whatever you've been doing for the last few weekends. My activities, or lack thereof, weren't a concern to you then, so they shouldn't be now."

Her eyebrows rose. "My man has to work this weekend, so I won't get to see him. Where's your guard dog been?"

"Assuming you are referring to Carbon, he's been in Croftridge."

Her countenance changed into what I could only describe as fake sympathy. She reached across the table to pat my hand. "Aw, sweetie. Did you guys break up?"

I jerked my hand back. "No, we didn't break up. I told you we weren't a couple. You have to be a couple to break up." That wasn't a lie. I did tell her we weren't a couple; I just never told her we had become a couple. I sighed, "Can we talk about something other than Carbon?"

"Of course," she smiled and changed the subject.

The rest of dinner was uncomfortable, at least

it was for me. She more or less admitted that she wanted to do something with me only because her man was busy. That just pissed me off. I cooled off on the drive home and decided that I would deal with Hilarie next week. Nothing was going to put a damper on my weekend with my man.

Hilarie avoided me the next two days at work, and I had no complaints about it. I didn't want to act like nothing was wrong, and I didn't want to discuss my issues with her either. As soon as the center closed on Friday, Titan and I drove straight to Croftridge. Chase told me to let myself in when I arrived because he wouldn't be home until after 7:00 pm. I was slightly disappointed at that news but figured I could use the time to freshen up and maybe put on something cute for him.

Titan did his perimeter check of the condo while I headed upstairs to Chase's bedroom. I dropped my bags beside the bed and turned to go to the bathroom. My mouth was covered by a large hand before a scream could escape me. "It's me, baby," Chase whispered in my ear before trailing his lips down my neck.

I tried to turn around so I could wrap my arms around him, but he held me firmly in place. He

171

kept one hand over my mouth while he tangled the other in my hair. "Strip," he ordered. By the tone of his voice, I could tell he wanted to play. That was fine with me. I'd missed his dominating ass.

"Yes, sir," I mumbled against his hand and promptly began removing every stitch of clothing from my body. This was rather easy given my previous profession as well as the fact that I wasn't wearing a bra or panties. A tug on one string had my wrap around dress opening and sliding down my body to pool at my feet.

Chase's groan turned into a growl while his hand tightened in my hair. "Naughty, naughty little minx."

The hand covering my mouth slowly moved down to cup my breast before he captured my nipple between his thumb and forefinger. He used his hold on me to guide me to the bed and bend me over the end of it.

"When did you take your panties off?" he asked while smoothing his large palm over my bare backside.

Shit. He wasn't going to like my answer, but he would know if I didn't tell him the truth. "I didn't put any on when I got dressed this morning."

He squeezed my left butt cheek. "You're telling

me my pussy has been uncovered under this flimsy excuse for a dress all fucking day?"

"Yes, sir."

He chuckled darkly and slid his hand down to slip two fingers inside of me, finding me wet and ready. He moved them in and out twice and paused, seeming to get himself under control. "Did you do that knowing it would rile me up? Is that what you wanted, Harper?"

He called me by my name. I knew that was his way of asking if I was ready for what he wanted to give me. He wanted to play rough and wanted to be sure I was right there with him. "Yes, sir."

The fingers inside of me started pumping again, causing me to push back against him in a fruitless attempt to find the friction I needed. Suddenly, the fingers were gone and a loud smack resonated in the otherwise quiet room before heat bloomed across my ass. Smack after smack was delivered until I was begging for him to stop spanking and start fucking. After the last smack, he demanded, "On the bed. Hands and knees."

I quickly obliged, proudly sticking my reddened ass into the air. It had been so long since I'd been with him and I was more than ready for anything he wanted to give me.

Chase climbed onto the bed behind me and instructed me to spread my legs wider. The moment I did, he slid into me to the hilt and pumped twice before he pulled out completely. "Naughty pussies don't get rewarded," he growled while he pressed the tip of his dick to my rear entrance.

I tensed for a brief moment, but it didn't go unnoticed. It wasn't the first time for us, but we didn't do it often, and it had been a while since the last time. I definitely wasn't expecting it. He paused and gave my hips a gentle squeeze. "I'm good," I said softly.

Two quick slaps to my ass were followed by, "I want your ass, baby girl. Let me in." I took a deep breath and pushed back against him, allowing him to slide past the tight ring of muscles.

He continued pushing in with slow and steady pressure until he was fully seated inside of me. He groaned loudly. "Harper, your ass feels so fucking good. Are you ready for me to fuck it, baby?"

I wasn't sure if I loved it or hated it when he made me answer questions like that in the middle of our proclivities. Regardless, I responded with, "Yes, sir."

He thrust forward with more force than I'd

anticipated, eliciting a loud moan from me. Apparently, he'd put on a condom and coated himself in lube when I wasn't paying attention, easing the way for him. He slid in and out, building up his rhythm until he was fucking me hard and fast, just like we both liked it. "Do you like having your ass fucked?"

"Only by you, sir."

"Are you going to come from having my big cock in your ass?"

"If you will allow it, sir."

"One hand on your tit and one on your clit. Make yourself come. I want to feel your ass clenching around me while I'm fucking it."

I did as he wished and was coming within seconds. "Chase! Harder!"

He didn't disappoint. He thrust into me half a dozen more times before finding his release. He collapsed on top of me and quickly rolled to the side, cradling me in his arms. "I missed you so much, baby."

I turned to face him and placed my hands on his cheeks. "I missed you, too, Chase."

"Come on, let's have a shower, and then I want to fuck you as many times as I can before the sun comes up." I giggled and happily followed him to the shower. That sounded like a great plan to me.

***

I missed the bachelorette breakfast the next morning. Chase was true to his word and kept me up until the wee hours of the morning with his animalistic fucking, which led to me sleeping through the alarm I had set. I woke to Chase's head between my thighs as he enjoyed his own personal breakfast. "Took you long enough," he mumbled against my skin.

"Oh fuck, don't stop," I moaned, writhing beneath him.

A sharp slap to my outer thigh had me gasping and growing even wetter for him. "I give the orders, not you, princess."

"I'm sorry, sir," I replied, playing along with his little game. It was no hardship for me. I loved his dominant side and his penchant for role-playing and rough sex.

He crawled up my body and slid inside me in one fluid motion, eliciting groans from the both of us. "You're already an hour late, so this is going to be quick and dirty."

"Yes, please!"

An hour later, Chase dropped me off at the

spa with the rest of the girls attending the bachelorette party. I climbed off his bike, gave him a quick kiss, and turned to go inside. Suddenly, I was yanked back and turned. Chase covered my lips with his in a very inappropriate for the public kiss. "Enjoy yourself today, baby, but don't you dare let another man touch you."

I leaned back to look him in the eye. I could tell by the tone of his voice that this was not one of his games. He seriously did not want another man touching me. Archaic as it was, I kind of liked that he didn't want another man's hands on me. "I won't. I promise," I said, lightly rubbing his cheek with my thumb while keeping my eyes locked with his.

He grinned, his eyes sparkling with a hint of mischievousness. "Good girl. Give me one more kiss and then get your ass in there before I decide to take you back home with me."

I did as he asked and met the girls in the lobby of the spa, surprised to find all eyes on me. My cheeks instantly heated, but I tried to play it off. "What?" I asked, shrugging and feigning innocence.

Ember fanned herself with a spa menu. "Damn, Harper! That kiss was smokin' hot. Now we know why you missed breakfast."

Reese stuck her fingers in her ears. "I'm not listening. I'm not listening."

I glanced around uncomfortably at all the women staring at me. I didn't like being the center of attention. Well, not when I had to interact with the ones focused on me anyway. Ember seemed to sense my discomfort and provided a nice segue. "Let me introduce you to everyone. On the blue couch, we have Sarah, Emma, and Tara. They work at the organic farm. Alexis is on the love seat beside Reese. She works in the office at the dairy farm. Keegan is the one in the green chair. She works at the barn with your brother."

"My apologies," I said to Keegan causing her to laugh.

Ember linked arms with a woman who looked just like her and smiled widely. "And this is Annabelle, my mother."

I smiled brightly and extended my hand. "It's so nice to meet you. I've heard a lot about you. I'm Harper, Duke's little sister and Carbon's girlfriend."

"It's nice to meet you, too. I'm surprised I haven't seen you around before now," she said.

"That's because I live and work in Sugar Falls. Unfortunately, Carbon and I haven't been able to see each other the last few weekends due to our schedules."

Annabelle smiled a knowing smile. "I hope you had him for breakfast."

I grinned. "I did." I liked Annabelle.

After being massaged, wrapped, exfoliated, and waxed to within an inch of my life, we were finally ready to leave the spa. When it was time to pay for my treatments, the clerk told me it was taken care of and handed me a small envelope. Confused, I took it and pulled out the slip of paper inside.

Harper,
My treat. Be good tonight.
Love you,
Chase

I was falling more and more in love with that man every day. I pulled out my phone to send him a quick text when someone bumping my hip startled me. I looked up to see Reese waving a similar white envelope around. "What's yours say?" she asked.

I glanced around and noticed that Annabelle, Ember, Reese, and Sarah also had white envelopes. "It's just a note from Chase letting me know he paid."

Reese gasped. "He lets you call him Chase?"

I couldn't tell if she was surprised or somehow offended. Hesitantly, I answered, "Yes, he told me to call him Chase when we first started dating, but only when we were alone. He wanted me to call him Carbon if we were around other people. I assumed it was because we weren't ready to share our relationship with the club."

Her eyes dropped to the floor for a moment before she raised them to meet mine. When she did, they were full of unshed tears. Softly, she said, "He hasn't let anyone call him Chase since our family was murdered. He's been Carbon ever since that day, even to me."

I reached out and placed my hand on her shoulder. "I'm sorry, Reese. I didn't—"

"No, no," she interrupted, "it's a good thing, a little bittersweet, but I'm happy about it." She took in a deep breath and squared her shoulders. "Load up, ladies. It's time to head back to Ember's house and get ready for a wild night out!"

Claps and cheers erupted around the tranquil spa as we filed out the door and climbed into a stretch SUV limo. Reese popped open a bottle of champagne and started passing glasses around as she got them filled. I found it hilarious that we went through a drive-thru to pick up a late lunch on the way back to Ember's house. Champagne and Burger King, what a combination.

By the time we arrived at Ember's house, I had downed multiple glasses of champagne but managed to finish my meal. Thinking the food would help ward off some of the effects of the alcohol was a mistake. As we were getting ready, Reese handed everyone a shot glass filled with something fruity. She held her glass high in the air, "We shall start the night off with what we will all be tonight, a cockteaser!" We each downed the shot and returned to getting ready, but Reese wasn't done. She came back shortly with another shot for each girl. By the time we were ready to leave, I had downed a purple hooter, a buttery nipple, and a red-headed slut, in addition to the initial cockteaser.

I stumbled to the car in my five-inch heels and indecently short dress, and I started to wonder if I should bow out now. I wasn't a big drinker, and I felt certain I had already surpassed my limitations. I turned around to search for Ember and tell her I wasn't going to be able to go with them when Annabelle placed her hand on my arm. "You'll be okay, Harper. I'll make you a drink with no alcohol in it so you can sober up a bit and no one will be the wiser."

I looked at her incredulously, "How did you know?"

She smiled. "I spit the shots into an empty glass when no one was looking. I thought someone needed to stay sober and keep an eye on things tonight. As the bride's mother, I silently volunteered myself for the job."

I breathed a huge sigh of relief. "Thank you."

We had a great time dancing and playing silly party games. I was glad Annabelle convinced me to stay. After dancing and drinking non-alcoholic drinks, I had significantly sobered up and was starting to get tired. We were at the third club of the evening when I started wondering how much longer this party was going to last.

I was sitting at our reserved table talking with Keegan when Annabelle came running over to the table, dragging Reese and Alexis with her. Ember and Sarah were right behind them pulling Emma and Tara to the table. I straightened in my seat, panic already seeping in. "What's going on?"

Annabelle explained, "I noticed a guy following us. He's been everywhere we've been tonight, and he's been staring. So, I asked Phoenix about it. Come to find out, Shaker and Carbon have been following us, or were supposed to be, but Phoenix can't get a hold of them. He told me to gather up everyone and stay put. He's on his way now."

Ember and Annabelle continued to whisper to one another. Reese sat stiff as a board in her seat. And I felt like I couldn't breathe. Where the hell was Chase? Did something happen to him? Nothing could happen to him. I needed him. Now. I've had a man follow me before, and it didn't turn out well. This couldn't turn out like that did.

I was damn near in a full-blown panic attack when I felt Reese's fingers intertwine with mine and squeeze. "He's okay. I can feel it. Take a few slow breaths and calm down so you can feel it, too."

At first, I thought she was insane, but then I thought, "What the hell?" and decided to give it a try. To my utter astonishment, she was right. After getting myself under control, I could feel it somehow; an unexplainable knowledge that he was okay. She must have been watching me closely because she spoke the moment realization dawned. "There you go. Just hang in there with me until we find out what is going on." Reese and I sat quietly together, hand in hand, waiting for Phoenix to arrive.

CHAPTER SIXTEEN

Carbon

"Looks like the girls are getting ready to head to another club," I said to Shaker. We were posted up in the back corner of some lame ass dance club in Cedar Valley. Phoenix wanted the girls tailed by two brothers, and I readily volunteered for the job. I was desperate to see Harper and would take anything I could get, even if that meant watching her drunkenly dance around in a dress that accentuated every perfect curve of her body.

"We can't get past them without being seen, so we'll have to let them go first and slip out behind them." Shaker nodded his agreement and finished his beer.

When the girls started filing out the front door, we rose and slowly started making our way to the front door. By the time all of them made it outside, we were a few feet away. I only took a few more steps when one of the bouncers stepped in front of me. "Sir, I'm going to need you and your friend to come with me."

"I don't fucking think so. You're not a cop and have no authority to detain me or keep me in this establishment against my will. Now, if you will kindly step aside, I have somewhere to be."

He shook his head and grimaced. "I can't let you leave, sir. Please cooperate and follow me."

I turned to look at Shaker, who looked equally as pissed off as I was. "Fuck this shit," I said and made to push my way past the bouncer.

"Hold it right there. Keep your hands where I can see them." I knew without even turning around those words were spoken by an actual police officer.

I slowly raised my hands in the air and directed my attention to the two police officers ready to pounce should Shaker or I try to run. "What's the problem, Officer?"

"Turn around and place your hands behind your back."

Grumbling under my breath, I did as he said and cringed when I felt the metal cuffs bite into my thick wrists. I could easily get away from these two bozos and have the cuffs off in no time, but Phoenix would have my ass if I did that. Plus, I hadn't done a damn thing wrong, so I saw no reason to commit a crime by running from a crime I didn't commit, though I was getting sick of being arrested for something I didn't do.

"We were called when someone informed the bouncers that the two of you were spotted putting something in a woman's drink at the bar. Anything you want to tell us about that?" Dickhead Number One asked.

"Are you fucking serious? We haven't even been at the bar. We got our drinks from one of the waitresses. Get the receipt out of my wallet, get her name, and ask her. Then, check your security footage," I spat and nodded toward one of the cameras pointed directly at the bar.

They hauled us into an office near the back of the club. Shaker and I sat quietly while they reviewed the footage. While we were waiting, my phone started buzzing in my pocket. When I heard Shaker's phone buzzing seconds later, I knew it had to be Phoenix calling. He was going to be pissed that we weren't answering.

Almost an hour later, the security footage and our waitress confirmed our story. The police officers undid the cuffs and told us we were free to go. The club's manager profusely apologized and offered us multiple free passes to the club which included unlimited free drinks. We took them, but I had no intention of ever setting foot in the place again.

We successfully made our way out the front door. "Call Phoenix back. I'm going to text Harper and see where they are."

"Where in the fuck have you two been?" Duke bellowed from down the block. I looked up to see Dash and him rapidly approaching us.

"Where are the girls?" I asked. I didn't have time for his shit.

"Shouldn't you know that?" he spat.

"Yeah, but it's kind of hard to follow them when the cops have me in cuffs in some club manager's office over a bogus complaint. Now tell me where the girls are or so help me—"

Dash interrupted my threat, "Phoenix is with them at The Night Owl. They're fine, but we need to get back there."

"Why are the three of you here?" Shaker asked, breaking his odd silence of the night.

"Annabelle called Phoenix because she

thought they were being followed. He thought she was referring to you two. When she told him to get you two in there ASAP, he knew something was wrong. He was already out the door when he was trying to get you on the phone. He called Duke and me to come look for you while he went to look after the girls," Dash explained.

We were moving quickly, but when I saw the sign for The Night Owl, I broke into a jog. I knew Harper would be upset about some unknown person following them and Reese would be upset about my unexplained absence. I was consumed with the need to hold Harper in my arms and comfort my little sister. I pushed through the doors and shouted to the bouncer, "I'm with them," pointing to the girls.

Reese and Harper were sitting very close to each other. When I reached them, I saw that they were holding hands under the table. Wrapping my arms around their shoulders, I pulled them both to my chest. I placed a kiss on top of their heads and asked, "Are you two okay?"

Reese squeezed my waist and pulled back while Harper remained in my arms. "We're okay," Reese answered. "We were a little freaked out at first, but we were more worried about you than anything else."

I filled them in on why Phoenix couldn't reach us earlier. Harper sat up and asked, "Do they know who made the complaint?"

I shook my head. "No, and we didn't stick around to press them on it. As soon as we were free to go, we flew out of there so we could find you and call Phoenix. We ran into Duke and Dash, and they filled us in on everything we missed."

We talked with Phoenix for a few minutes before he grumbled about a headache and declared it time to go. "I'll pick you up at Ember's house. You can't ride on the back of my bike dressed like that."

When I picked her up from Ember's house, we went back to my condo and spent the rest of the weekend in bed. I didn't want to let her leave Monday morning, but knowing that she would be back on Friday made it easier to say goodbye.

***

It had been a long week. From the moment Harper left Monday morning, I had been busy from sunup to sundown every day. When I got home Thursday, I cleaned up my condo before hopping in the shower. I planned to wash off quickly and call Harper before crashing for the night.

I couldn't wait to see her, and I was thrilled that I would get to spend the entire weekend with her again. As my thoughts drifted to Harper, my hand drifted lower. Wrapping my hand around myself, I let out a groan as I began to stroke. When it came to Harper, it didn't take much to get me worked up.

Bracing one hand against the shower wall, I continued my ministrations, lost in one of my favorite memories of her...

Both of her hands landed on my head, clutching fists full of my hair. She yanked my head back, dropped her forehead to mine, and stared into my eyes while she came and little gasps escaped her parted lips. It was by far the most erotic thing I had ever witnessed. She rode out her pleasure while I watched in awe.

I was still admiring her when she put her lips on my ear again. She ran her hand down my chest to the bulge in my jeans, rubbing me through my pants. I intended to stop her, to tell her that this wasn't about getting me off, but it felt so damn good I wanted to enjoy it for a few more seconds before I stopped her.

I don't know how she did it, but before I knew what was happening, she had my cock covered with a condom and sucked into her mouth. All. The. Fucking. Way. "Oh fuck," I groaned, leaning forward. "You don't have to," I gritted out. But I fucking wanted her to. Damn, her mouth felt good around my cock, even with it sheathed. And she didn't even bat an eyelash at my piercings.

My fantasy was interrupted when a warm, wet mouth wrapped around my cock. I reacted on instinct and tried to pull away before realizing it was Harper kneeling in front of me in all her naked glory. "Oh, you're in so much trouble, you naughty little minx. Clasp your elbows behind your back. Knees spread wide. Mouth open." She immediately obeyed every command. I took a step forward and slid my dick to the back of her throat. "Suck." She did, and she did it with fervor.

With my previous stroking and her sinfully succulent mouth, it wasn't going to be long before I came down her throat. Deciding to give her a little punishment for sneaking up on me in the shower, because, let's face it, that's exactly why she did it, I grabbed her head with both hands and began vigorously thrusting in and out of her mouth. "Is this what you wanted?" I grunted. "Me to fuck your pretty little mouth?"

She responded with a muffled, "Mmm-hmm."

The vibrations from her moaned affirmation sent me over the edge. I held her head still while I emptied myself down her throat. She was breathtaking, kneeling on the floor of my shower with her mouth stuffed full of my cock. I slowly slipped out of her mouth and reached down to help her stand.

"What are you doing here, princess? I thought you weren't coming until tomorrow."

She smirked and tipped her head toward my semi-hard cock. "Yeah, I thought the same thing about you." She squealed when my hand landed on her ass. "Okay, okay. There was no way I would be able to make it to the rehearsal on time if I worked tomorrow, so I took the day off and drove straight here when I got off work today. Is that okay?"

I lifted her into my arms and covered her mouth with mine. "Hell yes, it's okay. Damn, baby, I've missed you."

"I've missed you, too, big guy."

I placed her back on her feet and turned her around. With a light smack to her ass, I said, "Dry off, go bend over the bed, and wait for the rest of your punishment."

I couldn't see her face, but I could hear the smile in her voice when she answered, "Yes, sir."

***

We had to force ourselves to get out of bed and get ready for the wedding rehearsal. I was dressed and had been waiting on the couch for over 15 minutes when Harper came down the stairs in a long-sleeved, rather modest, black dress. Don't get me wrong; she looked gorgeous, I was just surprised at her choice. I stood and grabbed the keys to my Mustang from the table. "You ready to go?"

"Yes, just need to grab my bag from the kitchen." When she turned, I sucked in a sharp breath and let it out with a hiss. Her entire back was bare, all the way down to maybe an inch above her ass crack. She whirled back to face me with a devilish smirk on her face. "Something wrong?"

"You know I'm not going to be able to keep my hands off of you tonight," I said in a low voice.

She grinned. "You'll have to. Don't forget, my brother and your sister will be there." She then proceeded to prance out the door.

The rehearsal itself went smoothly and

was over in just under an hour. Phoenix and Annabelle were late to the rehearsal, and it was very obvious as to the reason why. Annabelle's dress was slightly rumpled, and she had a dazed, just fucked look on her face. When Shaker was the first to call them out, Annabelle turned red from head to toe and tried to hide behind Phoenix's broad back. I pulled Harper closer to me and said loud enough for everyone to hear, "See, baby, we had time." She jabbed me in the gut with her elbow, but it was worth it to see Duke and Reese both wrinkle their faces in disgust.

The rehearsal dinner was at an Italian restaurant in downtown Croftridge, which was nothing more than one main street lined with locally owned shops and restaurants. Harper and I were the first to arrive, so I chose our seats strategically. We took the seats at the end of the L-shaped table that butted up next to the wall. She quirked a brow at my choice but didn't make a comment.

Once everyone arrived and we placed our orders, idle chit-chat amongst the guests began. I leaned over to Shaker, who was seated next to me, and said, "Keep your attention focused in the other direction." He smirked and nodded once before angling himself toward Keegan.

When the speeches began, I placed my hand on Harper's bare thigh. Slowly, I inched my way up her leg. When I gently pulled her leg closer to me, she visibly tensed and whispered, "No." She didn't mean that, so I continued working my way up her leg until I reached her panties. I could feel the heat from her core, and I hadn't even touched her yet.

Sliding her panties to the side, I lightly ran my fingers over her pussy, not at all surprised to find her soaking wet, which was perfect for my plan. I reached into my pocket with my free hand and pulled out the remote-controlled vibrator I ordered the week before. I slipped one end of the U-shaped device inside of her and nestled the other end against her clit.

She grabbed ahold of my wrist in a vain attempt to stop me. "Chase," she whispered, but the warning in her tone was loud and clear.

I leaned in to kiss her cheek and murmured, "Do you trust me, baby?"

She audibly swallowed and nodded her head.

"Good. Now, let's have some fun," I said as I slid her panties back into place and leaned back in my chair.

I spent the next two hours toying with Harper

by turning the vibrator off and on at random intervals as well as adjusting the speed. Twice, I let her get close to climaxing before I abruptly turned off the device. The glare she shot me both times would have been enough to have a lesser man cowering in his seat.

When the rehearsal dinner was finally over, we said our goodbyes and Harper all but sprinted to the car. I chuckled to myself and followed along behind her at a much slower pace. The moment I closed the car door, she was in my lap and reaching for my belt.

"What are you doing, baby?" I asked as if I didn't know.

"So help me, Chase, if you don't put your cock in me right now, I will make sure you regret it," she growled.

"No need for threats, baby. I would have fucked you in the restaurant. All you had to do was ask. Oh, fuck," I groaned as she engulfed me with her tight heat.

My hands landed on her hips, intending to guide her movements, but she swatted my hands away. "Not this time, big guy. You just sit there and take what I'm giving you."

I grinned. "Show me what ya got, baby."

And she fucking did.

CHAPTER SEVENTEEN

Harper

Ember arranged to have a team of hairstylists and makeup artists on site the day of the wedding. She had them set up in a vacant building on the farm property. We rotated through hair, makeup, and nails in sets of two. Some of the girls had gotten their nails done the weekend before at the spa, but I wasn't one of them. It was a miracle if my manicures lasted an entire day; I had no idea how some of these girls managed to keep them for a week.

I was a little nervous because I didn't know most of the girls very well. I wasn't opposed to making new friends; it just wasn't in my nature to initiate conversation with someone I didn't know. Lucky for me, I was paired up with Keegan who had no problem opening up to someone new.

She was a year younger than me and had recently moved to Croftridge to work at Ember's horse farm. Her step-father was a successful horse breeder and trainer in Kentucky, and she knew her way around a barn. Ember practically hired her on the spot.

"So, you work with my brother?" I asked.

"Yes, but don't believe anything you've heard him say about me," she replied.

"He's never said anything to me about you…" I trailed off, hoping she would fill in the gaps.

"We don't always get along. The ranches in Arizona are nothing like the ranches in Kentucky. We tend to butt heads over the best way to do things."

I giggled. "Duke always thinks he knows what's best. Don't let him walk all over you."

She grinned. "I don't."

We continued chatting as we moved from station to station. We had our nails done first, followed by makeup, then hair. I had been enjoying myself up until my stylist swept my hair up and gasped, which was followed by another gasp from Keegan. I didn't have long to figure out what to say, so I went with instinct and told the truth. Shrugging, I said, "I like my sex with a little kink in it. Do you think you can cover it with makeup or should we leave my hair down?"

The stylist blinked at me and then seemed to gather her composure. "Let me grab one of the makeup girls and get her opinion."

The moment she was gone, Keegan looked me up and down and shook her head. "It's always the quiet ones."

We both burst into a fit of laughter, which drew the attention of a few other girls, particularly Reese. "What's so funny over there?"

Keegan answered, "It's about your big kinky brother. You don't want to know."

"Truth," Reese replied immediately and turned back to her conversation with Ember.

When all was said and done, the finger-shaped bruises behind my ears that extended slightly down my neck were successfully concealed with a combination of makeup and wispy curls flowing down from my updo. I was impressed, but I was still going to kick Chase's ass for it.

By the time it was my turn to walk down the aisle, my anger had cooled significantly. I waited patiently for the coordinator to give me the cue to go. The wedding was taking place outside by the lake on the clubhouse property, and we were lined up inside the tent set up for the reception. When I exited the tent and rounded the corner, I looked up, and my steps faltered. Chase was standing beside Duke who was beside Dash at the altar, and he looked amazing dressed in a tuxedo. A harsh whisper from Reese to quit gawking at her brother and walk brought me out of my lust induced fog. I closed my gaping mouth as the crowd chuckled at my expense, but I didn't care one bit because Chase was smiling from ear to ear, his eyes locked on me.

I couldn't tell you one thing about the wedding ceremony. My attention was solely focused on the man standing only a few feet away from me. My eyes didn't leave his for one second while our friends professed their love for one another. Chase nodded once and then started toward me. That was when it registered to me that the wedding was over. I stepped toward Chase and slipped my arm through his, walking by his side as he led me down the aisle. That moment was and would always be one of the happiest of my life. I don't know what happened between us during the ceremony, but I returned down the aisle feeling an even deeper connection to Chase. Judging by the look in his eyes, he was feeling the same.

Upon exiting the ceremony, we were immediately whisked away by the photographers for pictures. Thankfully, they made quick work of it and got us to the reception within half an hour. We were called into the tent one by one and introduced before the bride and groom were announced. Then, we were led to the table set up for the wedding party which had groomsman on one side and bridesmaids on the other. It felt like a forced separation again.

Finally, the DJ called for the first dance of the bride and groom, followed by the father/daughter dance and the mother/son dance. Since Dash's mother wasn't present, he danced with Annabelle, which lasted about 30 seconds before Phoenix cut in. At that point, the DJ invited the rest of the guests to the dance floor. I met Chase in front of the table and released a sigh of content when I was in his arms on the dance floor.

Chase leaned down and placed his mouth next to my ear, "Baby, there are no words to describe how beautiful you look tonight."

"You don't look so bad yourself," I breathed. I

was a hot, horny, needy, flustered mess.

His lips lightly grazed my jaw before capturing mine in a soft kiss. "I love you so much, Harper Jackson."

"I love you, too, Chase Walker."

"One day, I think—"

He didn't get to finish his sentence because he was interrupted by a shockingly familiar voice. "Harper! I had no idea you would be here!" Hilarie excitedly exclaimed from my side.

My surprise easily masked my annoyance at being interrupted. "Hilarie! What are you doing here?"

"The guy that I've been seeing was in the wedding. He invited me to attend as his plus one earlier this week."

"Who?" Chase and I asked at the same time.

"Jay Markus," she replied with a dreamy lilt in her voice.

Confused, I turned to Chase. His forehead wrinkled for a second before he shook his head and gruffly uttered, "Shaker."

"Shaker?" Hilarie asked.

"Nickname," Chase explained.

Right on cue, Shaker joined Hilarie on the dance floor. "Do you two know each other?" he asked flatly, looking back and forth between the two of us, but I got the distinct feeling he was pissed.

Hilarie laughed loudly. "I would say so; she's my best friend."

Shaker's face remained impassive. "Small world," he clipped.

"How did you two meet?" I asked.

"We met at a bar a while back and hit it off so we started hanging out when we could on the weekends," Hilarie explained.

"Why didn't you tell me he was from Croftridge?" I asked, failing to hide the hint of accusation in my voice. I don't know why, but her being at the wedding didn't sit well with me.

Hilarie glanced at Shaker. "Because I didn't know; it never came up." She directed her full attention to Shaker. "You're from Croftridge?" Shaker nodded uncomfortably. "How do you know Harper and her non-boyfriend boyfriend?"

Shaker's eyes widened, and Carbon said in a low voice filled with warning, "Tell her how we met."

"We met in the Marines. When I was discharged, I didn't want to go back home, so I called him. He invited me to come to Croftridge and invited me...to, uh, stay with him until I got on my feet."

"Oh, so that's how you know Harper?" Hilarie pried.

"No, I met Harper through her brother. I didn't even know these two were a thing until he cla—"

"Excuse us, please," Chase interrupted, pulling Shaker away by his arm, which left me standing in an awkward silence with Hilarie.

"I don't think your guard dog likes it that I'm here," she said, a hint of something unpleasant in her voice.

"I don't think he gives a shit one way or another that you're here. You're the one who doesn't like him. You've made that very clear from the first time you met him."

Her shoulders slumped, and her voice softened. "I'm sorry, Harper. I got the feeling that he didn't like me, so I wanted to not like him first. But then it wasn't so hard to not like him because I felt like he was trying to take you away from me. I'm pathetic, I know." She sniffled, her eyes full of unshed tears.

Well, shit. I hadn't expected an emotional confession from her. Reaching out, I pulled her into a hug. "Nobody is going to take me away from you, but it would be easier if you could try to get along with him, especially if you're seeing Shaker. If you and Chase could put aside your differences, we could all hang out together sometime."

She sniffled a few more times. "I would really like that."

"I would, too."

CHAPTER EIGHTEEN

Carbon

"Excuse us, please," I blurted, interrupting Shaker's loose lips and yanked him away by his arm. "You haven't told her about the club, have you?"

"No. I'm just fucking her. I didn't see the need to tell her my life story," he replied.

Well, that was good. Before I pulled him away, he was about to say, "...until he claimed her as his Old Lady." Harper had managed to keep her affiliation with the Blackwings hidden from her friends and coworkers in Sugar Falls, and for right now, I was okay with that. "How were you going to explain Harper being my Old Lady if I hadn't stopped you?" I growled.

Realization washed over his face. "Sorry, brother. It didn't even occur to me what I was about to say. I don't usually have to watch what I say on my own turf, you know?"

"Yes, I know. So I have to ask, what possessed you to invite a civilian piece of pussy to a club wedding?" I asked, genuinely curious.

He shrugged. "I knew no one would be wearing their cuts and she lets me fuck her however I want to. Saved me the trouble of having to go out and find a piece when the festivities were over."

"And the fake name?" I asked. His real name was Jacob Marks, not Jay Markus.

He laughed. "That's nothing new, brother. I've been using that name since I rolled into town. I thought you knew."

I shook my head, not believing this shit. I didn't care for Hilarie, and I had no interest in having to deal with her for the rest of the night. Unfortunately, Shaker was also in the wedding party, which meant he wouldn't be leaving anytime soon either. Sighing, I clapped his shoulder. "Just try to watch what you say. No one outside of the club knows the truth about my relationship with Harper, including Hilarie, and I would like to keep it that way for the time being."

"Is there a reason behind that?" he asked.

"Yes, but I'm not going to share it with you right now. Just know it wasn't ordered, but heavily suggested by Badger when he was standing in for Phoenix."

"Understood, brother." He turned and headed toward Hilarie and Harper, who were now standing to the side of the dance floor talking.

I stood there for a bit longer, just taking her in from afar. She was like a multifaceted jewel, beautiful and captivating from every angle, inside and out. Staring at her from across the dance floor, I decided I was going to ask her to marry me in the very near future.

Startling me, Duke asked, "Who's that with my sister and Shaker?"

"You don't know who that is?" Surely, he'd met Harper's best friend.

"No, should I?"

"Yes, you should. That's her best friend, Hilarie. They went to college together, and they work at the counseling center together. Hell, they even worked at The Booby Trap together."

I still hadn't taken my eyes off of Harper, so I missed Duke's jaw clenching and his fists balling. "The Booby Trap?" he asked.

"Yeah, the strip club she used to work at. It's where I met her," I replied offhandedly.

A flash of shimmery gold whizzed by me and slammed into Duke's chest. "Dance with me, handsome," my sister said and began pulling him to the dance floor.

She was still facing me as she pulled him with her. She glared at me over his shoulder and mouthed, "You owe me." Moving my gaze to Duke, I could practically see the fury rolling off of him. Oh shit. He must not have known Harper worked at The Booby Trap. And he didn't know about Hilarie. What the fuck else had she hidden from him?

I would have to tell her about my slip up eventually. For the time being, I pushed it to the back of my mind, tried my best to ignore Hilarie's presence, and spent the rest of the evening with my arms wrapped around my girl.

***

"Chase! Wake up!" I felt Harper's little hands trying to shake me while she called my name.

"What is it, baby?"

She pointed to the nightstand. "Your phone keeps ringing."

I snorted. "You could've answered it."

Picking up the phone, I saw that it was way too damn early for us to be awake after the night we had. I also saw that I had three missed calls. Before I could look to see who called, my phone started ringing in my hand.

"Carbon," I answered.

"It's Coal. Phoenix wants you at the clubhouse now," he said and disconnected. Coal's frantic voice coupled with Phoenix's early morning order to call the troops in caused an uneasy feeling to wash over me.

I climbed out of bed and began quickly dressing. "I've got to go to the clubhouse. I don't know what's going on or how long I'll be, but I'll be back as soon as I can."

"Be safe, Chase. I love you."

"I love you, too, baby."

We were supposed to stay at the clubhouse after the wedding because Phoenix didn't want anyone who'd had even a drop of alcohol driving, but we hitched a ride in the limo when Ember and Dash left. Now, I wished we'd stayed.

I walked into utter chaos when I arrived at the clubhouse. I didn't live far from the clubhouse, but somehow, I still managed to beat Phoenix there, and he lived on the same damn property.

"Somebody tell me what the fuck is going on!" he bellowed as he plowed through the front doors.

When I learned that our one and only prisoner had escaped from the makeshift jail we had hidden away in our basement, I knew I wouldn't be getting back to Harper anytime soon. Sighing, I pulled my phone out and sent her a text letting her know that I would be gone for the better part of the day. I felt torn. I wanted to spend the day with Harper, especially since our time together was limited, but I also wanted to be there for my brothers.

Harper replied back and let me know that she was going to meet Hilarie for lunch and some shopping. I turned to Shaker who was seated to my right. "You left that girl in your apartment alone?"

"I didn't have much of a choice. Besides, I keep anything of importance here."

"What excuse did you give her for running out the door this morning?"

He smirked. "Told her I had to go and I would be back when I got back. She wasn't happy with me this morning, but some of that was probably left over from last night."

"Do I even want to know?" I hesitantly asked.

"You tell me. She was pissed because I would

only fuck her ass."

"For the record, I didn't want to know."

"Noted."

Color me surprised when we ended up back at the clubhouse before 4:00 pm. Once again, I turned to Shaker. "Your girl has been hanging with my girl all day. You want to do a brother a solid and occupy her time for the rest of the evening?"

"Not really, but I guess I can take one for the team. Send the bitch back to my place." With that, he stood and left the room. I sat there for several minutes, shocked by his comment. His whole attitude toward Hilarie was out of character for him. Just like the rest of us, he had his fair share of one-night stands or sex only arrangements, but I had never known him to be openly disrespectful about it.

Badger's voice broke into my musings, "I've got my eye on him. I'll bring it to attention if need be. Go home and see your girl."

"Thanks, Veep."

I entered my condo to find Harper, Hilarie, Reese, and James in my living room. Like the big badass I was, I bypassed the ladies and went straight for James. "Hey, Little Man. Have you been good for your momma today?" He squealed and giggled when I blew raspberries on his onesie covered belly.

"When did you guys get back?" Reese asked.

"Just now, Reesie Piecie. Duke was talking to Phoenix when I walked out so he should be calling you any second now." I turned to Hilarie. "Shaker wants you to meet him at his place."

I helped my sister get James in the car and sent her on her way, followed by tactfully shoving Hilarie out the door. Back inside, I didn't see Harper in the living room where I had left her. I found her upstairs in my bedroom, and the anger in her eyes shocked me.

"What's wrong, baby?"

"Gee, Chase, I don't know. Maybe the fact that I had to explain to your sister, as well as Hilarie, how I got the bruises behind my ears and down my neck when she showed up here unannounced to question me about my previous job as a stripper!" she yelled.

"Bruises? What fucking bruises? Who hurt you?" I demanded. I could feel myself getting worked up and I wasn't in a place where I could get a handle on it myself.

She yanked her hair into a ponytail and turned to the side, pointing toward her ear. "These are from you, you big beast!"

I couldn't believe what I was seeing. My fingers were bruised into her skin from where I had held her in place while I was fucking her. "Harper," I croaked. "Baby, I'm so sorry. I didn't know I was hurting you. I would have stopped if I knew. I-I-Fuck!" I turned away from her, shame consuming me. I loved our rough fun together, but I never meant to hurt her.

Her little arms snaked around my waist from behind and squeezed. I could feel her cheek against my back. "You didn't hurt me, big guy. I didn't even know they were there until the hairstylist found them yesterday. After my moment of mortification in front of Keegan, I forgot about them, until Reese showed up here and my hair was in a ponytail. But, that's not what this is about. This is about me having to explain to your little sister about working at The Booby Trap. Apparently, someone, as in you, blabbed to my brother last night."

Fuck. "I was going to mention that, but we were having such a great night, I didn't want to ruin it. I planned on telling you today, but I got called to the clubhouse before I had a chance to. Honestly, Harper, I had no idea that Duke didn't know you were a stripper. He also didn't know about Hilarie. Is there anything else you've kept from him that I should know about?"

She sighed and took a step back. "After my ordeal, Duke was beyond overprotective of me, even years later. It's part of the reason I moved to Sugar Falls. I couldn't do anything without him hovering over me and scaring away anyone who got too close for his comfort. He had the best of intentions, but he inadvertently kept me from moving forward. I didn't tell him about working at The Booby Trap because I knew he would find a way to make me quit or get me fired. And I didn't tell him about Hilarie, because I met her at The Booby Trap and I didn't want him to scare her away. She was the first friend I made who knew nothing about my past. The only other thing I kept from him was how you and I met, but now he knows that, too."

Everything she said made sense, but there was one thing I had to ask—as much as I didn't want to—before we could put this behind us. I took her hands in mine and gently asked, "Are you afraid of me?" Watching her closely, I studied her eyes and looked for changes in her breathing pattern. I even discretely felt her pulse while I held her hands.

Her eyes never left mine, her breathing didn't change, and her heart rate remained the same.

"Of course not. Why would you even think that?"

"I didn't really think that, but I had to ask. I know I can be a bit much in the bedroom, but I don't want you to ever feel pressured to do something you don't want to, and I never want to hurt you. Promise me you'll tell me if we ever get to one of those points." I could feel the tears starting to well in my eyes. If that made me a pussy, so be it, but I couldn't bear the thought of causing her harm.

"I promise I'll say something. We've never talked about this before, but would it make you feel better about things if I chose a safeword?"

"Yes, it would."

"Okay, it's artichoke," she said, completely serious.

"Artichoke?"

"Yes, I hate them, and it's not something I would accidentally say. Artichoke."

I scooped her into my arms and covered her mouth with mine. "I love you, baby."

"Love you, too, big guy."

She pulled back and wiggled, letting me know she wanted me to put her down. Reluctantly, I released her. "Do we have to go back to keeping our distance after this weekend?"

"I don't know. I don't want to, that's for damn

sure. I haven't had a chance to talk to Phoenix or Badger about it. Nothing else has happened, so maybe it was just a random coincidence. I say we go back to spending our weekends together and see how things go. If shit starts happening again, we'll cross that bridge when we come to it."

She grinned. "That was the right answer. I was prepared to withhold my pussy if you didn't answer correctly."

CHAPTER NINETEEN

Harper

The next few weeks went by smoothly. During the week, I worked my regular schedule and alternated eating lunch and dinner with Hilarie. On the weekends, I was with Chase from the minute I got off work on Friday until I left to return to work on Monday. I still loved my job, but I hated saying goodbye to Chase on Monday mornings. I was certain he hated it as much as I did.

As per our usual, Hilarie and I went out to eat for dinner on Monday. We opted to try a new restaurant with a Tiki hut theme. The relaxed and upbeat atmosphere of the place inspired an idea.

"Are you still seeing Shaker?" I asked. She hadn't mentioned anything about him in at least two weeks, but she hadn't tried to invade my weekend time with Chase either.

"I wouldn't call it 'seeing him,' but yeah, we still meet up and fuck on the weekends," she replied.

"Oh," I said, deflated. "I guess I kind of thought it was more than just casual sex."

"Is there a reason you sound disappointed?" she asked.

"Yes. The summer is almost over, and we have a four-day weekend coming up. I was thinking the four of us could get one of those cabins and spend the long weekend at the lake."

"I'm game if Shaker is. Just let me know," she replied, not one ounce of excitement in her tone.

"It doesn't sound like it."

She huffed. "I'm not going to get excited about something that probably won't happen. I doubt Shaker will go, and I'm certainly not going to sit in a mountain cabin and listen to that behemoth screw your brains out all weekend."

I called Chase when I got home and told him about my idea. He said he would talk to Shaker and let me know, but either way, he and I could still go. When he called me back an hour later to tell me that Shaker agreed, I had a hard time containing my excitement.

The next day, I made our reservations and started mentally planning our activities. To my surprise, Chase called me while I was at work to ask if Ember and Dash, as well as Duke and Reese, could join us. One quick phone call to change the reservations and we were set.

Hilarie rode with Titan and me to Croftridge Thursday after work. I was almost to the clubhouse when Hilarie said, "This doesn't seem right. Did you miss a turn or something?"

"Sorry, I think you're right. I was thinking about our vacation, and I must have zoned out." Shit. She still didn't know about the club. How in the hell were we going to keep that from her for the next four days?

When we pulled up to Chase's place a few minutes later, both him and Shaker were standing on the porch waiting for us. Chase came down to help me with my bags while Shaker went back inside. I glanced at Chase and started to say something, but he subtly shook his head. I bit my tongue, but I would be asking him about it later. Chase smoothly reached over and grabbed Hilarie's bags in addition to mine and carried them to his car.

After a quick bathroom break for Titan, Chase unlocked his car and instructed us to climb in. I looked at the car, then back at him. "Uh, Chase, dear, this isn't going to work. Where is Titan going to sit?"

"Fuck!" he cursed and rubbed the back of his neck. "I'll call Dash and see if they have room for him."

"They would need to come here to pick him up," I said, widening my eyes slightly in an attempt to make him understand what I wasn't saying. We couldn't take Titan to Dash because he was probably at the clubhouse with Duke and Reese to drop James off with Phoenix and Annabelle for the weekend.

"Fuck this," Shaker said in annoyance. Jabbing a finger in Hilarie's direction, he went on, "I'm not going to keep hiding who I am just because she is around, and it was fucking wrong of you to ask me to."

"I didn't ask you to do anything you weren't already doing. You didn't tell her because you didn't want a 'cut slut.' I only asked you to keep your mouth shut for a few more weeks, but go ahead, brother, be who you are," Chase spat, making a grand hand gesture toward Shaker.

Titan had been silently standing in front of me while they shouted over the car, but he started a low growl when Shaker grabbed something from his bike and stomped back toward us.

Glaring at Titan, he roughly slid his arms into his cut and proudly displayed himself in front of Hilarie. "I'm a fucking Blackwing."

Hilarie smirked. "I can see that. What's your point?"

He eyed her suspiciously. "You don't seem surprised to find out you've been hanging out with a bunch of bikers. Oh, and fucking one of them."

"Shaker," I admonished, but it fell on deaf ears.

Hilarie let out a humorless laugh. "Seriously?" She pointed over her shoulder at Chase. "He is the very essence of a biker. You both ride motorcycles. Hell, over half the parking lot was filled with bikes at that wedding that took place at a very compound-like place. Several times you received a phone call and had to run out the door, saying you were called into work. So, the only thing I find surprising is that you thought I didn't know."

Shaker growled at her, "You won't get my cut."

She scoffed. "I don't fucking want it."

"Enough!" Chase bellowed. "You two will not ruin my girl's weekend. You have two minutes to decide if you're coming or staying. We'll wait in the car." He opened the car door for Titan and me to get in before he walked around the car and climbed into the driver's seat.

"Sorry, baby," he said, reaching for me.

"Shh! I want to hear what they're saying," I whisper-yelled, shooing him away with my hands.

Shaker grunted and stalked toward his bike. "Get on."

Hilarie glanced over her shoulder at me, rolled her eyes, and followed Shaker to his bike.

"That was strange," I commented as Chase pulled onto the road.

"It was, but let's forget about it and enjoy our weekend."

A little over two hours later, we were the first to arrive at the lake house I had booked for the next four days. "Are you sure this is the right place?" Chase asked.

"Yes, why?"

"It's huge, Harper. We didn't need a place this big for four couples."

I cleared my throat. "I have no desire to hear my brother giving it to your sister nor do I want them to hear us. I assumed you felt the same."

He grinned mischievously. "Indeed, I do. I'll reward your foresight later tonight."

We took a quick tour of the house before unloading his car. It was a lot bigger than it looked from the outside, but I got a good deal on it, and it was too late to get a refund anyway. I had chosen this particular house because it had bedrooms on all three levels and each bedroom had an adjoining bathroom. "I thought we could take the bedroom on the third floor and let our siblings choose one of the rooms on the first floor."

He pulled me in for a hug. "Whatever you want, baby."

I jolted when someone rang the doorbell, causing Chase to laugh. "Holy shit that was loud. I didn't hear anyone pull up, did you?"

"Nope. It's probably my surprise. Stay put," he threw over his shoulder while he strolled to the front door. I could hear male voices and then, "Harper, I'll be right back. Stay in there and don't ruin it by trying to peek!" Damn him for knowing me so well.

What seemed like an extremely long period of time later, Chase yelled for me to come downstairs. I flew down the stairs and didn't see him anywhere. I heard him laugh and then he yelled for me to come all the way downstairs. Descending to the lowest level of the house, I found Chase standing in the game room. "Follow me."

He led me through the sliding glass doors, onto an impressive deck, down the paved driveway, to the floating dock, which had a wicked looking boat in it. Chase held up a set of keys and jingled them. "Surprise!"

I squealed and launched myself into his arms. "I can't believe you rented a boat for the weekend! Thank you!"

He chuckled. "I didn't rent it, baby; it's mine."

Still in his arms, I leaned back so I could see his face. "You bought a boat for a four-day weekend at a lake?"

He shook his head. "I've had it for five or six years, but I don't get to use it as much as I would like. I keep it at a marina at a different lake, but I arranged to have it delivered here for us to use this weekend."

I held his gaze and murmured. "That was very thoughtful. Thank you."

It was almost a whisper, "I would do anything for you, baby." His lips met mine in a deliciously soft and sweet kiss, a rarity from Chase. Our tender moment was short lived due to the sound of a rumbling engine approaching.

By the time Duke, Reese, Ember, and Dash were settled, Chase and I had been at the lake house for well over two hours, but Shaker and Hilarie had yet to arrive. They pulled out right behind us when we left Croftridge. Even if they stopped a few times for food and bathroom breaks, they still should have already been there. Chase didn't seem the least bit worried, but I was. Something was off with Shaker, and they weren't on the greatest terms when we left.

Excusing myself to the restroom, I ventured upstairs and grabbed my phone before locking myself in the bathroom. I dialed Hilarie and crossed my fingers. When her phone went straight to voicemail, I debated whether or not to call Shaker for a good five minutes before I said 'screw it' and dialed him. When his phone went straight to voicemail, my worry kicked up several notches.

Trying to maintain an even tone, I opened the bedroom door and called out for Chase to come upstairs. Clearly, I was not successful in hiding my trepidation when Chase, Duke, and Dash crashed into the room. "What's wrong?" the cavemen triplets barked in unison.

Any other time I would have answered with a sarcastic remark, but I was too concerned about Shaker and Hilarie to dispense with my usual smartassiness. "Shaker and Hilarie should have been here by now. I tried to call them, and both of their phones went straight to voicemail. They left when we did, and we've been here for over two hours."

Chase nodded and pulled out his phone. "Yo, need a location on Shaker's bike." Chase pulled the phone away from his mouth and used his hand to guide me, "Come on, let's go back downstairs."

"Thanks, brother. Send those to my phone," Chase said before placing his phone in his pocket. He looked to Duke and Dash, "Byte is sending the location of his bike. He said it appears to be stationary. I'm going to go check it out. You two coming or staying?"

Ember rose from the couch. "You boys go. We'll be fine until you get back."

The boys looked unsure until Reese added, "Go make sure they are okay. We've got Titan, Ember, and two guns. Now go."

I lightly coughed out, "Three guns."

Convinced we would be safe in their absence, they piled into Dash's Hellcat and drove off into the night.

CHAPTER TWENTY

Carbon

The entire time we were driving to the location Byte sent us, I assumed we would roll up to find Hilarie bent over Shaker's bike while he plowed into her from behind. It wasn't until the headlights illuminated Shaker's bike propped up against a tree that a sense of unease set in. His bike didn't appear to have a scratch on it, but the thing that didn't sit well with me was its location. Instead of resting on the kickstand, Shaker's bike was leaned against a tree. Why hadn't he used the kickstand?

"What the fuck?" Duke uttered to no one in particular.

"Don't know, but let's go find out," I said, pushing open the passenger door.

Surveying the surrounding area and the bike itself, I didn't see anything that would help clue us in as to what had happened to Shaker and Hilarie. The bike had plenty of gas in the tank, and both tires were fully inflated. Turning to see if Duke or Dash had found anything, I noticed Dash had gone back to the car and had his phone to his ear.

"He's talking to Phoenix," Duke answered my unasked question. "I didn't find shit. You?"

"Nothing."

We continued to look around while we waited for further instructions from Prez. "Come on, brothers. I'll explain in the car," Dash yelled, sliding into the driver's seat.

I shoved Duke back a step and yelled, "Shotgun!" before sprinting to the car. Immature as it was, my big ass was not riding in the back seat. Granted, Duke wasn't much smaller than me, but he *was* smaller.

"They're both fine, but they're in jail. Phoenix wants us to go by there and get Shaker's keys so one of you can ride his bike back to the lake house. After that, he said to go on about enjoying our weekend. They likely won't be out until later tomorrow, and he said he would take care of getting them from the jail to the lake house," Dash informed us.

"What were they arrested for?" I asked.

Dash shifted in his seat, "From what Phoenix said, the police said they received a call about a girl being raped on the side of the road. When the cops showed up and found Shaker balls deep in Hilarie bent over his bike, they went nuts." He started laughing and took a few moments to get himself under control before he could continue. "Sorry. So, Hilarie tells them that it was consensual and that she's a bit of a screamer. By doing that, she saved Shaker from getting slapped with a rape charge, but her admission got them both arrested for a slew of charges including indecent exposure, committing a lewd act in public, disturbing the peace, something about obstructing the flow of traffic, and littering."

"Littering?" Duke and I asked in unison.

Dash managed to get out, "The condom wrapper," between laughs.

When our laughter finally died down, Dash added, "One more thing, Phoenix doesn't want the girls to know about it unless Hilarie decides to share it with them."

"Fuck. I was looking forward to a weekend of busting his balls about this," Duke grumbled from the back seat.

***

Walking into the lake house, the sounds of loud music and boisterous laughter coming from downstairs filled my ears. I quietly retreated and closed the door. "Let's go around back and see what they're up to," I suggested. Peering through the sliding glass doors, words failed me as I took in the scene before me.

Duke hissed, "What the fuck are they doing?"

Dash snickered. "Looks like Harper is teaching Reese and Ember how to give a proper lap dance."

"Oh fuck no," Duke spat.

"Hey, my sister is in there, too. Come on, let them have their fun," I said, walking back to the front of the house.

Duke dropped into a rocking chair and pinched the bridge of his nose. "I can't believe my little sister was working as a stripper and I never knew it. If she needed money, she should have come to me."

I sat in the chair beside him and considered his words. "I don't know why she was doing it, but I don't think it was for the money."

"What makes you say that?"

"Because she didn't do private dances. Hell, I had to pay $2,000 to get one with her. After the second one, she started charging me the standard price. If she was in it for the money, she would have ridden me all the way to the bank."

Duke growled and narrowed his eyes at me. I held up my hands. "Look, brother, I love your sister. I know how we met was less than conventional, but it all worked out in the end."

"I still don't like it," he grumbled.

"Now you know how I felt."

We sat outside on the front porch shooting the shit until Harper sent a text to my phone asking if everything was okay and if we would be back soon. We walked around back while I replied telling her we had been back for over an hour and were well aware of what they were up to downstairs. All three girls turned to the sliding glass doors, blushed, and promptly turned away. That was when I saw the red mark on Harper's arm that looked suspiciously like a hand.

"What happened to your arm?" I asked her, moving into the room to get a better look.

She slapped my hands away when I reached for it. "Calm down, caveman. Ember taught us some self-defense moves, and we were practicing on each other. I'm fine. Anyway, did you find Shaker and Hilarie?"

I grimaced. She was not going to be happy with my answer, but there was nothing I could do about it. "Yes, we did, and they're fine. They'll be here sometime tomorrow."

"What? Where the hell are they?" she asked, placing her hands on her hips.

"It's club business, Harper," Duke said, shooting a quick glance at me before stepping closer to his sister.

"Don't give me that shit. It might be club business for Shaker, but Hilarie is my friend, and I want to know where in the fuck she is," she yelled.

"Sorry, Sis, she was with him, so that makes her part club business, too. They are safe and will be here tomorrow, I promise. Please don't let this ruin your weekend. I know how much you've been looking forward to it," he said softly.

She sighed and dropped her shoulders. "Fine. I don't like not knowing the details, but as long as they are safe, I can let it go for now. But if she tells me that Shaker was still being a complete asshole to her, I will not be held responsible for my actions," she said, then promptly turned and pranced her sexy little ass to our bedroom.

I clapped Duke on the shoulder. "Thanks for taking the heat off me. I owe you one."

He shrugged. "No worries, I'm sure I'll need to be saved from the wrath of Reese at least once over the course of this weekend."

After making myself something to eat and drinking a beer with the boys, I went upstairs to find Harper soaking in the jetted garden tub, neck deep in bubbles. She slowly opened her eyes when I cleared my throat. "Is there room in there for one more?"

She smirked. "Yes, but your size counts as two."

I ignored her and began stripping out of my clothes. Glancing up, I caught her intently watching me disrobe. "See something you like?"

She raised one brow and quirked her lips. "Keep going, and I'll let you know." She was in the mood to bicker because she was pissed about Hilarie, but I had other plans for us.

I finished removing my clothes, lifted her up, and lowered us both into the water, placing her between my thighs with her back to my front. When she started to protest, I closed my arms around her and trailed kisses down her neck. "Show me what you taught the girls while we were gone."

"You want a lap dance in the bathtub?"

Sucking her earlobe into my mouth, I nibbled with my teeth before sliding my mouth down her neck. With my lips against her skin, I said, "Mmm-hmm. It's been a long time since you've danced for me." Switching sides to give her other ear the same attention, I continued, "Some of my favorite memories to jerk myself off to are of you dancing for me at the club."

"Is that so?"

"Yes, now show me what you were teaching them while we were gone."

She turned around and straddled my lap. "Since I'm already naked, we'll have to fast forward to that part of the dance." She then proceeded to seductively rub her body all over mine. I watched with glee as she got herself just as worked up as I was.

"Chase," she whined as she continued to move her hips against me. I kept my hands by my sides, just like I had to at the club, and she clearly didn't like it. "Touch me, please."

When she rose up on her knees, I latched onto her nipple and sucked. Her hands went around my head as she ground herself against me. She could have easily taken what she wanted, but I knew she wouldn't. She always waited for me to enter her, or for me to tell her to put me inside of her, and I fucking loved it.

"You want my cock?"

"Fuck, yes," she groaned.

I switched to her other nipple and lifted her hips just enough to line myself up with her entrance. Gently closing my teeth around the hard bud in my mouth, I brought her hips down as I thrust up.

She gasped and writhed against me. "Oh, Chase, please move. I'm coming!"

I let go of her nipple and covered her mouth with mine as I used her hips to move her up and down my shaft. "Fuck, baby," I rasped against her lips. "I'm not going to last. You feel so fucking good." With that, I followed her over the edge.

When I returned from bliss, I held her securely against my chest and stood. "I hope you didn't think we were finished."

I felt her grin against my skin. "Of course not."

***

"No fucking way! Your father would kill me if I let you do that," Dash said to Ember.

She turned away from him and crossed her

arms, seeming to accept his decree. She glanced at me, then Duke, and whirled around to face Dash again. "You'll just have to tell him you couldn't stop me," she said before diving off the front of the boat and swimming like an Olympic medalist toward the shore.

"Fuck!" Dash yelled, diving in after her. He was in great shape, but there was no way he was going to catch her in time.

"I can't wait to show this shit to Phoenix," Duke said distractedly.

Looking back over my shoulder, I saw him holding up a phone with his hands, aiming it in the direction of Ember and Dash. He chuckled. "I've been recording since the second time she said she wanted to go with Harper and Reese."

We watched as Ember made it to the shore and sprinted uphill toward Harper and Reese, waving her arms and yelling, "Wait for me!"

"You think she's going to make it?" Duke asked.

"Yep."

"You think Dash will jump in after her?"

"Not if she pops back up in a few seconds," I guessed.

She reached Harper and Ember with only 100 feet or so separating her and Dash. We could hear her yelling, "Go! Go! Now!" The three girls held hands and leaped off the 40-foot boulder into the water below. Dash came to a screeching halt, just barely missing her. He stood there with his arms crossed, silently waiting for their heads to pop up. Harper surfaced first, grinning from ear to ear. Reese popped up mere seconds later, but Ember had yet to come up. Dash took a step closer to the edge, and we could see him scanning the water below. Harper and Reese started frantically turning in the water trying to spot her.

We heard a loud curse and looked up to see Dash plunging toward the water. His body entered the water at the same time Ember popped up, alarmingly close to our boat. She heaved in a few deep breaths, then threw her hands in the air and yelled, "Wooooooo! That was fucking awesome!"

"Hope it was worth it," Duke teased, reaching for her hand to help her into the boat.

Ember turned her head to see Harper and Reese making their way to the boat and a furious Dash just behind them. She pushed past Duke and took a seat in the front of the boat. "It most definitely was."

Harper and Reese climbed into the boat and

knowingly moved to the side. Dash hit the swim platform fuming and stomped his way to his wayward wife. "Have you lost your fucking mind Ember?! What made you think it was okay to jump off a 40-foot rock?"

She jumped to her feet, hands on her hips. "Did you forget that I ran through the woods at night and scaled trees to escape Octavius? Do you remember when we were in the lake and I swam to shore after being shot not once, but twice? Jumping off a freaking rock was a piece of cake."

"You weren't fucking pregnant when you did any of those things!" Dash screamed. He obviously realized what he'd just blurted out because his expression and his tone instantly changed. Taking a step closer to her, he murmured, "Sorry, darlin'. You scared me."

"You're pregnant?" my little sister asked, her voice an octave higher than usual.

Ember smiled shyly. "I guess we're telling people now."

Harper and Reese rushed toward her with their arms outstretched. Duke and I took turns giving Dash a handshake and a slap on the back. "Congratulations, brother! Does Prez know?" I asked.

"Uh, no, he doesn't. You guys are the first to know besides us..." he said, stumbling over his words.

"Got it. We'll act like this never happened," I assured him.

The relief was evident on Dash's face. "Thanks, brothers. I didn't mean to disrespect Prez by blurting it out like that, but she scared the shit out of me."

Duke gave him a sad smile. "Enjoy this time with her. I would give anything to have been able to experience it with Reese." He would never know it, but that statement earned him a world of respect from me.

Clearing my throat, I spoke loud enough for all on board to hear, "Congratulations, Ember! I'm so happy for you, but you are hereby banned from all water activities except for basic swimming until further notice." As I had hoped, my declaration lightened the mood.

We stayed on the water for several more hours, until everyone agreed it was a good time to head back for dinner. I couldn't speak for the others, but I couldn't recall a time in recent years when I'd had more fun. Judging by the smiles on the faces of some of my closest friends as well as the woman I loved, I would venture to say they felt the same. I stopped Harper on the dock and pulled her into my arms for a kiss I poured my whole heart into. "I love you, Harper, so fucking much."

She grinned. "I fucking love you, too, Chase Walker."

CHAPTER TWENTY-ONE

Harper

Entering the lake house after our day on the water, I screamed when I spotted a man standing by the kitchen island. The next few seconds were a blur of activity. I'm not sure how it all happened, but in the blink of an eye, Chase, Duke, and Dash were in front of me, shielding me, but they weren't doing anything.

I heard Titan growling and snarling, but I couldn't see anything. Then I heard a familiar voice request, "A little help, brothers."

The boys parted like the Red Sea revealing none other than Phoenix, badass president of The Blackwings MC, standing on top of the kitchen island while Titan stood on his hind legs, front paws on the countertop, snarling and snapping at his motorcycle boots.

"Calmati," I sternly commanded Titan. He silenced and came to stand in front of me.

Phoenix jumped down, eyeing Titan warily. "Tell me that's one of Ruben's dogs."

Chase proudly answered, "Of course, Prez. I wouldn't have anything less for my Old Lady."

I rudely interrupted, "What are you doing here, Phoenix?"

He laughed. "Don't worry, Harper, I'm not staying. I just wanted to stick around long enough to say hello after dropping off Shaker and Hilarie."

"Oh, no, you're more than welcome to stay. We were just about to get dinner started," I replied.

"As tempting as that sounds, I've got to get back. Annabelle hasn't been feeling well, and I don't like leaving her for too long."

"Is she sick?" I asked.

"No, it's just worse with twins," he answered, then instantly slapped his hand over his mouth.

"Daddy?" Ember hesitantly asked, standing hidden behind Duke and Dash.

"Fuck. Your mother is going to kill me," Phoenix said, swiping his hand across his forehead.

"Mom's pregnant?" she asked.

Phoenix sighed. "This isn't how we wanted to tell you, or your brothers, but yes, she's pregnant with twins."

Ember smiled so wide it was a wonder her face didn't split. "Me, too! I mean, we're not having twins..." she trailed off, realizing what she'd just said to her father.

"I guess we're telling people," Dash mumbled.

"Okay, this conversation did not happen," he looked pointedly at Ember, then to Dash. "Announcements can be made when you two get back, yeah?"

"Of course, Daddy," Ember answered, wiping a tear from the corner of her eye.

Phoenix opened his arms wide for her. She didn't hesitate to run to him and be engulfed in a hug. "I've got to get back to my wife. You guys enjoy your weekend, but please behave. I really have no desire to bail anyone else out of jail in the near future."

"Jail?" I screeched. "Is that where they were?"

Phoenix cursed under his breath. "Yes, but that's all you're getting out of me."

"Where are they now?" I demanded.

"They both wanted to shower and sleep. Shaker was too wound up to get any sleep last night, and Hilarie was too scared," Phoenix said.

Phoenix seemed anxious to get back to Croftridge, so we said our goodbyes and started preparing dinner. Between the smell of food and the noise we were all making, I thought for sure we would see Shaker or Hilarie make an appearance, but by the time Chase and I were climbing the stairs for bed, we still hadn't seen them or heard a peep from either one.

I sat up in bed and glanced around, unsure of what woke me. Titan was awake, but he wasn't barking or growling, which put me at ease. I was just about to lay back down when I heard the sounds of someone moving around downstairs. Curiosity got the better of me, and I found myself tiptoeing down the stairs in my pajamas to see who was doing what in the middle of the night.

When the kitchen came into view, I saw Hilarie bent over with almost half of her upper body in the refrigerator rummaging around for something. "If you're looking for the leftovers from dinner, they're in the bottom drawer," I said.

She squealed and jumped, banging her head on a shelf. "Shit, Harper. You scared the hell out of me!" She closed the refrigerator and turned to face me, shoving her hands into the hoodie she was wearing.

I giggled. "Sorry, I didn't mean to." I made my way into the kitchen while she fidgeted and shifted her weight from foot to foot. "Hey, are you okay?"

She cleared her throat but didn't meet my eyes when she spoke, "Yes, I'm fine. I was hungry and looking for a small snack. I didn't mean to wake you."

"I meant with everything that happened last night. We weren't given any details; I only know that you two were arrested and kept overnight. Do you want to talk about it?" I asked.

"Would you be offended if I said no? It's so embarrassing. I'm still coming to terms with the fact that it even happened," she replied.

"No worries. I just wanted to make sure you were okay. You know I'm here if you decide you do want to talk about it," I assured her.

"I know. Thanks, Harper. I'm going to go back to bed. I'll see you in the morning," she said before descending the stairs.

It wasn't until I was drifting off to sleep that I realized she never got anything to eat. And why the hell was she wearing a hoodie in the middle of summer?

***

I sat in the front of the boat, casually observing my friends. Something was off, and I couldn't put my finger on it. The fun and carefree feeling surrounding us the day before had all but disappeared. We had spent most of the day tubing and swimming. While the activities were fun, the interactions between the guys seemed stilted, and Hilarie wouldn't say more than one or two words at a time. There was also an obvious rift between Hilarie and Shaker.

I continued my casual observations for the rest of the day. Not once did I see Hilarie and Shaker interact—no touching, no talking, nothing. Shaker didn't seem to have any trouble talking to Reese or Ember, but he said little to nothing to me, and he only acknowledged the guys when they spoke to him first. What in the hell was going on? Surely, I wasn't the only one who noticed the odd behavior.

Back at the lake house, Chase and I finally had a moment alone. "Did you notice anything odd about Shaker and Hilarie today?"

He carefully answered, "No, but I'm aware of what happened Thursday night, so their behavior made sense to me."

"You mean Shaker's behavior made sense to you. You don't know Hilarie well enough to make that judgment call."

He gave me an appraising once-over and stepped closer. "What's this really about, Harper?"

I sighed, exasperated with the whole thing. "I wanted this weekend to be a fun getaway, not a weekend full of unspoken tension and awkwardness."

"Okay, baby. I'll take care of it. Let's get showered and get dinner started. I'm starving." He finished that with a quick slap to my ass before he sauntered into the bathroom. Cocky bastard. How did he think he was going to take care of it? I rolled my eyes and followed him to the shower.

After dinner, I was in the kitchen loading the dishwasher when I felt a presence behind me. I glanced over my shoulder to see Shaker standing by the kitchen island. I arched a brow. "Did you need something?"

He cleared his throat and looked everywhere but directly at me. "Uh, yeah. I wanted to apologize for my attitude today. I can be pretty grumpy when I'm tired, plus I'm still pissed about what happened yesterday. But, none of that is anyone's fault but my own, and I'm not going to let it ruin the rest of this awesome weekend you planned for us." Then he went in for the kill with his puppy dog eyes and his killer grin. "Forgive me?"

"Of course, I will," I said, opening my arms for a hug.

"Do you need any help?" he asked.

"No, I'm almost finished. Thank you for offering. I'll be downstairs in a few minutes."

It was obvious to me that Chase made Shaker apologize to me, and it was sweet of him to do it, but I wondered if his attitude would change. I wasn't going to get my hopes up.

I found the whole group waiting for me downstairs. To my surprise, they were chatting with one another, and the tension from earlier seemed to have vanished. Chase noticed me first. "All right, ladies. Do any of you know how to fish?" Of course, Ember and Reese did. Me and Hilarie, not so much. With a promise to teach us, we followed the rest of the group down to the dock.

Chase magically produced fishing poles, tackle boxes, bait, and a host of other things that were apparently required to fish. He briefly explained how to cast and then handed me a pole with a hunk of something nasty dangling from the end of it. "Do I even want to know what that is?" I asked, pointing to the nastiness with a scrunched-up nose.

He laughed at my theatrics. "It's Ember's homemade bait. None of us have ever used it, but she said the people on some fishing forum swear by it."

Shrugging, I followed his instructions and tossed the dangling chunk of yuck into the water. I flopped into my chair and watched everyone else toss their lines in and get situated. "Now what?" I asked.

"Now you wait," Chase said.

"Wait for what exactly?"

"You'll know when it happens."

"I love your vague answers."

I have to admit. He wasn't wrong. When it happened, there was no question. The end of my rod started bouncing and bending, so I did what anyone else who was new at fishing would do. I jumped to my feet squealing, "Help! What do I do?"

Four male voices shouted, "Reel!"

I started reeling, and my pole just kept bending, to the point I thought it was going to break. It also felt like the thing was trying to pull me into the water with it. "Help me! It's going to snap this rod in half or yank me in with it!"

"You need to adjust the drag," my brother added.

"Like I know what the fuck that means."

Duke reached in front of me and did something on the reel. Suddenly, the reel started making a strange noise, and the pole wasn't bent nearly in half anymore. "Keep reeling," he instructed.

I was starting to get excited. This fish had to be huge if it was this much trouble to bring in. Grinning from ear to ear, I reeled my heart out. When it got close, Chase used a net to scoop my fish out of the water. "What is that little thing? Where is my big fish?" I asked.

Chase chuckled as he removed the hook and held up my fish. "This is your fish, baby. It's a decent sized catfish, maybe two or three pounds."

"That little thing was what I had so much trouble trying to reel in?" I asked, not believing a word he was saying.

"Yes, baby. Now you know how fishing stories get started," he replied.

"Well," I huffed, "that's disappointing."

"Do you want me to put some more bait on your hook?"

"Yes, please. I have no desire to touch whatever that is," I said, eying the jar of nastiness with disgust.

Ember laughed. "It's just hot dogs."

"No way. Hot dogs don't look like that."

"They do when they've been fried in butter and dumped into a jar of apple cider vinegar, strawberry Kool-Aid, and garlic," Dash added with a shrug. "It makes the whole house stink when she makes it, but it works better than any bait I've ever used."

To further prove his point, his pole started bouncing, and he reeled in another catfish about the same size as the one I caught.

By the end of the night, everyone in our group had caught at least two fish. Ember pulled in the biggest fish I'd ever seen firsthand in the wild. The thing was huge and ugly. I had no idea creatures like that lived in the lake. The boys, and Ember, assured me that the 35-pound beast, otherwise known as a flathead catfish, and his comrades didn't bother humans, but I would be googling that fact for myself when we got back to the house.

Despite the rough start, the rest of our long weekend getaway was perfect. The weather was beautiful, and everyone was in a good mood. It was perfect to the point that I didn't want to leave. Unfortunately, I found myself saying goodbye to Chase, yet again on a Monday. He asked me to stay, but I had laundry and grocery shopping to do before the work week started, and I needed to catch up on the sleep I missed due to our late-night activities.

With a promise to call him as soon as I got home and tears in my eyes, I pulled onto the road and pointed my car toward Sugar Falls. I was glad Shaker had driven Hilarie home from the lake house because I needed the time to myself to think. As much as I didn't want to admit it, leaving Chase and living our lives in completely different states had been getting harder and harder for me and I wasn't sure that I wanted to keep doing it. I also didn't know if I was ready for the changes ending our weekend-only romance would bring to my life.

CHAPTER TWENTY-TWO

Carbon

I watched her drive away. Usually, I was the one leaving, but it wasn't any easier being on the other side, and I was at a loss as to what to do about it. My life, the one I worked hard to rebuild after it was destroyed years ago, was in Croftridge. She knew as well as I did that I couldn't and wouldn't leave Croftridge. My only living family members lived in Croftridge. My club was in Croftridge. She was the only thing missing.

Sleep eluded me that night. My mind was in overdrive trying to figure out a way to get Harper to Croftridge. As the sun slowly began to light the sky, the answer to my problem finally came to me. I jumped out of bed, showered, and started the coffee. I waited as long as I could, but by 7:00 am, I was on my bike speeding to the farm.

I found Duke in the barn, getting one of the horses ready for a training session. His head shot up when he heard me approaching. The scowl on his face relaxed when his eyes landed on my face. "Morning, brother, I wasn't expecting you. Everything all right?"

"I wanted to talk to you about something. Do you have a few minutes?" I asked.

"I do if you don't mind talking while I'm getting Jelly Bean ready. I'm the only one here so you can speak freely."

"Jelly Bean?" I asked.

He scoffed. "Yeah. Happens all the time. These rich fuckers pay thousands of dollars for a quality horse and let their kid name it. That's how you end up with a champion named Jelly Bean."

"Right. So, I wanted to talk to you about your sister."

That got his attention. Duke stood and turned to face me. "What about my sister?"

I explained the situation with Harper to him and then shared my idea. Thankfully, he thought it was a great idea and even offered some suggestions to help. We spent over an hour talking out the details. By the time we finished, I was more than ready to get the ball rolling.

As I was stepping out of the barn, Keegan slammed into my chest, screamed louder than a banshee, and stumbled backward covering her mouth. "Keegan! What's wrong?" I barked, harsher than I intended.

Her eyes were wide, her breathing was labored, and her little hands were shaking. She was terrified of something. "N-n-nothing. I'm just running late, and you scared me." She was still panting and held a hand over her chest as if that could magically slow down her breathing.

Duke came barreling around from the side of the barn. "What the hell is going on?"

Keegan's eyes widened even more at the sound of his voice. Was she afraid of him? I narrowed my eyes at Duke when I spoke, "Nothing. We ran into each other, literally, and I scared her."

Duke looked at his watch and back to Keegan. "You're late."

She visibly swallowed and lowered her head. "I'm sorry. It won't happen again."

I reached for her chin and tilted her head up. "Don't bow your head to him or any man for that matter." I studied her for a few moments before I spoke again, choosing my words carefully. "You know you have the club's protection if you ever need it, right? All you have to do is ask."

She smiled, though it was forced. "Thank you, Carbon. I'm fine, really. I was running late and didn't expect to run into King Kong in the barn," she said, gesturing to me.

I chuckled lightly at her remark. I didn't believe her for one second, but there wasn't much I could do if she didn't want the help I offered. We said our goodbyes and I went in search of Ember.

After checking her office and the organics farm, I doubled back through the stables. At a loss, I pulled out my phone and called Dash. He informed me that Ember wasn't feeling well when she woke up and was probably still at home. It briefly crossed my mind that I should wait until she was feeling better, but I decided to let her tell me that herself and was soon knocking on her front door.

"Carbon? Is everything okay?" she asked, clearly surprised to see me standing on her front porch.

"Everything is fine, Ember. I wanted to talk to you about a new project of sorts. Is now a good time?" I asked.

"Sure, come on in." She made coffee, and we took a seat in her living room. I explained my idea and the reasoning behind it. Just like the bleeding heart she was, Ember jumped all over it. "I think that's a great idea, Carbon! I'm a little disappointed in myself for not thinking of it first..." she trailed off and started rubbing her palms together, her tell that she was nervous.

"What is it, Ember?"

"Well, if she says no, can I still do it?"

"Of course. But I don't think she'll say no. At least, I hope she won't," I muttered.

"For what it's worth, I don't think she will either."

***

The week flew by. I was busy busting my ass with Ember to get things moving. She already had over half of the resources we needed, so we were well on our way to achieving our goal. The next step in my grand plan was to get Harper on board.

When I arrived at her house on Friday evening, I was ready to burst with excitement until she opened the door. One look at her face had my elation deflating faster than an uncapped air mattress. Scooping her into my arms, I asked, "What's wrong, baby?"

Females baffled me from time to time. This being one of those times. If I hadn't asked what was wrong, she would have been pissed off and claimed I didn't care about her. I did genuinely want to know what was wrong, so I asked, and that one question had her sobbing into my shirt.

Taking quick strides to the couch, I sat us down and held her tighter to my chest. "Harper, baby, you're freaking me out here. Did something happen? Are you hurt?"

She shook her head and mumbled, "No, nothing like that." Then, she raised her head and said the words no man ever wanted to hear, "You know I love you, right?"

I froze, unsure of how to respond. She wouldn't do this to us. She couldn't do this to us. "Don't do this, Harper," I whispered.

Her eyes widened. "Do what?"

"What are you trying to tell me? Yes, I know you love me. Keep going," I snapped. I was scared, and just like every man I knew, I used anger to hide my fear.

She took in a deep breath and sniffled. "I can't keep doing the weekend only thing anymore."

"What the fuck do you mean by that?" I

barked, sliding her off my lap so I could stand and move about the room, a vain attempt to keep my temper in check.

"It's too hard when we have to leave each other every week," she cried.

"So, you'd rather not have to leave each other at all?" I asked through clenched teeth.

"Yes," she answered.

I felt every searing slice as the metaphorical blade cut my still-beating heart from my chest. I stared at her, not believing the words that just escaped her lips. Reality slammed into me with the force of a train. "Fuck you, Harper," I spat, spinning on my heel and stomping toward the door.

"Chase! Wait! Please!" she screamed, chasing after me. Fuck that and fuck her and fuck everything in the whole fucking world. I loved her with everything I had in me, but I would never, ever fucking beg and plead for anyone, not even her.

"Jason Chase Walker, stop and listen to me!" she yelled, seconds before launching herself into the air and landing on my back like a damn spider monkey. "I didn't do a good job of putting it into words, and you misunderstood me. I was trying to say that I want to see you during the week, too, but I haven't been able to find a job in or near Croftridge."

I grabbed her by her ass and slid her around to the front of my body. "Are you serious?" I asked, unsure what to make of her at this point.

She smiled shyly. "Yes."

"Then why were you crying?"

"Because I can't find any job prospects. I love the center I work at now, but after giving it some thought, I realized there are kids everywhere that need help, Croftridge included."

I carried her back to the couch but kept her straddling my lap when I sat. "You're willing to move to Croftridge?"

She nodded. "If I can find a job—"

I grabbed her face and slammed my lips to hers. She had mortally wounded my heart and healed it in a matter of seconds. My emotions needed an outlet and said outlet was currently straddling me. I stood, still kissing her, and started moving us to her bedroom. Against her lips and between kisses, I managed to tell her, "Ember is opening a counseling center in Croftridge. Wants you to be in charge of it. Say yes."

She moaned loudly when I worked my way down her neck and lightly bit down on her shoulder. "Yes. Oh, Chase. Talk later. Fuck now."

I grinned against her skin. I couldn't argue with that.

Once we made it to her room, I dropped her onto her bed and followed her down. Holding myself up with one arm, I shoved her skirt up to her waist and ripped her panties from her body with a firm yank.

"Chase," she gasped. "I just bought those."

"Hush and get your tits out unless you want the same thing to happen to your bra," I ordered as I undid my jeans and shoved them down far enough to free my length.

As soon as I had my dick free, I pushed into her and looked up to see her tits bouncing freely as she let out a sigh of contentment.

I brought my face down to hers and stared into her eyes. "You really upset me," I told her as I continued to move my body against hers.

Her hands came up to cup my cheeks. "I know, baby, and I'm sorry. I would never do anything to hurt you like that. I love you."

"I love you, too," I said before I covered her mouth with mine and showed her just how much I loved her.

***

"Why is Ember opening a counseling center?" she asked, lazily drawing circles on my stomach with her finger while her head rested on my chest.

"She felt like it would be beneficial to the community, and because I asked her to."

"You what?" she screeched.

I grinned. "I asked her to. I know how important helping children is to you and I wanted you to be with me in Croftridge. She already has some programs in place to help the community, and she has several buildings on the property that aren't in use, so I asked, and she said yes. And before you say anything, you should know she's opening the center whether you take the job or not, but she really wants you to take it, and so do I."

She pushed herself to a sitting position and met my eyes with her watery ones. "You did all of that for me?"

"Yes, baby. I love you. I would do anything for you."

"I love you, too, big guy."

***

"How long do you think it will take Ember to get the center open and ready for business?"

"I have no idea. Do you want to call and talk to her about it?" I asked.

"Yes, I probably should before I start making plans," she giggled.

"What kind of plans are you making?" I asked, still feeling off-kilter from our misunderstanding the night before. I don't think she realized it, but she had the power to destroy me with a few simple words. I hoped like hell that day never came.

She placed her hands on her hips and cocked one to the side. "Are you serious right now?" The dumbfounded look on my face told her she needed to continue. She started ticking things off on her fingers. "I have to give my notice at work. I have to pack and schedule movers. I need to find a place to live in Croftridge, and my house needs a little work before I can put it on the market."

"Hold it right there," I interrupted. "Did you just say you needed to find a place to live in Croftridge?"

"Yes."

I snorted. "Baby, you're living with me. Problem solved."

She glared at me. "I am not living with you, and I don't take orders from you outside of the bedroom."

The last part clued me in to the error of my ways. She was pissed because I didn't ask her. "You don't want to live with me, baby?"

"I didn't say that," she sighed, exasperated.

"I would like for us to live together. Will you move in with me, please?" I asked, trying to sound sincere. I did want us to live together and we would, but me asking her was total bullshit.

"I don't know how I feel about living at your condo. I mean, we've stayed there from time to time, but I don't want to make a home where you've had who knows how many whores in your bed."

I couldn't help it. I tried, I really did, but the laughter just wouldn't be contained. "Is that your only issue with my place?"

She seemed caught off guard by my question. "Uh, yeah, I think so."

"Baby, first of all, we've been together for a long time, and I haven't fucked anyone except you since the night I met you. Secondly, I haven't fucked anyone in my condo other than you. Ever. Club whores are just that, whores at the club. Any other pussy I picked up, I fucked at the club."

"I don't know if I should hug you or hit you right now!" she fumed.

"Why?"

She pointed her finger in my face. "You will get a new room at that clubhouse, and you will replace anything and everything that may have been fucked on."

"Okay, baby. I can do that for you," I said, wisely choosing to keep any details of fucking on the couches, pool tables, bar stools, etc. to myself. "So, is that a yes for living with me at my place?"

"Yes, it is. Now, call Ember so I can talk to her," she demanded.

"Keep it up, Harper. You're earning yourself one hell of a spanking later," I said, right before Ember answered my call.

Ember and Harper stayed on the phone for almost two hours. Had my phone battery not died, they would have talked longer. I couldn't complain though. Harper was excited about the new center and her new job which is exactly what I had hoped for.

"How'd it go?" I asked.

"Great!" she beamed. "It will be at least a month before the center is ready for business.

That will give me plenty of time to turn in my notice and transition my patients over to the other counselors. Now, I just have to tell my brother."

"He knows." I grinned at her stunned expression. "I talked to him about it before I brought it up to Ember. He was the one who suggested the horses as an alternative therapy method."

"And he was okay with it?" she asked.

"Yes, why wouldn't he be?"

"I don't know. I guess I just remember the Duke who would have gladly placed me in a protective bubble if the option had been available," she mumbled.

"You're a grown woman now. He knows that. Speaking as an older brother, it is hard to accept, but little sisters do grow up. Besides, you can't blame the man for being protective of you, especially after everything the two of you have been through."

"Okay, we've ventured far enough down memory lane for me." The tone of her voice changed, and she squealed, "Oh, my gosh, Chase! I'm moving to Croftridge, and we're going to live together!" She threw both hands in the air, wiggling her fingers, and did some sort of little dance in a circle. Even Titan hopped around in a circle as best he could.

Her excitement was contagious. I laughed. "Yeah, baby, we are. Hell, if this is how you react from moving in together, what's going to happen when I propose?" It was a foregone conclusion. We would be getting married, but I hadn't intended on bringing it up just yet.

She froze, mid crazy dance. "What did you just say?"

Confused, I repeated what I had just said. She didn't say anything for several long beats. Finally, she uttered, "You want to marry me?"

I rose to my feet and shook my finger in her direction. "That's not how this works. I ask you. You do not ask me."

"I wasn't asking, caveman," she sassed. "I just didn't know you'd thought about it."

"Of course, I have. I love you, Harper. You're already my Old Lady, and now we're moving in together. The next logical step is to get married," I said, placing my hands on her hips. "Is that something you want?"

She blushed and cast her eyes toward her feet. "What little girl doesn't dream of getting married to the man of her dreams?"

"I'm the man of your dreams? Hot damn!" I

joked, trying to lighten the moment.

She slapped my chest. "You're such an ass sometimes."

For the life of me, I don't know what came over me, but it seemed right, so I went with it. I captured her hands in mine and dropped to one knee. "Harper Jackson, you're the woman of my dreams. Will you marry me?"

Her jaw dropped. "Are you serious right now?"

"I'm down on my fucking knee, and you're asking if I'm serious. Fuck yes, I'm serious," I growled.

"In that case, fuck yes, I'll marry you!"

"Wait! Stay right there. I mean it. Don't move, baby," I said, getting to my feet and bolting from the room. I ran to my bag, found what I needed, and sprinted back to the living room. I resumed my position in front of her, down on bended knee and held up the diamond ring I purchased for her weeks ago. "Harper Jackson, you are the woman of my dreams. Will you marry me?"

She slapped a hand over her mouth as the tears started streaming down her face. She nodded her head several times, but that wouldn't do. "I need the words, baby."

"Yes," she croaked, extending her left hand to me.

I slipped the ring on her finger and stood, capturing her in my arms and pulling her mouth to mine. I held her like the prized possession she was and made sweet, slow love to her right there in her living room. It was by far the happiest day of my life.

CHAPTER TWENTY-THREE

Harper

Chase and I spent the weekend working on my house. I cleaned out closets and started packing things I wouldn't need before the move. Chase began working on a few minor house repairs that needed to be taken care of before putting my house up for sale. I was in a state of euphoria for the entire weekend, blissfully floating from task to task. Before I knew it, it was time to say goodbye to Chase yet again. However, knowing it was one of the last times made it a lot easier.

He rented a truck the day before to haul the boxes I had packed as well as some furniture and his motorcycle back to Croftridge. We both agreed it would be easier to make repairs and showcase the house if it was empty. For the time being, he was going to store my belongings at a building on Ember's property to prevent me from having to rent a storage space. When I arrived in Croftridge to stay, we would sort through my things and figure out how to mesh our stuff to turn Chase's condo into our home.

My giddiness was replaced by nerves when I pulled into the parking lot of the crisis center. Every part of me wanted to move to Croftridge and be with Chase, but I did not want to turn in my resignation. I knew, without a doubt, breaking the news to the kids I had come to love would be the hardest part. Titan must have picked up on my apprehension and tried to comfort me by nuzzling my hand with his nose. I took in a deep breath and willed myself to go inside and get it over with.

I didn't have a chance to ease into my news or prepare myself to deliver it once I stepped foot through the door. Jackie noticed the ring on my finger immediately. "Harper Jackson! Is that an engagement ring I see on your finger?" she more or less announced rather than asked. By the time she finished, she was at my side with my

Carbon

hand held up to her face, as if she was a trained jeweler inspecting my ring. "Wow! That's one hell of a rock. Congratulations girl! Who's the lucky guy? Is it that biker that I've seen you with a few times?"

Holy crap. I didn't know which question to answer first. "Uh, thanks," I said, trying to gently pry my hand from hers. "Yes, it's an engagement ring. His name is Carbon Walker, and he is a biker. He's probably the one you are referring to. The other biker that has been around here is my cousin Judge."

She smiled. "I know who Judge is. Well done, Harper. Your Carbon sure is one hottie. I bet he rocks in the sack, too."

I covered my face with my hand and shook my head. "I'm not going there, Jackie." When I looked up, I realized her overzealous interrogation had garnered the attention of most of the staff. "Good morning, everyone." I held up my left hand and wiggled my fingers. "I guess you all heard the news."

My co-workers instantly bombarded me with hugs and words of congratulations. The women fawned over my ring, and the men commented on what a lucky guy Carbon was. Everyone seemed genuinely happy for me. Everyone except Hilarie.

She was the last to approach me, and she did so with her arms crossed over her chest. "So, I guess this means you're leaving us?"

"I was going to do this later, but I guess now is as good a time as any. Yes, I will be turning in my written resignation today. I've enjoyed my time working here, and I'll miss all of you dearly, but I was presented with an opportunity that I couldn't pass up. Over the next three weeks, I would like to work with the other counselors on smoothly transferring the care of my patients. I plan on breaking the news to the kids one by one as they come in for their sessions," I announced, managing to keep my voice steady and my face free of tears.

Again, everyone in the office warmly received my announcement. Everyone except Hilarie. She huffed. "I guess I'll get to work on finding your replacement. Best of luck to you, Harper." Then, she stomped off to her office, leaving me standing in the reception area with my mouth hanging open.

Jackie patted my shoulder. "Don't worry about her. She's just upset about you leaving. She'll come around."

I headed to my office and got started with my day. I emailed my written resignation to Hilarie and as expected, did not receive a reply. When lunch rolled around, I wasn't sure if Hilarie wanted to eat lunch with me. I didn't have to wonder long. Jackie knocked on my door and told me that Hilarie had already left for lunch, saying that she wouldn't be back until after 2:00 pm. Since I was not in the mood to socialize, Titan and I picked up lunch at a drive-thru, and I ate alone in my office.

The rest of my day was a constant repetition of me telling a patient I was leaving, them telling me how much they would miss me, and then we discussed transitioning their care. By the end of the workday, I was emotionally exhausted. How was I going to survive two more weeks of this?

Assuming Hilarie wasn't interested in having dinner with me, I packed up my things and headed to my car, with Titan dutifully trotting along behind me. One glance around the parking lot confirmed my assumption. Her car was nowhere to be seen. Maybe she just needed some time to get used to the idea of me leaving. Crossing my fingers and hoping for the best, I went home to work on packing.

Hilarie successfully avoided me all week. She came in and left early, and she took her lunch breaks while I was in a session. I didn't try to call or text her. If she wasn't talking to me at work, there was no reason for me to think she would try to talk to me after work. She was going to have to get over it. I was moving to Croftridge, and there was nothing she could do about it. We could part ways on bad terms, or she could suck it up and be happy for me like a true friend would. It wasn't like I would never see her again. We could still talk on the phone, and we could even double date if she was still seeing Shaker. Her immature behavior was really starting to piss me off.

The woman ignored me for the rest of my employment at the crisis center. I had gone from resigned to pissed off to hurt by her actions. The staff members had a going away party for me during lunch on my last day there, and she didn't even show up to that. I smiled and did my best to pretend my feelings weren't hurt, but I'm sure they were able to see through my act.

After the party, I went back to my office and started the process of packing up my personal belongings. I didn't have any sessions scheduled that afternoon since all my patients had been transferred to the other therapists. I was still fuming about Hilarie's behavior when someone knocked on my office door.

"Come in," I called out and placed another book into the box at my feet. I turned to find Hilarie standing just inside the door with a sad look on her face.

"I'm sorry I missed the party," she said, her voice thick with emotion. She sniffed, and her chin trembled. "I'm having a hard time with this. I don't want you to go," she croaked and burst into tears.

I went to her and wrapped my arms around her. "Oh, Hilarie," I said and squeezed her tighter. "We'll still see each other. Croftridge isn't that far away. We could even meet halfway for dinner once a week if you wanted to."

I felt her nod against my shoulder. "I would like that," she said and pulled back, wiping the tears from her eyes.

"I would, too."

"I'm sorry for being such a bitch the last few weeks. I really do want you to be happy," she said and reached for a box I hadn't noticed. She picked it up and lifted the lid. "Peace offering?" she asked and held out the box filled with lemon squares from my favorite bakery in Sugar Falls.

I grinned. "I'm stuffed from the party, but I can always make room for a lemon square," I said as I surveyed the box and shamelessly reached for the biggest one. I pointed to one square in the corner. "Is that one different?"

"Oh, I almost forgot about that one. Yes, it's a peanut butter treat for Titan. Is it okay for him to have?"

I nodded and swallowed a mouthful of goodness. "Yes, he's had them before, and he loves them."

"I know you said he's friendly, but I think I'll let you give it to him," she said with a nervous laugh.

I took the treat from the box and held it out for Titan who swallowed it instantly. "Did you even taste it, boy?" I asked with a giggle.

Hilarie laughed, too. "I don't see how he could have." She glanced at her watch. "I have a conference call starting in five minutes. What time are you leaving?"

"I'm staying until the end of the day, just in case anyone has any last-minute questions about my previous patients."

"Oh, good. I'll come back and help you finish packing once I finish my call."

"Thank you," I said and hugged her again before she left.

With Titan sleeping in the corner of my office, I turned on some soft music and got to work. I was halfway through filling the third box when I decided to take a break. Yawning, I made my way over to the small sofa in my office. I collapsed onto the leather, closed my eyes, and fell into a dreamless sleep.

I don't know if it was just luck or some subconscious instinct for self-preservation, but my mind seemed to wake up before my body did. The moment my mind was back online, I knew something was wrong. I was cold and lying on something that was decidedly not the sofa in my office. My head was throbbing, and my hands and feet felt tingly like they weren't getting enough blood flow. That was when I realized my hands and feet were tied to something. Willing myself to maintain a steady breathing pattern, I cracked one eye open enough to get a glimpse of my surroundings, but I couldn't see anything. Slowly, I opened both eyes and realized there was nothing for me to see because I was in total darkness.

Don't panic.

Don't panic.

Don't panic.

No matter how many times I said it to myself, it didn't work. After dealing with anxiety issues for years and years, somewhere along the way, I learned that sometimes it takes more time and energy to fight off a panic attack instead of letting it run its course. So, I surrendered to the panic, the fear, the helplessness, the overwhelming sense of doom. I cried; I writhed; I felt like I couldn't breathe. I let it all happen, and when it was over, I started trying to figure out where in the fuck I was and what the fuck had happened.

The first thing that occurred to me was that Titan wasn't with me. If he was, he would have tried to comfort me during my panic attack. How had someone gotten to me with Titan around? He was sleeping in my office when I fell asleep. That's when I realized someone had drugged me, and likely Titan as well. Fuck.

Before I could analyze my situation any further, the door to the room opened, and someone stepped inside.

CHAPTER TWENTY-FOUR

Carbon

I barreled through the front doors of the clubhouse and ran straight for Church. I called Duke first and told him to get his ass to the clubhouse and bring my sister and nephew. Then, I called Phoenix and told him I needed him to call an emergency Church. He didn't ask questions and didn't give me any shit about it. He just said, "Okay," and disconnected the call.

When I arrived, everyone except Shaker was already there. I wasn't going to waste time and wait for him. "I can't find Harper, and I know something is wrong," I blurted, trying to catch my breath.

Duke was instantly on his feet. "What the fuck

do you mean you can't find her?"

"Today was her last day at work. She was going to leave from there to come here. She should have been here over an hour ago. Her cell phone is going to voicemail, and she's not answering her office phone. I had Judge tap into the camera feed at her house, and there's no sign of her. We have to find her!" I screamed. I was losing my shit. After what had just happened to my sister and Harper having been kidnapped before, my mind was flooded with worst-case scenarios that could be playing out that very minute.

"Lock it down, Carbon. We'll find her, but wrestling with you will take time away from searching for her," Phoenix said sternly.

"Say no more, Prez. I'm good," I replied. He said the right words to have me reining in my temper. I didn't want to do anything to take away from finding Harper. I knew, in my gut, that she was in trouble and it was killing me.

"Byte, see if you can get a location on her phone or her car if she has any kind of tracking on it. Somebody find Shaker and get his bitch on the phone. Carbon, call Ruben and see if Titan has a tracking chip," Phoenix ordered.

We scrambled to carry out our assigned tasks as fast as possible. Byte couldn't get anything on her phone or car, but Titan had a tracking chip, and it was showing him at the crisis center.

"Gear up and round up as many sober members as you can. We're rolling out in 10 minutes. Duke, call Judge and your Aunt Leigh to let them know what's going on. I'm guessing Copper and his boys will meet us there," Phoenix said.

"Do you think Boar would send some boys out? They're closer than either of the Blackwings clubs," I asked.

Phoenix nodded, his eyes full of understanding. "I'll call and ask. Just keep it together. We'll find her."

We left the clubhouse in exactly 10 minutes, leaving Ranger, Badger, and a handful of prospects behind to watch over the girls. Boar agreed to help us out and send some of his boys to the crisis center. As expected, Copper and his crew were on the way to Sugar Falls as well.

About halfway there, Phoenix signaled for us to pull over. "Boar's boys arrived at the crisis center. The place is empty from what they can tell. Titan is inside the building and, according to Boar's VP 'is on a rampage.' They looked through all the windows, including Harper's and didn't see anyone. Her car isn't there either. They're going to wait at the crisis center until we arrive. Carbon, do you think you can get that dog under control, or do we need to call Ruben to come down?"

"Let's get back on the road. I'll call Ruben and ask him what we should do," I replied.

Phoenix nodded and pulled back onto the road. Fuck. I knew something was wrong, but Titan flipping out inside the crisis center confirmed it. Nothing made sense. She wouldn't have left him there, so where was her car? Fuck, where was she?

The rest of the ride was a blur. I managed to keep my bike on the road, but I couldn't tell you how. The only thing on my mind was finding Harper.

When we pulled into the parking lot of the crisis center, I could hear Titan barking and snarling as soon as we turned our bikes off. Following Ruben's instructions, I walked to the door and called his name. When he focused his attention on me, I gave the command Ruben assured me would work. "Cessare!" Titan closed his jaws and dropped his butt to the floor, sitting still as a statue. "Good boy!"

A few of the guys behind me muttered their surprise that it worked. Ignoring them, I got to work picking the locks. It took several minutes, but I finally got the doors open. Byte and Judge had already disabled the security system. I slowly opened the door and eyed Titan warily. He was a good dog, and I trusted him completely with Harper, but Harper was missing, and I wasn't sure how he was going to react to me. He whimpered when I took a step inside the building. I patted my leg with my hand and called him to me. He eagerly came to me and started nudging me in the direction of one of the offices. One that was not Harper's.

He took the lead when I started walking toward her door. I heard Phoenix, Duke, Copper, and Judge following behind me. Titan walked behind a desk and stopped. He barked once and tapped the floor with his paw like he was pointing at something. I bent down to retrieve a small plastic bag lined with a white powder residue. Holding it up for my brothers to see, I bellowed, "Motherfucker!"

"No. Fuck no," Duke groaned. The sound of something being destroyed had me turning to see Judge pull his fist from the wall.

"Brothers! She needs you to keep your shit together. Carbon, I can see the red haze in your eyes. Focus, boy. We'll find her," Phoenix demanded.

"Get the computer guys in here. I installed a few cameras here when I installed the ones at her house. Spazz checked the live feed for the office and her house when we first got here, but we didn't have time to go back and look through the recordings from earlier today. One can pull up the feed from here, and the other can get the feed from her house," Judge said, shaking his hand out and pacing the room.

"I'll take the office, and you get the house," Byte declared, sitting down at Harper's desk with Spazz setting up his laptop on the opposite side.

"What the fuck?" Byte shouted at his computer. He sounded pissed, which was a rarity for our laid-back resident computer geek.

"What is it?" I demanded.

Byte motioned for us to come closer and turned his computer screen around to face the room. He clicked play, and the screen showed Harper packing her personal belongings from her office. He skipped forward to show Harper talking to someone at her office door. We saw her reach for something, eat it, and then feed something to Titan. Byte skipped forward again, and we saw Harper yawning and curling up on her sofa to take a nap; Titan snoozing on the floor beside her. Then, the screen went black for a few beats before a message filled the screen. "Carbon and Duke, here's your only hint." The screen filled with a bunch of dots, then lines started connecting the dots to make a picture that roughly resembled two stick figures holding hands.

"That's what was painted on her living room wall," I stated. "What the fuck is it?"

"I have no idea," Phoenix muttered.

"I haven't found anything on the recordings from her house, but if the office feed was jacked, there's a good chance the feed from her house has been tampered with as well," Spazz interjected.

"We'll have some of the guys stay here while we go check out her house," Phoenix said, already heading toward his bike.

Copper pointed toward Titan. "What about the dog?"

"He'll be fine here. Byte, can you watch him while we're gone?" I asked.

"Sure. Jot down the commands to get his ass under control in case I need to, and we're straight," Byte said, not the least bit worried about the dog.

When we arrived at Harper's house, I immediately knew something wasn't right. I could feel it. I crept closer to her front door, and the hairs on the back of my neck stood on end. I turned back to the guys. "Something's not right."

They all murmured their agreement. Copper added, "My gut is telling me we should go around back."

Halfway to the back side of Harper's house, our phones started ringing, all of them. I pulled mine out and accepted the call. My ear was filled with Byte shouting, "Get away from the house! Now! Go! Go! Go!" The five of us started running as a group. We hopped on our bikes and peeled out of the driveway. I was about to stop and ask where we were going when the sky brightened, and I felt an intense heat warm my back. Stopping in the middle of the road, I looked back over my shoulder to see Harper's house in flames.

"She wasn't in there!" Phoenix shouted. I felt his hand clasp my shoulder and shake me. "She wasn't in there! Byte had the true live feed up. That's how he knew the house was about to go up in flames. She. Was. Not. In. There!"

I nodded and turned my head to find Duke staring up at the house. Copper was in between Judge and Duke, a hand on each shoulder, I assumed having the same conversation Phoenix just had with me. "We have to find her, Prez," I said, the desperation evident in my plea.

"We will. Let's get back to the crisis center before the pigs show up and try to pin this on us," Phoenix said, climbing back on his bike.

Back at the crisis center, I didn't know what to do. Only one thought was on my mind, and it played over and over.

We have to find her.

We have to find her.

We have to find her.

We used Harper's office as a makeshift command center. The small space was cramped with everyone piled in there, but we made it work.

"Has anyone heard from Shaker? And what about her little friend that's been fucking him? Anybody else think it's strange that they seem to have vanished as well?" Phoenix asked the room.

I jumped to my feet. "You think he has something to do with this?" I growled.

Phoenix pinched the bridge of his nose and shook his head. "I don't know what to think. Harper's missing. He's missing. Hilarie's missing. That can't be a coincidence, brother." He directed his attention to Byte. "Find anything yet?"

Byte never took his eyes from his computer. "I can't find shit on a Hilarie Thaxton in Sugar

Falls. Are you sure that's her name?"

"Yes, I'm sure, but screw the computer search. She works here. There has to be something in this place with her address listed on it," I replied.

I was right. Less than five minutes later, we had the address of Hilarie Thaxton and were heading to her house.

Her house was empty, as in completely fucking empty. No clothes, no food, no furniture. If she had lived there, she sure as shit didn't anymore. I clenched my jaw and balled my fists, feeling my control slowly slipping from my fingers. We had nothing. Not a damn thing to go on. Anyone could have her, and they could be doing...I couldn't even complete that thought.

I turned to face my brothers. "What do we do now?"

Phoenix looked at me pointedly and opened his mouth to speak, but his phone ringing stopped him. Phoenix answered, and Byte's voice traveled through the silence surrounding us. "Get back here now. I've got something."

Byte stood when we entered the room. Spazz had moved to the other side of the desk and continued pounding furiously on the keyboard in front of him. He made eye contact with Phoenix and ever so subtly lifted his chin in my direction. Before Phoenix could make a move in my direction, I held up my hand. "I'm good, but I won't be if you don't spit it the fuck out."

"Does the name Valarie Vine mean anything to you?" Byte cautiously asked.

"She's the daughter of Vincent Vine, the fucker that kidnapped Harper," Judge exclaimed.

Duke furrowed his brow in confusion. "She's dead. Why are you asking about her?"

"What?" Byte asked. "How do you know she's dead?"

"Because I had a private investigator keep tabs on her and her aunt and uncle. Not long after she went to live with them, she tried to kill herself and was placed in a psychiatric hospital. She was released when she turned 18 and seemed to be making a life for herself. She stayed in the same town, got an apartment, and found a job. A few months later, she was found dead in her apartment. The private investigator called to let me know and even sent me copies of the newspaper with the obituary," Duke explained.

"What about the aunt and uncle?" I asked.

"They're both deceased," Spazz said. "The uncle died five years ago, and the aunt died two years ago. Both from natural causes. I also have Valarie Vine's obituary pulled up."

"Again, why are you asking about her?" Duke demanded.

"Because that name keeps popping up. Valarie Vine is listed as the owner of this building as well as Hilarie Thaxton's house. The property taxes are mailed to Valarie Vine at a PO Box in Arizona, not far from where you and Harper used to live."

"So, what? We think someone is impersonating Valarie Vine?" I asked.

"Byte and Spazz, keep searching. Brothers, let's lay out what we know," Phoenix said and began writing out the facts on Harper's bare office wall.

Harper is missing.

Shaker is missing.

Hilarie is missing.

Harper's house exploded.

Hilarie's house is empty.

Harper's car is missing.

Valarie Vine owns the building.

Valarie Vine owns Hilarie Thaxton's house.

Valarie Vine is dead.

"No fucking way!" Byte shouted.

"What?" we all asked in unison.

Byte turned his computer screen around to face us. "The picture on the left is Valarie Vine's driver's license photo from years ago. The picture on the right is Hilarie Thaxton's mugshot from last month."

I couldn't believe what I was seeing. Valarie's picture looked like a young Harper. They could be, well, twins. Hilarie's picture, however, looked completely different.

Before I could ask, Byte enlarged the pictures and continued, "The eye color is different, probably contacts, but the size and shape of the eyes are the same. Also, note the mole on the upper left cheek as well as the faint scar along the right jawline. The preliminary result from my facial recognition software is a 77.58% chance of these two photos being a match."

"Other than those three things you pointed out, they look completely different," Phoenix stated the obvious.

Byte nodded in agreement. "They do, but everything else could be surgical, such as the cheekbones, nose, and chin, or cosmetic, like eye color and hair color. Moles can be removed, but I don't believe anyone adds them...same thing with scars."

Suddenly, a horrible thought came to mind as a rock settled in my gut. "How did she try to kill herself as a child?"

Duke's face paled, and I assumed he was following my line of thoughts. "She jumped off the roof of her aunt's house...and landed face down on the walkway."

Fuck me. I rasped, "Hilarie Thaxton is Valarie Vine."

CHAPTER TWENTY-FIVE

Harper

I froze in fear as the footsteps came closer to the bed. I felt a pinch as something pierced the skin of my arm. The footsteps retreated, and I faded into the darkness.

When I woke the next time, my head felt groggy, and I was extremely thirsty. For a brief moment, I wasn't sure why I felt so bad, but the reality of my situation came flooding back to me the very next second.

My breathing increased, and my heart beat frantically in my chest as sheer terror tried to consume me once again. With an inner strength I didn't know I possessed, I forced myself to calm down, and I opened my eyes. To my surprise, the lights were on. I moved my hand to shield my eyes from the bright lights and realized my hands and legs were free.

A shot of adrenaline coursed through me as I got to my feet and started exploring my surroundings. I was in a small room with concrete walls, no windows, and two doors, one open and one closed. I immediately went to the closed door to find it locked. The open door led to a bathroom, also with concrete walls and no windows.

I made use of the facilities and rinsed my mouth out with some water. I stood there for a moment, braced on the sink, and tried to gather myself. I could have a meltdown later, after I found a way out. Taking in a deep breath, I slowly released it and returned to the room to see if I could find anything useful.

The room held no furniture, other than the bed, which was somehow affixed to the floor. On the floor beside the bed, I found a few stacks of folded clothes, a loaf of bread, a jar of peanut butter, packets of jelly, a large bag of chips, and several bottles of water. What I didn't find was something I could use as a weapon.

I took a seat on the bed, pulled my knees to

my chest, and cried. It wasn't my intention to fall asleep, but I had, and I blamed the drugs that were obviously still in my system. It was a fitful sleep with dreams filled with voices and sounds instead of images.

"Sister dearest, my plans are coming together perfectly. Soon, it will be just you and me, together again in our new home. No one will bother us, and no one will be able to find us. I wish it could be like that now, but I haven't finished getting everything ready. It won't be much longer. Until then, you'll stay here, where you're safe. I love you so much, Vanessa."

Vanessa.

Vanessa.

Vanessa.

My eyes flew open, and I shot to a sitting position with my hand pressed to my chest and sweat beading on my forehead. I gasped in breath after breath as flashes of the past flooded my mind in vivid color, one after another.

When I opened my eyes, I saw a little girl sitting on a bed staring at me. She looked like me, almost exactly like me. Her eyes widened when she saw me look at her. She gasped and covered her mouth with her hand. "Vanessa?" In a flash, she was across the room hugging me. "I'm so glad you came back. I thought I would never see you again. I've missed you so much."

"Your name is not Harper! It's Vanessa. The sooner you learn that, the better off you'll be. Time for another lesson," he screamed before I felt the streak of fire across my bare back.

"What happened to you, Vanessa? You don't act the same as you did before the accident. Why don't you remember our secret handshake or our favorite hiding places?"

"If you would do as you're told, I wouldn't have to keep doing this," he spat. Then he whipped me with his belt over and over and over.

"You motherfucker! What the fuck are you doing to my sister?" my brother bellowed. My brother! Oh, thank you, thank you, thank you. Duke was there to save me. "Close your eyes, Harper! Now!" I did as he asked. Sounds of flesh meeting flesh and bones being broken followed. My bound hands prevented me from plugging my ears, so I started humming to try and drown out the noise. Suddenly, Duke was in front of me,

removing the ropes and sliding a shirt over my head. "He's dead. Take one look at him, and then I'm getting you out of here."

I ran to the bathroom, dropped to my knees in front of the toilet, and vomited what little bit of bile and acid was in my stomach.

"It was just a dream," I repeated to myself. They were all dead, and there was no way the Vines had anything to do with abducting me this time. The dreams were to be expected given my history.

With my elbows propped on the toilet seat and my hands cradling my face, I recalled something Ember said when she was teaching us some self-defense moves. *"Use whatever you can as a weapon."* I looked up and knew exactly what I was going to use.

I had no idea how much time passed before I had an opportunity to put my plan into action. It had to have been hours, possibly even a day, but I couldn't be certain. It was enough time for me to eat a sandwich and some chips and become hungry enough to eat again.

I was starting to get sleepy, but the moment I heard someone at the door, I jumped to my feet, grabbed my weapon, and got myself into position. The door slowly opened, and a woman stepped into the room carrying bags in each hand. I didn't hesitate. I moved from behind the door and swung the toilet tank lid as hard as I could at the back of her head.

She went down to her knees with a groan of pain. She started to turn her head toward me as I swung the lid again, causing me to hit the side of her head. She went down, and the sound of her head bouncing off the concrete floor had me close to puking all over her. I managed to contain it and swung the lid one more time for good measure.

I thanked the lucky stars above that her keys flew out of her hand when she fell and landed not far from my feet. I grabbed the keys and ran out of the room, slamming the door behind me. With shaky hands, I found the correct key and breathed a sigh of relief when the lock slid home.

Judging by the concrete walls, lack of windows, and set of stairs, I was in a basement. Unsure of what I may find beyond the walls surrounding me, I picked up a piece of wood and quietly climbed the stairs. I pressed my ear against the door and listened. When I didn't hear anything, I unlocked the door and cracked it open. That's when I heard something.

Clank.

Clank.

Clank.

What the hell?

I remained frozen to the spot, unsure of what to do. What if there was someone else in the house? Would I be able to get out unnoticed? Would I have to fight them off with only a piece of wood? It didn't matter. I couldn't stay in the basement with a psycho. I took a deep breath and slowly pushed the door open. The noise was significantly louder.

Clank.

Clank.

Clank.

I waited and listened, but I couldn't tell where the noise was coming from nor did I have any idea what it could possibly be.

Clank.

Clank.

Clank.

Creeping forward, I tried to ignore my fear and find a door or window. Every time I heard the strange sound, it felt like my heart stopped for a few beats.

Clank.

Clank.

Clank.

"Let me out of here, you crazy cunt!" a male voice shouted.

I gasped. It couldn't be, could it? I knew that voice.

"When I get my hands on you, you are going to wish you never met me. I don't give a fuck that you have a pussy. I am going to carve you like a holiday turkey!" he bellowed.

Clank.

Clank.

Clank.

Hesitantly, I called out, "Shaker?"

"Harper?" he asked, sounding hopeful.

"Yeah, it's me. Where are you?"

"Locked in a room. Are you okay? Where's the cunt?" he asked.

"I'm okay. She's locked in a room in the basement," I hedged. "Keep talking so I can find you."

"Harper, you need to get out of here. She's fucking crazy! Go, now, while you can!" he yelled.

"I'm not leaving you here. She's knocked out and locked in a room. I took her keys. I'll be fine," I said. I found a door underneath another set of stairs and jiggled the handle. "Are you in this room?"

"Yes."

"There are a lot of keys. It might take me a minute to figure out which one goes to this door."

He cleared his throat. "Uh, just so you know, I'm cuffed to a bed...and I'm naked."

I felt my cheeks heat and I let out an uncomfortable laugh. "Thanks for the warning. I'll try not to look."

He chuckled. "Doesn't bother me, sweetheart. Just didn't want to shock you."

I rolled my eyes. Only Shaker would be flirting while trying to escape from a kidnapping.

It took forever to get the damn door open. Of course, I went through every key on the ring before I found the one that unlocked his door. I pushed it open and went straight to him, keeping my eyes on his face, his battered and bruised face. "Shaker," I gasped.

"That bad, huh?" he joked.

I quickly undid his handcuffs, easily finding the correct key due to the difference in shape and size. He casually rose from the bed and strolled across the room, seemingly not concerned about his nakedness. I couldn't keep from looking at his firm ass when he bent over to pick up a pair of jeans. Before sliding them over his hips, he wiggled his butt and asked, "Like what you see?"

"Oh, shut it, Shaker. Now is not the time," I playfully scolded. I was so glad to see a familiar face.

"You're right. Are you okay? Did she hurt you?" he asked.

"Physically, no, other than drugging me at least twice. Other than that, I didn't see anyone until a few minutes ago. Do you know who took us?" I asked.

His forehead wrinkled, and he looked at me with an expression I couldn't place. "You don't know?"

I shook my head. "No, when a woman came into my room, I hit her, and she fell to the floor. Her hair was covering her face. I didn't stop to look; I just grabbed the keys and ran."

He visibly swallowed and came closer, placing his hand on my shoulder. "It's Hilarie."

My hand flew to my mouth as I tried to process what he said. I shook my head and met his eyes. "It can't be. She wouldn't— She couldn't— Why would—" I trailed off as my face crumpled.

"She would, and she did. I'm sorry, Harper. I know she was your friend, or made you think she was your friend, but she's not who you think she is," Shaker said gently.

"What do you mean?"

Shaker blew out a slow breath and looked to the ceiling for a moment before he answered me. "I've been here for a few days, and during that time, she shared a lot of secrets."

"Spit it out!" I yelled, frustrated with his hedging.

"Fine," he gritted out. "Hilarie Thaxton is actually Valarie Vine."

My heart pounded in my ears, and my vision started to blur. No. It couldn't be. She was dead. Oh, fuck. I couldn't breathe.

A light slap to my cheek brought me back to the present. I looked up to find Shaker's dark eyes fixed on me and filled with concern. "I know about your past, Harper. I'm not going to pretend to know how you're feeling right now, but I need you to box those feelings up and push them to the side so we can focus on getting out of here. Can you do that for me? For Carbon?"

I took in a deep breath and squared my shoulders. I could and would do anything for Chase. "Okay, I'm good," I said with a sharp nod.

Shaker grinned. "Good. I'm going to go down to the basement and make sure she can't escape. Then, we need to get the fuck out of here."

"No, let's just go," I countered as I followed him through the house.

He stopped when he found the kitchen, opened a few drawers, and pulled out a large knife. "But I have a threat to make good on," he said with an evil smile, holding the knife in one hand and his handcuffs in the other. I hadn't seen him pick those up.

"Wait here. I'll be right back," he instructed.

"Fuck that. I believe I'll stay with the big man holding the knife."

Following him down the stairs that led to the basement was one of the hardest things I've ever done. Everything in me told me to go the other way, to flee, to not return to the dungeon, but I wasn't leaving without Shaker and the odds of her taking down the two of us at one time were slim to none.

We paused outside the door and listened. When we didn't hear anything for several minutes, Shaker unlocked the door and cautiously pushed it open. The woman I still couldn't believe was Hilarie, or Valarie, was exactly where I left her. He looked at me over his shoulder and back to her; then he did it again.

"What?" I asked.

He didn't say anything and entered the room. Kneeling beside her, he moved her hair to the side and pressed two fingers to the side of her neck. I got a clear look at Hilarie's face, but what had me gasping in horror was Shaker rising to his feet and dropping the handcuffs on the bed. "Is she…" I trailed off, unable to ask the question.

Shaker pulled me to his bare chest and wrapped his arms around me. Softly, he said, "You're not going to be upset about this. You did what you had to do to save yourself, and you saved me in the process. She was going to keep you locked away for the rest of your life, and she was going to kill me in a matter of days."

I started to shake in his arms. "She's dead?"

"Yes, sweetheart, she is."

I couldn't help it. I burst into tears. A part of me was relieved, and another part of me was scared. "What am I going to do? I killed her. I'll be in prison for the rest of my life," I wailed.

"That won't happen. It was self-defense, plain and simple. We have a decision to make. We can leave the house as is until we can notify the police or we can torch the place and leave the police out of it. It's up to you, but you've got to make a decision right now so we can get the fuck out of here," he said as he closed the door and locked it.

I thought over those options for a few minutes while we went back upstairs and searched through the house for a phone or any means of communication. "Do I have to decide now?" He looked at me quizzically, so I continued. "I would rather Phoenix make that decision."

Shaker smiled brightly. "Good answer. Your man and your brother will love hearing that."

Our search of the house turned up jack shit, so we headed outside. I had hoped for some sort of recognition upon exiting the house, but that wasn't the case. The house was situated in the middle of a small clearing surrounded by what appeared to be dense forest. There were no sounds of traffic or civilization nearby.

"Do you have any idea where we are?" I asked.

He looked around and shook his head. "Not a clue. I was at my apartment, and then I woke up here, cuffed to a bed."

"She has to have a car or something around here," I pointed out.

One trip around the perimeter of the house and a quick search along the edge of the wooded area revealed that she indeed did not have to have a car around there. "What do we do now?" I asked Shaker, trying to hide the desperation in my voice.

He stood tall and faced me. "We're going to get the fuck out of here, car or no car, phone or no phone."

Reluctantly, I followed him back inside the house. "I remember seeing a backpack in the room I was in. I'm going to grab it and see if I can find some shoes. While I'm doing that, can you grab us a few bottles of water and see if there are any snacks we can take? I'm not sure how far we will have to walk to get out of here. Oh, and grab anything else you think might be useful."

He disappeared around the corner while I got to work rummaging through the kitchen. When he returned, he had the backpack, but no shoes. I had a pile of supplies on the kitchen counter, including water, snacks, paper towels, matches, knives, and a wad of cash. He looked at my collection and smiled. "Nice job. Where did you find the cash?"

"It was crammed in one of the drawers. Cash always comes in handy," I replied.

"Oh, almost forgot." He reached into the backpack and produced a roll of duct tape. "I couldn't find any shoes. Tear off a couple of strips and put them on the bottom of your feet."

I gratefully took the roll of tape and started placing pieces on my feet. Hopefully, the duct tape would provide enough protection for our feet to get us back to civilization. With our loaded backpack and taped feet, Shaker and I ventured outside once again.

"This looks like the beginning of a path," Shaker said, pointing to a slightly worn area on the ground. "Shall we start here?"

I shrugged. "Your guess is as good as mine."

Shaker led the way, and I dutifully followed him. We walked in a comfortable silence for at least an hour. I think we were both trying to process the events of the last few days. That thought had me breaking the silence. "How long did she have us?"

"I was there almost five days. I'm guessing you were there around three. She disappeared for over six hours on my second day, which is probably when she nabbed you," he answered.

"Do you know what time it was when she came back?" I asked.

"I don't know the exact time, but it was starting to get dark." He glanced at me over his shoulder. "Why does it matter?"

"Because she took me from my office on Friday. She would've had to wait until everyone else left to get me out of there. That puts her leaving with me no earlier than 6:30 pm. If she was here by the time it was starting to get dark, we're not that far away from Sugar Falls," I excitedly told him.

He nodded. "Yeah, you're probably right."

We continued walking, for hours. Every so often, Shaker would stop and listen for the sound of cars in the distance. My feet enjoyed each small reprieve, but the feelings of hopelessness grew with each stop. How could we have walked so far and still be in the forest? My feet were killing me, and all I wanted to do was sit down and cry. Everything was starting to catch up with me, and an emotional breakdown was looming on the horizon.

When he stopped again to listen, I couldn't hold it in any longer. I dropped my ass to the ground and let the tears flow. "We're never going to find our way out of here! She's dead, and she's still torturing us!" I balled my hands into fists and screamed to the sky, a deep, guttural sound filled to the brim with emotion.

Shaker dropped down beside me and placed his hand on my shoulder, giving it a gentle squeeze. He sat quietly with me, giving me time to compose myself. I was just about to tell him I was ready to keep going when I heard it. Shaker obviously heard it, too.

"A car!" we shouted at the same time and took off running, hopefully toward the sound.

He was much faster than me, and for a few terrifying moments, I was afraid I would lose him and be stuck in the woods by myself. The sound of tires screeching had me moving faster. "Shaker!" I called out, but he didn't answer.

A burst of adrenaline appeared out of nowhere and pushed me forward even faster. Voices. I could hear voices. "Shaker!" I screamed, panting and running and hoping I didn't die before I could make it back to Chase.

"Harper! Over here!" Shaker yelled.

I slowed my pace once I heard his voice. He was okay, and he wouldn't leave me. Breaking through the trees, I saw the car pulled over on the side of the road first. Shaker was standing beside the car smiling like a loon. Then, I saw the last person I expected to see.

"Harper!"

"Hey, Shannon," I said between gasps for breath, completely shocked to see my brother's ex-wife talking to Shaker.

Shaker opened the car door and motioned for me to get in. "Shannon is going to drive us back to Croftridge. Get a load of this shit. The Manglers' clubhouse is about five miles from here."

I looked at him like he had grown two heads.

"How in the fuck can you run that fast? And why aren't you gasping for air? I feel like I could keel over any second."

He chuckled. "I run five to seven miles almost every day. You didn't know?"

If I could have, I would have smacked the smug look right off his face. Instead, I opted to collapse into the back seat of the car and concentrate on the difficult task of breathing.

"Here. Take a couple sips of water. Slowly," Shaker said, thrusting a bottle of water at me.

Shannon climbed into the driver's seat and started the car. She glanced at me in the rearview mirror and then I saw her eyes dart to Shaker. She put the car in gear and glanced at both of us again. I laughed. "What did you tell her, Shaker?"

"Nothing. When she pulled over, I asked if she could give us a ride to Croftridge."

That made me laugh even more. Clearly, I was losing my mind. "I can't imagine what you're thinking right now. What a sight the two of us must be." I was laughing so hard my eyes were watering.

Shaker turned in his seat to look at me. "Harper!" he barked. "Not yet. If you lose it, I'll lose it, and we can't do that right now. Got me?"

Something in his eyes had my laughter dying instantly. I pushed myself to a sitting position and nodded. "Got you."

"Are you guys okay?" Shannon asked, eyeing us both warily. "Should I call Boar or Phoenix?"

"No!" we both shouted, and she flinched.

"Sorry," Shaker continued. "We're okay right now. We just need to get back to the clubhouse. It's not a story to be shared over the phone."

Shannon nodded knowingly. "Enough said."

She kept us occupied with idle chatter for the entire drive to Croftridge. I would be forever grateful to her for that. If she hadn't kept us talking, I wouldn't have been able to hold it together. I almost broke down when I saw the gates to the clubhouse come into view.

Shaker turned again, his eyes locked onto mine. "Not yet. We're going to be rushed the moment we walk through those doors. Then, Phoenix is going to call Church, and you'll have to come in there to tell your part of the story. He'll decide what the next steps will be. Once we've told them everything and he dismisses Church, you can let it go."

I sucked in a deep breath and nodded. "For the record, I'm damn proud of you, Harper."

Shannon pulled up to the gate, and I heard

Kellan say, "Holy shit!"

"Not a word, prospect. Open the gate and keep your mouth shut," Shaker ordered.

Kellan nodded. "Glad you two are okay."

When the gates opened and Shannon drove through, I felt like I could breathe again.

CHAPTER TWENTY-SIX

Carbon

Three fucking days and we still hadn't found her or Shaker. We were assuming that Hilarie had done something with both of them, but we didn't have any proof of that. Phoenix had a prospect basically living at Shaker's apartment in case he or anyone else happened to show up there. The club was on lockdown. Ember, Reese, Aunt Leigh, and a few of the other girls were always crying. Duke, Judge, and I had put more miles on our bikes in those three days than we did on some of our longest runs.

I hadn't slept more than the minimum

necessary for my body to continue functioning. The same could be said for Duke and Judge. Phoenix was the only thing holding us together. He let us lose our shit when we needed to, he let us ride out when we needed to, and he sat us down for reality checks when it was warranted.

Walking into the clubhouse after spending several hours out searching for Harper, I went straight to Duke's room in search of my sister. She opened the door to their room and pulled me in for a hug. I couldn't hold it together any longer, and she knew it. She didn't say a word while I cried on her shoulder. Giant, body-wracking sobs shook me and my little sister. I could hear her sobs mixed with mine, yet neither one of us uttered a word. Exhaustion took over, and before I knew it, I had fallen asleep on my little sister's shoulder.

"CARBON!!!" my sister shrieked. "Carbon! Carbon! Carbon!"

I jumped to my feet and started running, slightly disoriented until I realized I was in Duke's room instead of mine. She continued screaming my name as I ran toward the sound of her voice. I rounded the corner to the common room at a full sprint and immediately dropped to my knees when I saw Harper standing between Duke and

Judge. I didn't give a shit who was watching. I shamelessly let the tears run down my face as she walked to me. "Baby," I croaked and yanked her to me as soon as she was within reach.

"Are you okay?" I asked, running my hands all over her.

"Yeah, I'm okay. I missed you so much. I love you, Chase."

"I love you, too, baby. I was so fucking worried. We haven't stopped looking for you. Oh, I can't believe you're standing right here in front of me," I rambled, holding her tightly to my chest.

"Church!" Phoenix bellowed.

I rose to my feet to protest. There was no way in hell I was letting go of her for Church. Hell, I probably wouldn't let go of her for the next month. Phoenix stopped me before I could get started. "Relax, big guy, she's coming, too."

Phoenix cut right to the chase. "We're all happy as fuck to have you two back. First, are either one of you hurt, other than what we can see?" he asked, gesturing toward Shaker's beat up face. When they both said they were fine, he continued, "Before we get to the details, do we have any loose ends that need attention?"

Shaker nodded and opened his mouth to speak, but Harper rising to her feet had him closing his mouth. "Yes, we do. I killed someone, and we left the dead body in the house."

No other words could have shocked me more. "What?" the room collectively asked.

Harper cleared her throat and explained. "The woman who kidnapped us. I killed her. I didn't mean to. I was trying to knock her out. Anyway, I found Shaker on my way out and freed him. He said we could leave her and let the police handle it, or we could not involve the law and torch the place. I suggested we let you make that decision."

I pulled her back into my lap and gave her a squeeze. "Damn proud of you, baby." I looked up to see every brother in the room looking at her with pride in their eyes.

"Damn fine woman you are, Harper Jackson," Phoenix told her, smiling broadly. His smile faded with his next question. "Did you kill Valarie Vine?"

She couldn't hide her surprise. "Y-yes, how did you know?"

"Carbon can explain the details, but when you and Shaker turned up missing, we started digging. It took some doing, but we finally pieced together that Valarie Vine was posing as Hilarie Thaxton." He cleared his throat and addressed the room. "I think we should let the law enforcement officers handle this one. It isn't directly related to the club or club business, and it was clearly a case of self-defense. They've only been here for a few minutes, so if we call now, there won't be any gaps in the timeline."

"We didn't file a missing person report for either of them," Dash added. "How are we going to explain that?"

Phoenix grinned. "Oh, but we did. Byte filed them online."

The room erupted in laughter, and Harper turned to me with confusion on her face. "I'll explain later," I whispered in her ear.

"I'll place the call now. Until further notice, the club is still on lockdown. Dismissed," Phoenix said and pulled out his cell phone.

I pushed open the door and stepped into the common room. Suddenly, Harper's hand was ripped from mine, and she let out a yelp. I spun around quickly, ready to defend my woman when I heard her giggle. She was on the floor with Titan standing over her, licking all over her face. She wrapped her arms around his neck. "I missed you, too. Yes, I did," she cooed at Titan.

"Sorry, I didn't know how to stop him," Annabelle said, looking sheepish. She had volunteered to look after Titan while we were out searching for Harper.

When Titan calmed down, Harper got to her feet and asked, "Do you think I have time to take a shower before the police officers arrive?"

Three loud knocks on the front door answered her question for me. Phoenix gestured for one of the prospects to open the door. Phoenix greeted the officers and led them to our Church room. Shaker and Harper followed Phoenix and the officers while Duke, Judge, and myself followed Harper. Phoenix stopped us at the door. "You can wait right outside this door if you want, but you three aren't coming in there." Before any of us could say a word, he slammed the door, and I heard the lock slide into place.

Oh.

Hell.

No.

President or not, he was not going to lock me away from my woman, especially when I had just gotten her back only minutes ago. A small body hit me from behind, and arms circled around my waist.

Reese.

She knew I was about to rage. "Stay with me, big scary brother. She's going to need you when they finish in that room, and you can't be there for her if you're locked up in jail or sedated by Patch."

She didn't let go of me until my breathing returned to normal. Once I had calmed, she led me to one of the couches and placed James in my arms. I couldn't help but grin at the little guy. He was so damn cute. "Smart move," I mumbled.

She dropped down beside me and didn't leave my side until the locked door opened. She scooped James into her arms and leaned down to kiss the top of my head. "Call if you need me, either one of you. Love you both," she said and carried her son toward Duke.

I stood when I caught sight of Harper. She said something to Duke and Judge, hugged each one of them, and came straight to me. "Can we go now? If I can't shower and sleep in the very near future, I will not be held responsible for my actions."

I took her hand in mine and led her to my room. "The club has been on lockdown since you and Shaker went missing. Phoenix hasn't officially given the all clear, so we have to stay here for the time being," I said, hoping she wasn't going to be pissed about it.

"I don't care where we stay, as long as you're

there, and I get to shower and sleep."

I was already in bed waiting for her when she finished her shower. She crawled under the covers and nestled against my chest. Neither of us said a word before almost instantly falling asleep.

***

Pounding on my door woke us. "Carbon! Open up, brother," Duke shouted.

I yanked on a pair of jeans and stumbled to my door. Pulling it open, I stretched and yawned. "What do you want?"

He pushed against my chest in a weak attempt to move me to the side. "I want to make sure my sister is okay!"

"She's fine. Why wouldn't she be?"

He looked at me incredulously. "Do you have any idea what time it is?" I shook my head. "It's almost 1:00 pm. You've been asleep for 16 hours."

My brows rose at his words. "Shit, brother. I guess we were both exhausted." I moved out of his way so he could see Harper.

She was sitting in my bed looking sexy as hell in one of my t-shirts. She gave a little wave to her brother. "Hi, Dukie."

"You two should get up and make yourselves presentable. Phoenix said one of the officers called and they'll be here soon to discuss what they found at the house," Duke informed us.

Right on cue, there were three crisp knocks on the door as soon as we entered the common room. Again, the officers were led to our Church room; however, this time I was allowed to tag along.

The officer began, "We were able to locate the property where Mr. Marks and Ms. Jackson were held. It was roughly a seven-mile hike to the property from the point where Mrs. Anderson picked you up. We did find the body of a young woman we believe to be Hilarie Thaxton, aka Valarie Vine. A search of the house turned up plenty of evidence to support your claims as well as other evidence that will need to be further investigated. Ms. Jackson, this was a clear case of self-defense, and no charges will be filed against you."

Harper let out an audible sigh of relief and sagged against my chest. Then, I felt her body stiffen as she straightened. "What else needs to be investigated?"

The officer cleared his throat and glanced

at his partner. "I don't want to cause you any unnecessary distress after what you've been through, but in the interest of your safety, you should be aware that we believe Ms. Thaxton was not working alone."

Phoenix was quick to ask, "Why do you think that?"

"We can't explain how Ms. Thaxton could have possibly carried two unconscious bodies seven miles through the woods, particularly one the size of Mr. Marks. We found no evidence of any means of transportation on the property or anywhere in the surrounding area."

"Do you have any suspects?" I asked.

"Not at this time. We do have a few questions for Mr. Marks and Ms. Jackson in regards to a possible suspect. Shall we take care of those now?" Harper and Shaker both nodded in agreement. "Did either one of you ever see or hear anyone else in the house?"

"No, I didn't even know Shaker was there until I escaped from the basement," Harper answered.

The officers perked up. "Who is Shaker?"

Shaker answered, "Me. Shaker is my road name. I didn't see or hear anyone else in the house, either."

"Ms. Jackson, you were friends with Ms.

Thaxton for several years prior to this event, correct?"

Harper explained her recent history with Hilarie. I wondered if they were aware of Harper's kidnapping by the same family in Arizona, but I wasn't going to ask in front of everyone. Harper said Hilarie never mentioned any other friends in the Sugar Falls area, and she never shared many details about men she dated or hooked up with. "I didn't even know she had been seeing Shaker until I ran into her at Ember's wedding. Shaker and I were both in the wedding party, and she came as his date. At the time, I thought it was just a coincidence..." she trailed off.

"That's all we have for now. The investigation is still open, and a team is still on site processing the house. We'll be in contact when we have more updates," the officer said and pushed his chair back to stand, his partner mimicking his actions. We shook their hands, and they handed us a card with their contact information and the case number.

As we filed out of the room, I heard one of the officers say, "Phoenix, I need to speak with you privately before we leave." I made a mental note to ask about that, too.

Not even five minutes later, the officer and his

partner left, and Phoenix called Harper, Duke, Shaker, and me back into Church.

"Harper, what I'm about to share with you cannot be shared with anyone outside of this room. Is that going to be a problem for you?" Phoenix asked sternly.

Harper grinned and said in a deep voice, "Club business, right, Prez?"

Phoenix threw his head back and laughed, his laughter echoing around the room. "Good one, Harper." When his laughter died down, he continued, "The two officers assigned to your case are friends with Luke Johnson, who is a good friend of mine. Luke is an FBI agent, but that's not relevant at the moment. Anyway, Luke got wind of the investigation and called in a favor on my behalf. He asked the officers to keep an eye out for anything that might be detrimental to the club."

Phoenix paused and lifted a file folder from the chair beside him. He placed it on the table and pushed it toward Harper. "This folder is a copy of a journal found at the house. It's assumed to be Hilarie's. I haven't read through it, but I was made aware of the highlights. In the back of the folder, you'll find some original pages from the journal. As far as anyone else is concerned, those pages were not a part of the journal when it was found. The officers removed them because they implicate Duke in the murder of Vincent Vine. I promised to destroy the pages, but I wanted to give you the option to read them. If you want to, you have to do it now."

Harper stared at the folder in silence for several beats and then shook her head. Her voice was quiet when she said, "I don't need to read them. I was there. I know exactly what happened."

"I don't want to see them either," Duke added, though I didn't recall Phoenix offering that option to him.

"Understood," Phoenix said, reaching for the papers. He pulled a thin stack from the back of the folder, dropped them all except one into a metal trash can, lit the remaining page, and dropped it into the can. "That takes care of that. Now, do you want to hear the highlights or do you want to find out by reading the journal?"

"I would like to read through the journal... eventually, but I would like to know the highlights now," Harper answered.

"Shaker?" Phoenix asked.

"Now is good."

"To clarify, I'm going to refer to the crazy bitch as Hilarie, since that's how we all know her. So, after Duke killed Vincent and rescued Harper, things got even worse for Hilarie. Her mother killed herself, and Hilarie ended up in the care of relatives who ultimately had her committed to a psychiatric hospital, where she remained until her 18th birthday. When she turned 18, she inherited the money from her family's estate, as well as her father's life insurance money. She used the money to find Harper and relocate to be close to her. She enrolled in the same college, always lived near her, and even managed to work at the same place as Harper. The officers said it seemed like she wanted to be close to Harper and have a relationship with her like one would a sister. Things were fine until Carbon and Harper went from casual to serious. Her attempts to tear them apart only pushed them closer together. Changing tactics, she thought dating one of the brothers would allow her to still be close to Harper, so she set her sights on Shaker. Shaker wasn't following the script she had in her head, so she had to come up with another plan. When Carbon and Harper got engaged, and Harper announced she was moving to Croftridge, Hilarie became desperate. In short, she kidnapped Harper and planned to keep her as her prisoner for the rest of their lives. As for

Shaker, well, whatever happened pissed her off, and she planned to kill him," Phoenix told us.

"How did she try to tear us apart?" Harper asked.

"She was the one who broke into your house. She was pissed about you being in Croftridge for a few weeks and thought it would scare you and have you running to her for comfort. She was also the one who broke into Carbon's condo and stole the gun that she somehow managed to link to a gang-related shooting, hoping to get him sent to prison for the foreseeable future," he explained.

"She was the one who tried to get Carbon and Shaker arrested for supposedly drugging a drink at Ember's bachelorette party. And she was responsible for getting herself and Shaker arrested on the way to the lake house," Phoenix added.

"What?"

"How?"

"Seriously?"

"No fucking way."

The four of us exclaimed at the same time.

Phoenix held up his hands. "I don't know the details. I'm guessing it's all in the folder. Like I said, they gave me the highlights, and I just gave them to you."

Harper was flipping through the copied pages, apparently on a mission to find something. "What are you looking for, baby?"

"I want to know about the peas and the damn dots," she answered distractedly. It didn't take her long to find what she was looking for. "Two peas in a pod!" she screeched. "There were no pods! That bitch covered my bed with frozen fucking peas. Oh, and get this, the dots on the wall was her rendition of the Gemini Twins constellation. I'm not her fucking twin!!"

"Baby, it's over now. She's gone. You don't have to worry about her anymore," I soothed.

"It's not over, Chase. You heard the officers. They think she had help. That means someone is still out there who may or may not be coming after me, especially when they find out I killed her! What am I supposed to do, hide out at the clubhouse for the rest of my life?"

I didn't know what to say to her, so I chose to say nothing at all. I held her in my arms and let her have her meltdown. She needed to cry and scream and get it all out.

Our moment of silence was interrupted by Duke's voice. "I think now would be a good time to tell her the rest of it," he said.

Her head shot up immediately. "What the hell else is there?"

"When we realized you were missing, we started looking for you. I guess Hilarie set a trap for us, or tried to, because your house went up in flames while we were there. No one was hurt, but your house was destroyed. Duke has touched base with your insurance company since he's your next of kin," I told her, hoping the news wouldn't be the straw that broke the camel's back.

She inhaled deeply and released it. "I'm glad no one was hurt, and I guess I don't have to worry about going through the hassle of selling it now."

I smiled. "That's my girl."

CHAPTER TWENTY-SEVEN

Harper

I was more than ready to put anything and everything involving the Vine family behind me for good. In order to do that, I had to read her journal. Hell, even a part of me wanted to read it, but I was scared of what I might find written on those pages.

I was already having a hard time dealing with certain aspects of the situation. Even though I knew Hilarie and Valarie were one and the same, to me, it still felt like I had lost the person who had been my best friend for the last few years. Up until a month before my kidnapping, Hilarie and I had never had a major argument, and I genuinely enjoyed the time we spent together. Once I remembered I was grieving for a fictitious friendship, I would get angry with myself. How could I have been so stupid not to figure out who she was? I knew her for years! Berating myself over and over for being an oblivious moron with zero self-preservation skills, I would start to cry and feel sorry for myself. Just like anybody else, I would automatically want to call my best friend and cry on her shoulder, bringing me back to missing my friend. The emotional merry-go-round wouldn't stop, and I couldn't figure out how to get off.

Chase was great about giving me space and not pressuring me to talk about it. He carried on as if it never happened, but I could see the worry in his eyes, and the anger lurking behind the worry. With no one to talk to and the club still on lockdown, I only left Chase's room in the early morning hours to get enough food and water from the kitchen to last me until the next day.

On the seventh day of my pity party, I slipped out of bed at o'dark thirty and made my way to the clubhouse kitchen. I flipped on the lights and nearly pissed myself. Sitting on top of the kitchen island with her arms and legs crossed was none other than the president's wife,

Annabelle, clearly waiting for me.

"Good morning, Harper," she said gently. "I'm sorry, I didn't mean to scare you."

"I wasn't expecting anyone to be in here," I blurted, still trying to compose myself.

She nodded knowingly. "Yeah, I figured. That's the reason I'm here."

"I'm not sure I understand," I mumbled, even though I was fairly certain I knew exactly what she meant.

"I think you do. You've been locked in Carbon's room almost the entire time you've been back. Hiding from everyone and keeping your feelings bottled up isn't going to do anything to help you. I'm not going to pretend to understand what you're going through, but I'm going to help you get through it whether you want me to or not," she said.

I was slightly taken aback by her bluntness. "I appreciate your concern, but with all due respect, I don't want your help," I said, hating the way my voice shook.

"I know, that's why I said I was doing it whether you wanted me to or not," she smiled. She hopped off the counter and carefully slid a steaming cup of coffee toward me. "Come take a walk with me. I want to show you something."

She picked up her own mug of coffee and started walking toward the back door. She just assumed I would follow her, never once looking back. She was right in her assumption as I dutifully followed her outside.

We walked in silence, quietly sipping our coffee, until we reached the small lake, or maybe it was a large pond. Anyway, she walked toward a bench and gestured for me to sit. "I was kidnapped once, a long time ago. Did you know that?" she asked. I shook my head. "I was younger than you are now. A man, who later turned out to be Phoenix's half-brother, took me from my home and wouldn't let me leave. I was there for over six years before I managed to escape." She was quiet for a moment, and then she continued. "In order to escape, I had to give up everything and start over, as in the witness relocation type of starting over."

"That must have been difficult for you," I said, unsure of what to say.

"It was. I had to give up Phoenix to protect him. I didn't have a lot of friends, but I had a few that were close, like Badger and Macy. I had to give up those friendships, too. I was in a new place with a small child, and I had no one to talk to. I was too scared to leave the house. In fact,

I didn't leave the house for almost two years. The point I'm trying to make here is you have a fiancé, family, and friends here to help you. Let them," she urged.

"It's not that I don't want to, Annabelle. I don't know how," I confessed.

"You can start by coming out of the room. No one is going to pressure you to talk or bombard you with questions. Is that what you're worried about?"

I shook my head, and despite my greatest efforts, tears started falling down my cheeks. Then, Annabelle did the worst thing anyone can do when someone is trying to stave off tears; she hugged me. "I'm embarrassed," I wailed into her shirt.

"Honey, what in the world do you have to be embarrassed about?" she asked.

"I miss her. Not *her*. Hilarie, or the persona presented to me as Hilarie. And I feel stupid for being kidnapped by that family twice. How did I not recognize *her*?" I hiccupped and semi-choked on snot. "And I don't feel bad about killing her, but I feel bad about killing Hilarie even though Hilarie isn't real! I'm so confused!"

"Harper, those feelings sound perfectly reasonable to me." She was silent for a few minutes, holding and comforting me. "Have you read the journal yet?"

"No. I know I need to, but I'm scared to read it," I admitted.

"I have nothing to do today. Do you want to read it together? Or I could just sit with you while you read it?" she offered.

The thought of having her there with me surprisingly made the task seem less daunting. "I think I would like that," I said, wiping snot and tears from my face with my shirt. Yuck.

"HARPER!" someone bellowed from a distance. I couldn't tell if it was Duke or Chase, but the voice sounded panicked. "HARPER!!"

Annabelle jumped to her feet, popped two fingers in her mouth, and whistled so loud I thought my eardrums would burst. "We're fine! Be right there!" she yelled, her melodic voice echoing in the quiet morning.

We started walking back to the clubhouse, much faster than our stroll to the lake. Chase nearly trampled us before we even made it halfway back. He yanked me to him, "You scared the fuck out of me. I woke up, and you were gone. Couldn't find you anywhere inside."

"Can't. Breathe." I grunted.

"Shit, sorry, baby," he said, quickly releasing

me. "What are you two doing out here anyway?"

Annabelle grinned. "We were just talking. She was keeping me company while I watched the sunrise."

Chase's wild eyes came back to me. "Let me know next time, okay?" he pleaded.

"I will. I'm sorry, big guy. I ran into Annabelle in the kitchen, and we decided to go for a walk. It didn't even cross my mind that you would wake up and be worried. It won't happen again, I promise," I said, meaning every word.

After breakfast, Chase headed out for the day, leaving Annabelle and I sitting at one of the tables in the common room. She smiled softly and reached for my hand. "Do you want to bring the journal over to my house? No one will be there other than me until later this afternoon."

I spent the better part of the day at Annabelle's house reading Hilarie's journal. We took turns reading it out loud and would frequently pause to discuss entries. Many of her entries were confusing. We ended up getting a notepad to jot down questions and make notes. What started out as an emotional journey for me quickly turned into an investigation of sorts.

"Is this the only journal the police found?" Annabelle asked.

"I don't know. It's the only one they gave me. At the time, I didn't think to ask if there were any others," I said, wondering how I could find out if more journals were discovered.

"There have to be more. Several times she wrote 'as I said before' in reference to something that wasn't in this journal," Annabelle said, tapping the folder containing Hilarie's photocopied journal.

"I could call one of the detectives and ask," I suggested.

After a quick phone call, we were informed that no other journals or items of a personal nature were discovered in the house, such as pictures, journals, keepsakes, etc.

"She had pictures and crap all over her house in Sugar Falls. She even had a framed photo on her desk at the crisis center. Where in the hell did all of that stuff go? It didn't just disappear," I said.

"Maybe she rented a storage unit or something," Annabelle suggested.

"Maybe, but how would I find that out? The detectives didn't mention anything when they were here, and they just told me they were about to close the case since no new evidence had been discovered. It's not like I can ask Byte to do some searches for me. I feel like there is more to the story and I'm having a hard time letting that go," I told her.

Annabelle straightened in her seat and grinned. "I know someone we can ask."

Keegan arrived at Annabelle's house with a wicked looking laptop and a smile on her face. "How much trouble am I letting you two get me into?"

"Not much, if any," Annabelle answered. "We are trying to locate the personal belongings of someone recently deceased, possibly in a rented storage unit."

Keegan nodded while she got her system up and running. She pushed a notepad toward Annabelle. "Jot down names, aliases, dates of birth, and any other information you have that might be useful."

The sound of Keegan's fingers hitting the keyboard was the only thing that could be heard for long minutes. "I'm not finding any kind of storage unit associated with either of those names. I did find some information on a recent property she purchased. Could the personal items be there?"

"No, the police said they didn't find anything when they searched the house," I said, disappointed.

"The police are involved in this?" Keegan asked, a hint of panic in her voice. "What's really going on?"

I sighed and gave her a short version of what happened to Shaker and me and the questions we were trying to answer.

"Holy shit, Harper! I don't even know what to say right now," Keegan stammered. "Uh, now that I know more about what I'm looking for, let me see if I can dig anything up." She went back to typing while Annabelle and I sat in silence. A few minutes passed, and Keegan snorted, "You guys need to talk. It feels like you're both staring at me while I'm working and it's distracting."

We apologized and began chatting about mundane topics. I tried to pretend like Keegan wasn't in the room, but I couldn't and found myself glancing at her every few minutes. Finally, her head popped up, eyes wide, "I think I found something."

Annabelle and I quickly joined her on the couch. Pointing at the screen, she asked, "Is this the house where you were kept?" When I nodded, she continued, "This house was built on top of an old coal mine. I was able to pull up an old map of the mine, and it looks like a mine shaft connects the house to another house several miles away."

"Who owns the other house?" I almost yelled.

"Well, that brings up another interesting point. The documents naming Valarie Vine as the owner of the house were fake. There're actually no records of the house that I can find. The other house and the land both are on are owned by William Anderson," she said and pointed to the documents she had pulled up on her computer screen.

Annabelle gasped and covered her mouth with her hand. She was white as a ghost, and I'm sure I looked very much the same.

"Do you know who that is?" Keegan asked.

Annabelle was already nodding her head.

"Boar."

CHAPTER TWENTY-EIGHT

Carbon

I had been at the garage busting my ass all day. We'd fallen behind schedule when we were searching for Harper, and we were close to being caught up. It was almost closing time when Phoenix called and told me I needed to come over to his house. Immediately, my mind went to Harper. Before I could ask, he assured me she was fine.

When I arrived at Phoenix's house, I was surprised to find Harper there, as well as Keegan. Both of them were seated on the couch with Annabelle, perched in front of a large laptop, looking nervous as hell. I eyed them warily and glanced at Phoenix. "What's going on?"

Phoenix ran his thumb and forefinger over his chin. "I don't know whether to be pissed or proud right now. Seems these three decided to play detective and managed to dig up something that Byte, Spazz, and the cops missed."

"Is somebody going to tell me what they found?" I asked, not bothering to hide my irritation.

Harper turned her body to face me. "Annabelle offered to help me get through reading the journal. That's what we were talking about this morning. Anyway, as we were reading it, a lot of things didn't make sense. Hilarie would refer to something she had previously written, but it was nowhere to be found in the journal we have. That led us to believe she had other journals. I wanted to find those as well as any of her other personal belongings because I want answers. I want to know why she did this to me. I want to know who helped her. I want to know how in the hell she got me and Shaker to that house!"

Annabelle placed a comforting hand on Harper's shoulder. "I knew Keegan's computer skills could rival Byte's, so I asked her to come over and help us. We thought maybe she had a storage unit in her name somewhere. Anyway, Keegan worked her magic and discovered that

Hilarie's house, the one she took Harper and Shaker to, wasn't actually her house and was built on top of an old coal mine with a shaft that connects to another house several miles away," Annabelle said, stopping abruptly, her eyes darting to Phoenix.

He sighed and pinched the bridge of his nose. "The other house and the property are owned by Boar."

I heaved in breath after breath, trying to keep my rage contained, at least until I knew more. "You talked to him?" I gritted out.

Phoenix shook his head. "I called you first. Do you want to do this on the phone or in person?"

"Phone," I said through my clenched jaw. In person, I might kill him if he didn't have the right answers. Who was I kidding? I would rip him apart with my bare hands before anyone could stop me if he said the wrong thing.

Phoenix shot Keegan a stern look. "What you hear in this room cannot be repeated. Do you understand?"

She nodded and met his eyes. "Yes, sir. I understand."

Phoenix dialed and placed the phone on speaker. When Boar answered, Phoenix got right to the point. "You got a property out on Cold

Creek Rd?"

"Yeah, what about it?"

"Who lives there?" Phoenix asked, though it wasn't a question.

"Phoenix, man, there's no need for an interrogation. Tell me what the problem is, and I'll tell you what I know," Boar replied, sounding a little put off by Phoenix's approach.

"Your Old Lady picked up my Road Captain and my Enforcer's Old Lady last week on the side of the road and brought them back to Croftridge. I don't know how much she told you, but they'd been kidnapped and held in a house hidden in the woods out there. That house is on your property and connects to your house by an underground mine shaft," Phoenix explained.

"What? How'd you find that out? I own the damn thing, and I had no idea," he said, blatantly sounding confused.

"A resident computer whiz found a map of the coal mine," Phoenix answered, smirking at Keegan.

"What do you need from me?" Boar asked.

"Do you live there or know who does?"

"I don't live there. I inherited the place when my father died. Since then, it's always been a rental property," he explained. "The current tenant is a man in his 30's. Can't remember what his name is. Oh, hell, I just remembered something, hang on a second." We heard him move away from the phone and call for Shannon. They exchanged a few words before he came back to the phone. "Sorry about that. Shannon was on her way out to the rental house to see why he hadn't paid his rent when she found Shaker on the side of the road. I'd forgotten about that and just asked her if she'd been out there to get the rent. She hasn't, so I'm going to have to ride out there. You fellas want to tag along?"

I didn't hesitate to give a sharp nod to Phoenix. "Indeed, we do. It'll just be three of us. We'll head that way now."

"Grab Shaker and let's roll. You three ladies stay put and stay out of trouble. We'll be back in a few hours," Phoenix ordered. He kissed the hell out of Annabelle and strolled out the front door. I gave Harper a quick peck and followed him.

We met Boar outside the gates of his clubhouse. Even though we were friendly with his club, it wasn't kosher for us to roll onto his turf sporting our colors. Boar pulled out of the gates and led the way to his rental property.

He turned onto what I thought was a gravel

road but turned out to be a long driveway. The house was tucked back behind a copse of trees, not visible from the street. Pulling up in front of the house, I could immediately sense something was off.

Boar rang the doorbell and knocked on the door several times. After a few minutes with no answer, he walked around to the back of the house and pressed his face to a window. "I haven't heard from my tenant in several weeks, and I'm going to exercise my right as the landlord to do a welfare check," Boar announced, producing a key from his pocket.

Once inside, it didn't take long to figure out Boar's tenant was long gone. "What was this guy's name?" I asked.

Boar snorted. "Ivan Ceven."

"Shall we check out the mine shaft?" Shaker asked.

"Sure, if we can find it," Boar offered.

"I don't even know what we're looking for," I added.

After thoroughly searching the house, Phoenix relented and called Keegan. Comparing the map of the mine to the blueprints of the house, she suggested we look outside near the southwest corner of the property. I pulled up the compass app on my phone and used it to guide us southwest. We found a large shed hidden behind a wall of trees.

We pulled the doors open to find a set of steep stairs. Using flashlights, we carefully descended to the bottom. I slowly rotated, shining my light along the walls. I froze when I saw it. "Holy shit," I uttered. The other three turned and remarked with similar statements of disbelief. In front of us was a bona fide mine shaft, complete with a waiting mine cart.

"You think this thing works?" I asked.

"I have no idea, brother," Phoenix mumbled.

"Ah-ha," Boar exclaimed, seconds before we were illuminated with fluorescent lights. He smiled proudly. "I found a breaker."

Shaker mumbled, "That's how she did it."

We turned to see what he was talking about. He had pulled the mine cart out of the way to reveal a utility vehicle with a flatbed on the back. Shaker climbed into the driver's seat and cranked it. "Let's see if Ms. Keegan's theory is correct."

Reluctantly, I climbed into the flatbed portion of the UTV with Phoenix while Boar got into the passenger seat. As we moved through the tunnel, it was clear it had been recently upgraded. Lights had been installed, and the walls and ceiling had been reinforced and covered with sheetrock. What was supposedly once a mine shaft now looked more like a subway tunnel.

At the end of the tunnel, we found two doors, both locked. "Stand back," Boar ordered and proceeded to shoot the locks off of both doors. "Problem solved," he said proudly. At least, I thought that's what he said seeing as how none of us could hear shit since he fired two shots back to back in an enclosed space.

The first door we opened appeared to be a storage space with a few cardboard boxes inside. Behind the second door was a set of stairs. The stairs led to a hinged door overhead. Phoenix and I had to use a bit of force, but we were able to push it open. We climbed out to find a house in the middle of the woods.

"How the fuck did we miss this?" Shaker asked.

Closing the door to the stairs, Phoenix pointed at the ground. "It was well hidden, brother. Hell, the cops didn't even find it." Looking down, I realized why it was so difficult for us to push it open. The crazy bitch had built flower beds around it and must have been covering the door with the small fountain that was knocked over.

"Shall we take a look inside the house?" I asked.

"No need. Harper and I went through it before we left and the cops have been through it. She really didn't have much in there," Shaker answered.

We went back to the mine shaft, loaded up the cardboard boxes, and drove the UTV back to Boar's property. "Now we know how she got us there and how she was getting supplies, but I still don't think she did it by herself. There's no way she could have carried my big ass up those stairs and up the stairs inside the house. My money is on the guy that was renting this place," Shaker said.

"You got any other information about this guy?" Phoenix asked Boar.

"No, sorry. He paid the first couple of months upfront in cash and then he paid in cash every month after. He was never late on the rent until this month. He seemed like he was going through a tough time, and he had the money, so I didn't press him for more info. I can give you a description of what he looks like, but that's about it," Boar explained.

"I'll get some of the boys to come out and change the locks on this place tonight and make sure everything, including the entrance to that mine shaft, is locked up tight. We'll put up a few cameras around the property, too. If he shows up around here, we'll grab him for you," Boar promised.

"Thanks, man," Phoenix said, extending his hand to Boar.

"Do you want me to have those boxes sent to you?" Boar asked.

It didn't even occur to me that we were on our bikes and couldn't carry them back with us.

"Yeah, that'd be great," Phoenix said. "Carbon, you want to look through them before we head out?"

After digging through the contents of each box, I found one journal that appeared to be from Valarie's childhood. I held it up for Phoenix and Shaker to see. "I think this is what we were looking for."

Phoenix nodded and turned his attention to Boar. "Appreciate your help, man."

"Hell, I ought to be thanking you for letting me know about a house I didn't even know I owned," Boar said with a chuckle.

"When we get back to Croftridge, I'll have Byte start digging into Ivan Ceven," Phoenix said.

I snorted. "Sounds like you might want to

have Keegan do the digging."

Phoenix laughed. "Nah, as soon as I tell Byte that she found something he missed, that boy won't miss shit ever again."

CHAPTER TWENTY-NINE

Harper

I knew they found something. I could tell by the look on Chase's face when he got back. Without a word, he held up what looked like a child's diary.

"Is that Hilarie's? I mean Valarie's?" I asked.

He nodded. "Yeah, baby, it is. I haven't looked at it, other than to see if it was what we were looking for," he said and handed it to me.

He cleared his throat and seemed to be nervous. "Just tell me what will make this easier for you. Do you want me to stay with you while you read it? Do you want to be with Annabelle? Your brother? Alone?"

I put the journal on the coffee table and walked to my troubled man. Reaching up, I cupped his cheeks in my hands. "Let's get something to eat first and then we can read it together."

Over dinner, we talked about their trip to Boar's property. He told me Hilarie used a UTV to get Shaker and me to the hidden house. "We think the guy renting Boar's house helped her. We went to the house, but he's long gone. We're trying to find him, but I need you to be extra careful until we do."

We cleaned up the kitchen and went upstairs to get comfortable. Once we were situated, I opened the journal and started reading aloud.

Dear Diary,

I am so mad. Mommy and Daddy made Ants leave today. And it's all Vanessa's fault. She told them something that made them mad at Ants. Ants didn't do anything. She's just jealous because Ants always liked me more than her.

Valarie

I handed the notepad we used at Annabelle's house to Chase. "Might as well take notes as we go. Who is Ants?"

Dear Diary,

I hate Vanessa. I thought Mommy and Daddy would let Ants come back when they weren't mad anymore, but they didn't. I miss Ants so much.

Valarie

Dear Diary,

I have a new friend. Her name is Ann, and she's all mine. No one else knows about her. I don't have to share her with stupid Vanessa. I like her a lot, but she's not Ants. I miss Ants so much.

Valarie

Dear Diary,

Vanessa told Mommy and Daddy she heard me talking to someone. She told them I wouldn't play with her or talk to her because I spend all of my time with my new friend. Daddy got mad, and Mommy cried. They sent me to my room and told me not to come out. Stupid Vanessa. We hate her. She took Ants away from me and now she wants to take Ann away, too.

Valarie

Dear Diary,

Mommy took me to the doctor today. I told

her I wasn't sick, but she said I had to go. She wasn't like the other doctor. She didn't take my temperature, and I didn't have to get any shots. She told me to sit on a couch, and she asked me so many questions. She asked me about my new friend, but I lied and told her I didn't have one. Just like I was supposed to. Mommy says I have to go see this doctor every week. Stupid Vanessa.

    Valarie

Dear Diary,

    I'm in trouble again. I was supposed to help stupid Vanessa clean up the playroom, but I fell asleep. I couldn't help it. Ann won't stop talking so I can go to sleep at night. She only talks to me when I'm alone and then she won't stop talking. She hates Vanessa as much as I do.

    Valarie

Dear Diary,

    I don't like Ann anymore, but she won't go away. I asked her to leave me alone, and she said she would, but she wants me to make Vanessa go away first. She said if I did that, she would leave me alone and promised to never talk to me again. Stupid Vanessa. She ruins everything.

    Valarie

Dear Diary,

Ann helped me come up with a plan to get rid of Vanessa. I'm going to do it tomorrow. I'll be so happy when both of them are gone.

Valarie

Dear Diary,

Today I acted like I liked Vanessa again. She was so excited to play with me. She said we could do whatever I wanted. I told her I wanted to show her a new secret hiding spot. Stupid Vanessa followed me up to the attic. We opened a window and crawled out onto the roof. I made her go first. She was scared, but she did it because it was what I wanted. I climbed out behind her and then I kicked her in the back as hard as I could. Stupid Vanessa screamed and then she stopped. Ann told me I did a good job and then she said goodbye. I'm back in my room, and I'm going to go to sleep.

Valarie

"Holy shit. She killed her sister. Did you know that?" Chase asked.

I was already shaking my head. "No, I had no idea. I don't think anyone did. I looked up a few articles about it, and everything said the girls were playing in the attic and Vanessa fell out of an open window."

"I just can't believe she would kill her own twin because her friend told her to do it. She should've known better at that age."

"Chase, I can't say for sure, but I think her friend was actually an auditory hallucination."

"A what?"

"An auditory hallucination. In other words, she was hearing a voice that wasn't real. It's actually not uncommon in children."

"You mean like an imaginary friend?"

"Yes, like an imaginary friend. Most of the time, imaginary friends are nothing to be concerned about, but I think this instance is different," I explained.

"Yeah, you're probably right. Let's see what else she wrote," Chase said and nodded toward the journal.

Dear Diary,

I don't have anybody to play with. Stupid Vanessa is gone. Ants is gone. Ann is gone. Mommy cries all the time and says she can't look at me. Daddy is always at work. I'm glad he's not here. He's always mad when he's at home.

Valarie

Dear Diary,

Daddy brought Vanessa home today. I thought she was gone forever. I know Mommy and Daddy told me she went to Heaven, but Daddy said they didn't say that. He said they said she went to the hospital. He said that she looks a little different because of her accident, but it was the best the doctors could do. I don't care if she looks different. She's back home. We're in the same room. Sharing everything. Just like we were before.

Valarie

Dear Diary,

Vanessa doesn't remember anything, like our secret handshake, or our favorite hiding places. Daddy said it's because of her accident. That her brain is still healing. I don't believe him. I think she's acting like she doesn't remember stuff because she's still mad at me. I don't care if she's mad at me because I'm mad at her.

Valarie

Dear Diary,

I hate Vanessa. Mommy and Daddy are always with her. Always talking to her. Always talking about her. Daddy even takes her with him sometimes, for hours or even a whole day. It's not fair. I don't know why they love her more than me. We're supposed to be the same. But, we're... shut up! Ann's talking again. I can't even write in my diary without her blabbing on and on and never SHUTTING UP!!

Valarie

Dear Diary,

I can't take it anymore. Ann was quiet when Vanessa was gone. She promised to be quiet if I made Vanessa go away, and she was. But she started talking again when Daddy brought Vanessa home from the hospital and every day she talks more and more. Especially at night. I have to make Vanessa go away again so she'll be quiet.

Valarie

I gasped. She was going to kill me, too. I sat there in total disbelief. After a few minutes, Chase asked, "Do you want me to read for a bit?"

I nodded and passed the book to him.

Dear Diary,
I did something I wasn't supposed to today,

and it was so much fun. A man was outside the gate to our house taking pictures. Nobody noticed him. Because they were paying attention to Vanessa again. So, nobody noticed when I went outside to talk to him. He said he was studying buildings in school and had to bring in pictures of houses he liked for his project. He asked if it was okay to take pictures of our house. I told him it was okay even though I knew Daddy won't like it. He doesn't let anyone come to our house. Not since Vanessa came back home. I told the man he could come back whenever he wanted. He asked me if it was okay with my parents and I told him it would be okay because they would be too busy with my twin sister to notice. He said he would come back at the same time tomorrow and I promised to meet him at the gate so he could come inside. Daddy is going to be so mad when he finds out, but I don't care. I'll tell him stupid Vanessa did it.

Valarie

Chase paused and looked at me curiously. I cleared my throat to explain. "That must have been the private investigator Duke hired to find me."

Dear Diary,

The man didn't come back. He was sick, so his friend came instead. I let him come inside the house. He pulled out a big knife and told me to go to my room and to not make a sound. I ran to my room and hid under my bed. I didn't come out until I heard Mommy screaming. Vanessa went to Heaven again, and this time she took Daddy with her. I didn't tell Mommy about the man with the knife. She told me to go to my room because she didn't want to look at me. Mommy is mad at me. Daddy is gone. Vanessa is gone. Ann is gone. Maybe Ants will come back this time.

Valarie

Chase paused again and studied me. "I'm okay. Keep going," I said.

Dear Diary,

Mommy went to Heaven today. I have to go live with Aunt Violet and Uncle Darrell. I don't want to go live with them. They live in Idaho. I wanted to go with Ants, but Aunt Violet said Ants was in some kind of bin and was never coming back. I want to go to Heaven with Mommy and Daddy and even Vanessa. I don't have anyone to talk to. Not even Ann. She won't talk to me, just like she promised.

Valarie

Dear Diary,

This is the last time I'll write. I'm going to Heaven to be with Mommy, Daddy, and stupid Vanessa. I'm going to go the same way Vanessa did.

Valarie

"That's it, baby. She didn't write anything else after that," Chase said.

"Yeah, that makes sense. The other journal started right after she was released from the mental hospital. It sounds to me like she was so upset by Ants leaving that she created Ann as a way to fill the void and express her anger toward Vanessa. She obviously blamed Vanessa. We need to know who Ants is and why the Vines made them leave."

"Did the other journal mention anything about Ants?"

I shook my head. "I don't think so, but it wouldn't hurt to read through it again."

Dear Diary,

I'm sorry for neglecting you. Aunt Violet found

my old diary when I was in the hospital after I jumped off the roof. After that, I thought it was best not to write things down until I could be certain no one else could read them. Since I've been in a mental facility for the last eight years, there was no way for me to have any kind of privacy. But today is different! Today, I turned 18 and signed myself out. With the money from my family's estate and my father's life insurance money, I'll be able to start my life over.

Valarie

Dear Diary,

They tried to tell me, but I refused to believe it, and no one ever showed me proof. And the proof wasn't hard to find. A simple search of my father's name brought up article after article about his murder and my mother's subsequent suicide. And of course, the numerous articles of my sister's death. The death that occurred a little over three months before my father's death. If Vanessa really died after her accident, then who in the hell did my father bring home from the hospital?

Valarie

Dear Diary,

Harper Jackson. My father kidnapped her and brought her home to replace Vanessa. Why did Ann start talking again if Vanessa wasn't really Vanessa? And what happened to Harper Jackson? My mother told me my father and Vanessa went to Heaven. Was Harper murdered the same day my father was? None of the articles mention anything about her.

Valarie

Dear Diary,
I found her.
Valarie

Dear Diary,
She hasn't recognized me. My face does look different, even after all the surgeries I've had to put it back the way it was. It will never be the same again, and I hate it. I want to look like I used to, like Vanessa did, and like Harper does. Seeing her has made me miss Vanessa so much. I wish my parents had recognized my problems when I was younger and had gotten me the help I needed. But they didn't, and now they're all gone. Maybe I can become friends with Harper. I haven't talked to her yet, but I've passed her a few times at the college she goes to, and I've

followed her into the grocery store once or twice. I'll keep watching and wait for my chance.

Valarie

Dear Diary,

I cannot believe what I did tonight. I followed Harper and a small group of girls to a club. A strip club! Where the girls strip, not the men. If that wasn't bad enough, the four of them entered the wet t-shirt contest, and Harper won!! It was like watching my very own twin doing something I know she never would have. I don't even know what to say right now.

Valarie

Dear Diary,

This has to stop. She went back again for another contest, and she won, again. There was a time when we could pass as twins. Maybe I should enter the next one and beat her. Ha! That would show her. Yes, I think that's exactly what I'll do.

Valarie

Dear Diary,

I hate Harper Jackson. I entered the contest as Hilarie Thaxton. I wanted us to sound like twins without being too obvious. Especially if we both won. But no, she won, and I got second place. Then the bitch told me to try again next week because she wouldn't be a contestant. Stupid me asked why. Because employees can't enter club sponsored contests. That's right, my twin's replacement twin is going to be a stripper.

Hilarie

Dear Diary,

I hate Harper Jackson, and I work at a strip club. As a stripper. This cannot continue.

Hilarie

Dear Diary,

I'm friends with Harper Jackson! At least, I think I am. She keeps to herself most of the time, but she's friendly to me at work, and she says hello to me when she sees me at the college. She thinks I'm a student there, but I'm not. I just hang around the campus in certain places I know she'll pass when she's between classes.

Hilarie

Dear Diary,

What a coincidence. Harper is the licensed clinical therapist just hired by the clinic where I work as the office manager. I suppose it helps that I own the building and set up the entire clinic so that we could work together. We'll be best friends in no time. Just like sisters should be.

Hilarie

Dear Diary,

She's got a boyfriend, and I don't like him. She says he's not her boyfriend, but he is. He's the same guy that used to come into the club to see her every Friday night. The only one she would do private dances for. We don't have room for a boyfriend in our relationship. It's supposed to be just me and her. I won't let her leave me, too. I just need to remind her of how much she needs me. We're two peas in a pod.

Hilarie

Dear Diary,

I can't believe this shit. She's been gone for two weeks and didn't call me once. My anger may have gotten a little out of control. I meant to just paint the mural on her wall, but seeing all those pictures of her stupid fucking family infuriated me. Her brother...ugh! Nope, not going there. Anyway, watching her pick up pea after pea while her 'friend' tried to decipher the painting on her living room wall was by far the most fun I've had in a long time. I should've brought popcorn to munch on while I watched. Seriously, they're mystified by the things I did to her house. I can understand the dots. Not everyone would recognize the Gemini Twins constellation without the lines connecting the stars, but come on...two peas in a pod? Not a hard one to figure out. I've been giving her hints all along. I always offer her Double Mint gum. I gave her Thing 1 post-it notes for her office, and I kept the Thing 2 post-it notes for mine. I bring her a Twinkie at least once a week. Was she always this stupid? I guess she was.

Hilarie

PS – Earlier tonight, I thought I was going to get lucky, and she was actually going to take care of her boyfriend for me, but, alas, Harper isn't a good shot. Actually, she's a terrible shot if she missed that big ass man at damn near point blank range. <sigh> I'll have to take care of him later.

Dear Diary,

Why is she making everything so difficult? A new security system, new locks, a guard dog, and a boyfriend. Is she trying to test me? To see if I'm willing to fight for her? I just want us to be

together. Time to try a different plan.
Hilarie

Dear Diary,
I can't take this much longer. I have stooped so low, just to spend time with her. It shouldn't be like this. I shouldn't have to spend my holiday weekend with her boyfriend's dipshit friend. I almost got out of it, but the dumbass small town cops arrested me, too! Then, she caught me when I was in the middle of trying to poison their food. Ugh!! It's okay though. She will be with me as soon as everything is ready. Until then, I have to put up with her boyfriend's friend so I can be included in her plans. Not much longer. Not much longer. Not much longer.
Hilarie

Dear Diary,
I thought I heard her today. I stopped what I was doing and waited to hear something, anything. If it was her, she wouldn't say anything else. Why won't she talk to me?
Hilarie

Dear Diary,
I've run out of time. Harper announced her

engagement today and turned in her resignation. In three weeks, she's moving to Croftridge to marry that monster of a man and leave me here in Sugar Falls all alone. I don't think so. Fuck her. Fuck her brother. Fuck her boyfriend. And fuck her boyfriend's friend. Fuck them all. Hahahahaha!

Hilarie

Dear Diary,

My plan is coming together perfectly. Tomorrow, I will bring Harper to the home I have made for us. No one will find us, and no one will bother us for the rest of our lives. Well, after I get rid of her pain in the ass friend. At least there's plenty of room to bury the body out here.

Hilarie

"That's it. There's nothing about Ants," Chase said and placed the folder on the nightstand.

"Can we ask Byte to look into it and see if he can find anything?"

"Yeah, I'll call him in the morning." Chase was quiet for a few moments before he asked, "Are you sure you're okay?"

I sighed. "Yeah, I think so. I was having trouble processing my feelings about everything that happened, but reading her journals has helped. She was obviously suffering from some significant mental health issues as a child, and no one was there to help her. I just hate that I didn't pick up on any of her issues as an adult."

"Stop right there, Harper. You're not going down that path. She was very good at hiding her truths. Not a one of us picked up on her being anything other than your friend or coworker who could be slightly clingy at times. And correct me if I'm wrong, but it sounds like she was fairly stable until recently."

"Yeah, I guess you're right."

Chase pulled me to his chest and gently kissed my lips. "Let's get some sleep, baby."

CHAPTER THIRTY

Harper

Several weeks had passed since Shaker and I were kidnapped, and we hadn't learned anything new. Byte was fit to be tied when Phoenix told him Keegan found a crucial piece of information he missed. However, when his searches turned up nothing for Ivan Ceven, he didn't hesitate to ask Keegan for help. Unfortunately, she was unable to find anything on an Ivan Ceven either.

They were both still trying to find something about Ants, but they weren't having much luck and the only people we could ask, Valarie's Aunt Violet and Uncle Darrell, were deceased.

A few days after the guys returned from searching Boar's property, the boxes they discovered in the mine shaft arrived at the clubhouse. I felt an odd mixture of excitement and dread upon seeing the boxes. Swallowing my fear, I bravely opened and rifled through box after box. To my disappointment, the boxes were full of items I was mostly familiar with as they were things from Hilarie's house in Sugar Falls and her office at the crisis center.

I knew the missing pieces to the rest of her story were out there somewhere, but I made the decision to let it go. I accepted the fact that some of my questions would never have answers. What's done was done and couldn't be changed. She was dead, and I was starting my new life with Chase.

Part of my new life was my job at Ember's new counseling center. It had been open a little over a week, and I was pleasantly surprised by the number of appointments we had. I assumed the first few weeks would be slow until word got around town, and we established a client base. Apparently, Croftridge and the surrounding areas had a great need for a counseling center. Until we had a better understanding of that need, I agreed to see adult patients as well as children.

"When is my next session?" I asked the receptionist.

"In 30 minutes. Oh, I made a note here that this one is afraid of large dogs," she informed me.

I looked at her quizzically. Did she tell the patient about Titan? Had she been asking all of the patients if they had a fear of dogs? She shrugged. "He told me that when he was making his appointment. I'm guessing that's what he's here to work on."

"Okay. I've got time to take Titan down to the barn so Duke can watch him while I'm in session. I'll be back soon."

I walked Titan to the barn, talked to Duke for a few minutes, and trekked back to the counseling center. It wasn't far enough away to drive, but it made for a decent walk. It would have been much shorter, but I had to go around the fences that separated the public portions of the farm from the private part of the property.

I rushed back into the building, trying to catch my breath and compose myself. "Sorry, that was a longer walk than I thought. Is my patient here yet?" I asked the receptionist.

"Yes, he's waiting for you in your office," she smiled.

I entered my office to find a man who looked to be around my brother's age sitting on the sofa. He was wearing a button-down shirt and dress slacks, his appearance clean and well-kept. I hadn't even introduced myself, and I was already assessing him. I cleared my throat and extended my hand. "Hi, I'm Harper Jackson. You must be Mr. Smith."

He shook my hand with a firm grip. "Yes, but please, call me Vance."

He held my hand in his for a beat longer than necessary. Slowly retracting it, I replied automatically, "Okay, Vance. What brings you in today?"

Sitting in the chair across from him, I listened to him tell me about being attacked by a dog at a young age and struggling to overcome his fear of dogs ever since.

"Do you mind if I stand? Sometimes I find it easier to talk if I can move around. A nervous habit I suppose."

"Not at all. Many of my patients find it helps to open up when they are moving about," I said.

He stood and began to slowly pace back and forth while talking. I studied him carefully and listened intently to his words. It didn't take long for me to be certain of one thing, he was lying.

"Vance, I understand that admitting the need for counseling is hard for many people, but there's nothing to be ashamed of." I softened my voice, "Instead of telling me this elaborate story, why don't you tell me why you're really here?"

His pacing came to a halt when he was in front of my office door. I fully expected him to open the door and bolt. To my horror, I heard the deafening sound of the lock clicking. He whirled around and peered at me with dark, soulless eyes. "Well, since you asked so nicely…"

In a flash, he was in front of me with his hand around my throat, squeezing. "I'm here because," he said through gritted teeth, "you were promised to me."

My eyes widened in shock. What the hell was he talking about? I reached up with one hand, wrapping it around the wrist of the hand he had clasped around my neck. With my other hand, I slowly placed it on my left thigh and felt for the bump. When my fingers found it, I pressed down several times in a row for good measure and then focused my attention on the psycho in front of me. "What are you talking about?" I rasped.

His grip tightened slightly. "Allow me to introduce myself. I'm Ivan Ceven, otherwise known as Vance Vine."

My eyes widened in disbelief, and he chuckled at my response. "I see you recognize the name. Yes, I am the older brother of Valarie and Vanessa Vine. Surprise!"

And then even more realization dawned.

Vance.

Ants.

Oh shit!

Oh fuck!

Oh shit!

Oh fuck!

Oh shit!

"Why are you here?" I croaked. He wasn't squeezing hard enough to cut off my air supply completely, but enough to make it difficult for me to speak.

"Like I said, because you were promised to me." He sighed at my expression and continued, "I agreed to help Valarie kidnap you and her little boy toy if you could be my little toy. She thought it was a wonderful idea. The three of us would live happily ever after with you being the sister she desperately missed and the hot piece of pussy I relentlessly fucked." His eyes darkened, and his grip grew tighter. "But then you had to go and kill her."

He raised his other hand and plowed it into my face. Pain radiated outward from my cheekbone. Suddenly, he released the grip on my throat, and I gasped for air. My reprieve didn't last long. He fisted my hair and yanked me from the chair, forcefully tossing me to the ground causing my head to bounce on the floor. I tried to roll to my side, but I wasn't fast enough. He came down on top of me, one leg on either side of me and ripped my shirt open.

No.

No.

No.

This wasn't happening. I opened my mouth to scream, but he stuffed a cloth in my mouth before a sound could escape. He grinned wickedly. "Now, let's see what you have to offer me." He held my wrists over my head with one hand and began tracing the swell of my bra covered breasts with the other. I heard the snick of a knife and froze for a millisecond before I started bucking and thrashing against him.

"Be still, bitch," he barked and struck me across the face again. Screw that, I wasn't going to make it easy for him, and I'd much rather have him knock me out than be awake and alert for any of his plans.

Before I could register what was happening, he leaped off me and yanked me to my feet, placing me in front of him with the knife held tightly against my throat. When my brain caught up to what was happening, I found myself staring into the furious eyes of Chase with an equally furious Titan at his side. The sight of them had tears leaking from my eyes.

"Let her go," Chase said, in a tone so icy it sent chills down my spine, and I realized this was Carbon, not the Chase I knew and loved.

"Why do you heroes always say that? Has it ever worked?" Vance asked rhetorically, chuckling to himself.

Carbon shrugged. "It's perfunctory."

What in the hell was wrong with him? He went from furious to stone cold to nonchalant. Carbon's eyes scanned me from head to toe and back up. His green eyes locked with mine and for the briefest of seconds, I caught a glimpse of the man I loved before he morphed back into his role as the club's Enforcer. It was all I needed to know that he had this. I kept my eyes trained on him and waited, trying my best to ignore the sharp knife digging into my throat.

"You have perfect timing," Carbon said, grinning maniacally.

I felt Vance's body tense and shift. I couldn't see his face, but I imagined his countenance conveyed confusion. "Why is that?" he asked, his voice not near as confident as it had been moments before.

Carbon made a face of disappointment and dejectedly replied, "You don't want me to ruin the surprise, do you?" I honestly couldn't tell if Carbon was being serious or if this was part of some act. One thing I did know, Carbon the Enforcer was a scary motherfucker.

"Shut the fuck up. I know what you're doing, and it's not going to work," Vance spat, taking a few steps back, dragging me with him.

Carbon feigned shock. "You do? Am I that transparent?" He focused his wide eyes on Vance and blinked several times, waiting for him to answer. When he didn't, Carbon bared his teeth and growled, keeping the corners of his lips turned up in a wicked smile. "You don't have a clue what I'm doing," he said, taking one step forward causing Vance to take another step back. Titan's eyes moved to the side and came right back to me. Vance must have seen it, too, and started to turn, but Carbon spoke again grabbing his attention, "...but you're about to find out."

There was a snarl and a flash of black fur before I felt a line of fire erupt down my leg. Then, I was on the ground being pulled across the floor. I could hear grunts and groans accompanied by the sound of flesh hitting flesh. Curses and swears sounded around the room. Before I could put the pieces together, worried green eyes appeared in front of me.

Chase gently cupped my cheek. "You're okay, baby. We got him."

"He's her brother!" I shrieked. "That's Vance Vine! Don't let him get away!"

"Duke's got him. He's not going anywhere."

"Duke?" I croaked.

Blue eyes, much like my own, appeared beside Chase. "I came in through the window and disarmed him from behind," my brother said, not at all looking happy about capturing the madman trying to harm me. "Patch is already on his way to look at your leg. I'm sorry, Harper."

I had forgotten about the pain in my leg until he mentioned it. "What happened to my leg?" I asked, trying to sit up.

Chase's hands gently pushed back against my shoulders. "Stay down, baby."

There was a commotion at the door, and I involuntarily flinched, despite being surrounded by Carbon, Duke, and Titan. "It's Phoenix and Badger. They're getting Vance out of here," my brother informed me.

"Why won't you guys let me sit up?" I whined.

Before either one of them could answer, Patch arrived. He knelt beside me and pointedly asked, "Are you hurt anywhere other than what I can see right now?"

I shook my head. "No, it didn't get that far."

He gently patted my shoulder. "Good. Good. I'm going to take a look at your leg first." He moved toward my feet. I felt the leg of my pants being moved and then heard several intakes of breath. "I'm going to wrap this in some gauze. We need to keep some pressure on it. One of you get a car from Ember and have it out front and ready to go." Redirecting his attention to me, he continued, "Your leg needs to be treated at the hospital. I'm going to wrap it, and then we're moving."

"What. Happened. To. My. Leg?" I demanded.

Patch looked at me then to Chase and back to me. "You have a significant gash on your upper leg that will require an extensive number of sutures and quite possibly a surgical repair. He missed your femoral artery, but it is bleeding significantly, and we need to get to the hospital as soon as possible."

"What?" I shrieked.

Carbon cleared his throat. "Duke grabbed Vance's arm from behind and pulled it away from your neck. As soon as Duke had his hands on Vance, Titan lunged and pulled you down to the ground by your pants' leg. It just so happened that Vance's arm was moving in a downward arc at the same time. The knife made contact with your leg as you were being pulled down and away. The momentum and the angle..." he trailed off and shook his head. "It's a nasty cut, baby. I'm so sorry."

"You, Duke, and Titan saved my life. There's nothing to be sorry for," I said. "Is Titan okay?"

"He's fine. He was on the other side of the knife."

"All finished. Let's get her out to the car," Patch announced.

Hours later I woke to the sounds of machines beeping and the smell of Band-Aids. I shifted my weight, and the crinkle of plastic beneath me confirmed my suspicions, I was in the hospital. But why? Oh, that's right, because the fucking Vines struck again. Cracking one eye open, I saw two large forms sitting in chairs off to the side. I opened both eyes and managed to croak,

"Water."

If I could have laughed, I would have, at how fast the big badass bikers jumped to their feet and scrambled to fetch me a cup of water. Chase gently placed the straw to my lips, and I swallowed a few small gulps of precious hydration. "Hi," I uttered stupidly, then rolled my eyes at myself.

"How are you feeling, baby?" he asked, his eyes full of worry.

"I'm okay. My leg is a little sore, but I think that's to be expected. Did the surgery go okay?" I asked.

"It went fine. The surgeon got the bleeding under control and repaired a tendon and a muscle that were damaged by the knife. Then, a plastic surgeon came in and closed the wound. You'll still have a scar, but it will be as pretty as it can be," he explained.

Duke stepped forward and placed a kiss on my forehead. "Do you need anything?"

I grinned and lowered my voice, "Don't kill that motherfucker yet. I have a few questions I want to ask him first."

"I think they gave you too much pain medicine, little sister," Duke said and winked.

"Are you up for some visitors?" Chase asked. "The waiting room is full of club members and

Old Ladies waiting to check in on you, but there are three that are going to cause a problem if they don't get to lay eyes on you soon."

Right on cue, I heard my Aunt Leigh's voice getting progressively louder as she told the nurses what they could do with their visitation policy. She burst through the door to my room with her hulking son blocking her from the security guards trailing after them. "Duke Jackson, I specifically told you to call me the second she woke up."

I giggled. "I literally just woke up, Aunt Leigh. I promise."

"Oh, my sweet Harper. How are you feeling?" she asked, tears welling in her eyes.

"I'm okay," I said. "Hey, what's happening out there?" I craned my neck to see around her. "Hey! Let them go. They're family," I yelled to the security guards who were trying, unsuccessfully, to escort Judge and Shaker away from my room.

Judge shook the guard's hands off his arms while Shaker stuck his tongue out and sauntered into my room. "Hey there, sweetheart. I won't stay long, but I had to see for myself that you were okay," Shaker said, bending down to kiss the top of my head. A low growl came from Chase. "Easy, killer. I know she's yours, but we were kidnapped together, so I'm allowed to kiss the top of her head. It's in the rulebook."

I laughed again, and Chase muttered a curse under his breath.

Judge stepped forward and squeezed my hand. "Clearly you've been trying to get my attention with your recent antics. You have it, so you can stop now."

"I'll do my best," I sassed.

"Glad you're okay, Sister Cousin," he murmured.

"Me, too, Brother Judge."

CHAPTER THIRTY-ONE

Carbon

I would forever be grateful to Byte for hooking Harper up with the device that saved her life. Since we hadn't found the man who had assisted Hilarie with the kidnappings, Byte suggested Harper keep a small device in her pocket that would alert designated parties when she needed help as well as her current location. All she had to do was press the button one time to send the signal. When I received seven alerts back to back, I couldn't get to her fast enough. In a stroke of luck, I was over at the stables. Duke had called and asked if I could get Titan because one of the horse owners had shown up at the barn unexpectedly.

When I found Vance with a knife to Harper's throat, I wasn't sure how I was going to get him away from her without her getting hurt. I was still trying to formulate a plan when I saw Duke peering in her office window. Between Titan's growling and my cryptic taunts to Vance, Duke was able to open the window and climb inside silently. Ultimately, she would be okay, but he hurt her, spilled her blood, and for that, he must pay.

It had been three days since he attacked Harper. She had been home from the hospital for two of those days, and she had not stopped asking me about going to see Vance. We argued about it the first day she was home until she finally agreed that it was too soon. She brought it up again the second day and refused to back down.

I threw my hands in the air and roared, "Fucking fine, Harper! I'll take you to see him!"

"Thanks, pumpkin. I just need to freshen up first," she sassed and hobbled away as haughtily as she could.

We drove to the clubhouse in silence. I was pissed, and she was strangely happy. Upon entering the clubhouse, I instructed her to wait in the common room while I spoke with Phoenix. She could bitch about it all she wanted, but if he said no, I couldn't go against my president.

Phoenix agreed to allow her to speak with him as long as the officers were present and she was separated from Vance by bars.

I sighed, exasperated when I didn't see Harper in the common room. "I told her to wait right here. Let me go see if she's in my room."

Returning to the common room after checking my room and Duke's room, I pulled out my phone to call her. When I heard her ringtone and saw her purse on the floor beside one of the sofas, a feeling of deja-vu hit me. "Fuck," I growled and stormed toward the door to the basement.

Sure as shit, it was wide open. Phoenix and I cursed again and rushed down the stairs. I pulled open the second door that should have been locked and stopped dead in my tracks, causing Phoenix to slam into my back.

"What. The. Fuck. Are. You. Doing?" I bellowed, causing everyone to startle, everyone except Harper that is.

She met my gaze with a devious look in her eyes. "Sorry, big guy. You would've never agreed, and I needed this," she said, punctuating "this" by driving the knife in her hand into the leg of the man strapped to the table.

Vance Vine released an ear-splitting scream that made my mouth water. At that moment, I was torn between wanting to carry Harper kicking and screaming from the room and kicking everyone out so we could work him over together. Regardless, her and her cronies had broken into the club's basement yet again to interact with someone we were holding.

I scanned the room and was not at all surprised to see my sister standing quietly off to the side. What did shock me was seeing Annabelle and Shaker leaned against the wall opposite Reese.

"Brother?" Phoenix growled at Shaker.

He stepped forward and held his hands up in surrender. "They were going to do this come hell or high water. If I had ratted them out, they could have ended up down here without a brother present. I wasn't going to—" Shaker stopped speaking when Phoenix's phone as well as mine dinged at the same time. As we pulled out our phones, Shaker smiled smugly and finished his sentence, "—keep it from you."

I looked down at the text telling me to get my ass to the basement immediately.

Phoenix pinned Shaker with a glare. "That text saved you from an ass-beating, but I'm by no means happy with you. Did you let them down here?"

He shook his head and pointed to Annabelle. "She had your keys. They were halfway down the stairs when I caught them."

Phoenix stalked toward Annabelle. "You're pregnant!"

She placed her hands on her hips. "Last time I checked, there are no restrictions on opening doors during pregnancy."

"We'll talk about this later." Phoenix turned to face Reese. "What do you have to say for yourself?"

Reese shrugged. "He hurt my soon to be sister-in-law and indirectly hurt my brother. I'm just here to watch." She reached behind her and produced Duke's .45. "Oh, and to shoot him if things went sideways."

Phoenix cursed low and turned to me. "She's your Old Lady. You want to let her carve him up, be my guest. Since I'm almost positive Duke will be barreling down those stairs any moment now, I'm taking Annabelle home. Clean up your mess, kids."

"You have got to be fucking kidding me!" Duke yelled, coming to an abrupt halt at the sight of his knife-wielding sister and his gun-pointing

Old Lady standing beside a man strapped to a metal table.

Phoenix guided Annabelle back upstairs, and I quickly caught Duke up to speed.

"Are you hens done with your clucking? I would like to get back to business," Harper snarked, causing Reese and Shaker to snicker.

I exchanged glances with Duke, and he gave a curt nod, his silent agreement to see how this played out. With an exaggerated gesture, I said, "Carry on."

I silently watched my woman taunt, tease, and torture Vance Vine like she was a pro. Not long after we gave her the go-ahead, I had to drop my ass into a chair to keep the room from seeing how hard she had my dick. It was sexy as hell to watch Harper face off with the last member of the family that had haunted her since she was 10 years old.

When she seemed to be satisfied, she looked directly at me and said, "Seems only fair to let you end him." I cocked my head to the side, and she continued, "Valarie killed Vanessa. Duke killed Vince. Vivian killed herself. I killed Valarie. You kill Vance."

I didn't know what to say. I didn't want her to have to kill him, but I didn't share this side of myself with anyone other than my brothers. Reese caught a glimpse of it once, but only a glimpse. If I let Harper see me kill, would it change the way she felt about me?

Shaker picked up on my turmoil and stepped forward. "Do you think I could exact a little retribution first?"

Harper smiled brightly and handed the knife to Shaker. "By all means!" I wasn't afraid to admit, Harper's exuberance was downright scary.

Shaker proceeded to make a show of punching and slicing Vance before "accidentally" slipping and driving the knife too deep into Vance's neck, effectively hitting one of the large vessels in his neck and killing him. I quickly mouthed "thank you" before anyone else could see.

He nodded in response and turned to face Harper. "Shit, Harper! I'm so sorry! I guess I got carried away."

She shrugged. "No worries. What's the protocol for clean-up?"

Who in the hell was this woman? "Uh," I stammered, "we'll take care of it, baby. There's a shower at the end of the hall. Leave your clothes on the floor outside the door so that we can burn them. Reese, can you bring down a change of clothes for Harper?" She nodded and headed for the stairs. Harper turned and walked toward the shower.

Duke started to speak, but I cut him off. "I don't want to talk about it right now. Let's get this cleaned up. I want to be available in case she needs me when it finally sinks in."

He nodded, and we made quick work of cleaning up our mess and disposing of what was left of the body. After trashing my own clothes and showering, I made my way upstairs, expecting to find Harper in bed in my room. I did not expect to see Harper, Reese, and Keegan posted up at the bar tossing back shots.

"What are you ladies doing now?" I asked from behind them.

"We're celebrating!" Harper cheerfully announced.

"What are we celebrating?" Shaker asked, entering the common room with Duke.

Harper hoisted her glass into the air and shouted, "Freedom!"

EPILOGUE

Harper

After partying too hard the night before, I was woken far earlier than expected by someone beating on the door to Chase's room. The knocks on the door matched the throbbing beat in my head. "What?" I groaned.

"Phoenix wants to see you in Church in 15 minutes," someone said. Kellan maybe?

It required extensive effort to force myself out of bed. I tossed back a few pain relievers, brushed my hair and teeth, and threw on some clothes. I didn't even bother checking my reflection in the mirror. I knew I was a hot mess and I didn't even care.

Staggering into the common room, I was surprised to see Annabelle and Reese seated on one of the sofas. Annabelle looked like the poster woman for recently married and pregnant. Reese's appearance mirrored my own. I moved my hand in a weak attempt at a wave. "Morning."

Reese snickered. "You look like shit."

"Back at ya, bitch," I retorted. "What are you two doing here?"

They didn't get a chance to answer. The door to Church opened, and Dash stuck his head out. "Come on in, ladies."

Neither Annabelle nor Reese uttered a word as they stood and moved toward the door. I wordlessly followed them wondering what in the world was going on.

Phoenix stood at the head of the table and gestured to three chairs in the front of the room. "Have a seat."

We sat. Looking around the room, I realized all of the club officers were present, setting off alarm bells in my mind.

"As you know, what is said in this room doesn't leave this room," he paused and made eye contact with each one of us. "Last night, the three of you stole my keys, let yourselves into the basement, which you know is off-limits, put yourselves in danger by releasing a prisoner, and topped it off by torturing and killing him. Had Shaker not caught you descending the stairs, all of this would have occurred on club property without a single brother knowing!" he yelled.

He pointed to Reese and me. "You two have already pulled this shit one time, and I let it go — not this time. This time there will be consequences. If a brother pulled the shit you did, he would have his ass beat and might even lose his patch. Each one of you is an Old Lady as well as a blood relative to at least one club brother, so I can't very well ban you from the clubhouse. However, you have broken my trust and the club's trust. You will earn it back similarly to how the prospects earn it initially. For the next year, the three of you will be responsible for planning and organizing all club runs and events, you will be responsible for cleaning up after major parties, and you will work out a schedule to make sure this clubhouse is thoroughly cleaned three days a week. Whatever time Annabelle misses later in her pregnancy and when she delivers will be made up when the doctor has cleared her. You drop the ball on any of your assignments, and you're out, I don't give a fuck who you belong to. Understood?"

A collective, "Yes, sir," was mumbled by the three of us.

"Good. You're dismissed," Phoenix barked.

No need to tell me twice. I jumped up and ran out of there like my tail was on fire.

Carbon

"I think you might've been a bit too hard on the girls, Phoenix," Badger said pointedly once the girls left the room.

"I don't," Phoenix huffed. "They could have gotten themselves seriously hurt or killed! Annabelle is pregnant and knowingly put herself in danger. That crazy fucker could have easily overpowered them."

Shaker snorted. "I get where you're coming from, Prez, and I don't disagree that they were in the wrong, but you did see the gun Reese had trained on him, right? And the shotgun propped against the wall beside Annabelle? Not to mention the 20-inch Bowie Harper was brandishing. That man wouldn't have gotten anywhere close to them. Annabelle and Reese are crack shots, and apparently, Harper has some untapped skills with a blade."

Phoenix glared at Shaker. "Be that as it may, they need to know they can't do whatever they want around here. Let's say you didn't discover them, and like you just said, they were able to handle themselves without issue. What do you think they would have done when they killed him? Do you think they would have been able to get rid of the body and all of the evidence? No, they wouldn't have. Hell, Harper didn't even know to burn her clothes and shower when she was done."

Shaker nodded. "Point made, Prez."

"Byte, I want new a lock installed on the basement door that requires a fingerprint to open it. I'll be damned if I have a bunch of girls get into my basement again," Phoenix barked.

I chuckled to myself. Like that would stop them. I was going to have my hands full with Harper, and I wouldn't want it any other way.

Also by Teagan Brooks

Blackwings MC
Dash
Duke
Phoenix
Shaker

41120941R00230

Made in the USA
Middletown, DE
04 April 2019